Devouring You

E.M. Eden

Emory Eden

To everyone who asked where the smut was in Book One—

thank you for your patience.

This one's for youuuu.

***

To my family, with love—

this is your official warning.

There's sexually explicit material in chapter 5.

And chapter 7.

And chapter 12.

And chapter 13.

***

I will not be discussing those at Thanksgiving <3

Content Warning

This novel is a mafia romance and contains explicit sexual content, violence, murder, and mature themes including obsession, power imbalance, traumatic childhood events, and pregnancy-related content. Reader discretion is advised.

Contents

Chapter 1

Sage

I wake in his arms.

And for just one moment, I forget why that should hurt.

Light hasn't dawned through the curtains yet. Instead, the morning stays suspended in a haze of exhaustion. It feels like my eyelids weigh a thousand pounds, just like my heart does.

The world might not yet remember what unfolded in my kitchen last night, but *I do*.

I do, and I'm not sure if it's for the better or worse.

Somehow, I made it through the night unscathed.

I half expected him to drag me from my sleep with hands around my throat, but instead, I slept fitfully in his arms. Arms that were strong, but relaxed, allowing me to move as I pleased.

I tossed and I turned and yet, he didn't so much as breathe as though he felt anger toward me.

Somehow, my heart continued beating even after the clock struck midnight.

He didn't do it.

He didn't kill me like Andrew instructed him to.

Which means I'm safe... at least for one more day.

Yesterday was the day that Ellison was supposed to kill me, and today is the day that my father-in-law will likely try.

But I can't think about that right now.

Not with his weight surrounding me.

Ellison's body is warm behind mine. The slow rise and fall of his chest presses against my back, his arm curved around my waist so naturally that it makes my throat tighten.

It aches... the familiarity of it all. The memory of every morning that I'd gotten used to. Of every morning I tried convincing myself that I was waking up in my husband's embrace.

The man I'm supposed to somehow love. The life I believed in. The future I thought was in my grasp.

But the man holding me isn't my husband.

He never was.

I can't believe I tried deluding myself into thinking he could be.

He isn't.

And I knew that he wasn't, didn't I? I knew he wasn't Adrian from the very first moment that I saw him through that phone screen, and yet...

...and yet, how badly I wanted him to be.

How badly I'd prayed he would be.

That's the truth of it all.

I wanted my husband to be this man. I wanted him to touch me and hold me like this, to want me this close.

The truth sits heavy in the room now, unmoving and suffocating. It sits right here out in the open, not even able to fit in the space between us.

Ellison Gray.

I didn't even have to push him.

He admitted everything to me. Every lie he sold me was to shorten the distance between us, and I played right into his hand.

He didn't even try to justify himself or soften the blow.

He simply told me the truth and tried to hold me together when I shattered. Quiet and steady. The way someone might hold a wounded animal that could bite at any second.

And I let him do it.

Maybe that says something worse about me.

I don't want to think about that yet.

I can't.

I slip carefully from his hold, and his hands stay limp as they fall to the bedsheets softly. He just exhales a slow, rough breath, like he's dreaming about letting me go and it pains him even during his sleeping hours.

My feet touch the floor and the cold travels up through my bones as if the house itself is trying to freeze me so I can't leave him.

Last night feels unreal, an echo of a nightmare I haven't yet woken from. Maybe my daylight hours are the same thoughts as Ellison's sleeping ones, both tormented by the decisions that brought us here.

But the cold under my feet is real. My heartbeat is real. This silence is real.

I pick up my phone as I step out of the room, casting one more look back at the bed. He still hasn't moved. His breath hasn't faltered, still deep and solid. Repetitive.

I force myself to turn away and pull the door closed behind me.

The hallway is dim, familiar to me but somehow all wrong, as if the house is wearing someone else's face. I wonder if it was ever really mine or if I just told myself that it was. Maybe now it recognizes that neither of its occupants belong here.

I dial without thinking, without breathing, holding the phone to my ear like it's a lifeline I don't want to admit I need.

Dallas answers with a voice full of sleep and immediate alarm. "Sage?"

I keep my voice low and steady even though I want to scream at him to come get me, like a child calling their parent after their first failed sleepover. At least I sound somewhat controlled, in the way one has to be when standing over a cliff.

"Wipe the feeds from last night," I rasp into the receiver. "Every camera. And end anyone who saw anything. Then come here. Right now."

There's a brief but weighted pause, and I know in that silence, he is imagining every version of why I would ask him to erase the evidence of my own life. From the cameras I made sure were here to capture every angle of my undoing.

"Don't watch the footage," I breathe out, and I know he won't listen.

"On my way," he says, and hangs up. No questions asked. No hesitation.

Maybe this is what Dallas meant when he said he valued loyalty.

I step outside while I wait, needing the cold morning air to clear my lungs even if it burns. It fills my lungs until it aches. But I pace the length of the patio slowly, like if I move too fast, the ground might crack apart beneath me.

I don't know if I'm angry or grieving or simply suspended somewhere between the two. But I know something feels broken inside of me.

I hear the car before I see it, tires grinding over gravel, the slam of the door and footsteps that are heavy and determined.

Dallas enters the house like a hurricane, tearing through the room until he locks onto his target. We turn to look at Ellison coming down the staircase at the same time, only Dallas has different plans from mine.

He pulls his gun before my next heartbeat has a chance to finish.

And I move.

My body is between them before my mind makes the decision to move. My palm flattens against Dallas' chest, my back slamming into Ellison as he tries to tug me out from in front of the gun. My heart is throbbing against my ribs, and I fear they might crack.

This isn't the first time I've been on this side of a gun, but it's the first time I've stepped in front of it willingly.

Dallas stops, but only because I told him without words that I would hate him if he didn't.

I know he can see it in my eyes.

I know he can.

"Sage," his voice is low and dangerous, all business and no pleasure. The voice he uses when he commands the guys at work. But I'm in charge here. "Move."

"No."

The word sits calm and immovable in the space between us.

Ellison doesn't move either, but his grip is tight around my waist, pressing me back against him like he'd be able to protect me if Dallas decided just to pull the trigger.

The same way he held me last night when everything was falling apart.

Dallas' gaze moves to him, sharp enough to cut to bone, and I pray to a God that I'm not even sure I believe in that he will listen to me. That he will understand why I need him to keep his finger off of that trigger. "Who the hell are you?"

Ellison's voice comes out low and rough, tugged from somewhere deep. It's not a voice I've heard from him before. As if he's somehow dropped his mask in the wake of me being in danger. "No one you want around," he rasps, and Dallas scoffs. "I know you won't believe it. But I am not your enemy. I only want Sage to be safe."

Dallas laughs once, dark and humorless, maybe the most genuine sound I've ever heard fall from his lips before. "You expect me to fucking believe that?"

"No," Ellison says, and his voice gains that subtle, razor-edged sarcasm he never used as Adrian. "But that doesn't make it any less true."

The silence that follows is a loaded weapon, like a hairpin trigger waiting to be pulled.

I can see it churning in Dallas' eyes. He's thinking. Weighing. Judging. Whatever happens next will likely traumatize me.

I don't see any world where it doesn't.

When Dallas decides to pull the trigger, it might break my heart.

It might destroy every ounce of strength that I've pretended to have these past few months.

It might kill me.

Unless a miracle happens. Unless, somehow, Dallas weighs the odds in Ellison's favor.

He doesn't lower the gun as his eyes drop to me, but this time, his voice is quiet and lethal, meant just for me. "Say the word, Sage, and I'll put him in the fucking ground."

And just like that, I understand the core of the problem.

If Ellison dies, I will break.

Not because I forgive him.

Not because I trust him.

Not even because I could possibly love him.

But because my heart already knows his hand.

And I'm not ready to live in a world where he does not exist.

"I don't trust him," my voice shakes wildly, and I have to swallow back the thickness in my throat. "But he's here. And we have work to do."

Dallas' jaw clenches.

"And the work is Andrew Hart," Ellison speaks up, his voice turning cold, lacking all of the warmth he's always spoken to me with. "You want power back in this house? Then we need to take it."

"And what's in it for you?" Dallas challenges, pushing the gun closer toward him.

"I don't want anything but Sage." He says it so surely, like it's not rupturing my blood vessels.

"You lie," Dallas practically spits the words out, jutting his gun forward like he wants to put a bullet between Ellison's eyes. Like he'd find pleasure in it.

"Believe what you want," Ellison retorts, not gently or apologetically, but like nothing said will change his answer. "Sage needs to be safe. You know that and I know that. The only way to make that happen is to eliminate all threats to her safety. And that doesn't include me."

Dallas stares at him for a long time. Then at me. And then at Ellison again.

Then he holsters his gun, and I take a breath that burns my lungs.

"We'll talk tomorrow. Just the two of us. You," he snaps his fingers in front of my face to make sure I'm paying attention. "You don't leave this fucking house today. Understood?"

"Understood," I whisper, and I take a few staggered steps forward as he starts walking toward the front door again. "Wait a second, where the hell are you going?" I call out, and he barely twists around to glare at me.

"It's four in the morning, Sage, and I'm fucking tired."

"You're going to just leave me here with him?" I shriek, and Ellison snorts like he's offended. I turn to glare at him before I start following Dallas to the door, leaving Ellison's fingers clutching at the spot I just occupied. "What if he plans to kill me after you leave?"

"Kill you?" Dallas sighs. "Be reasonable, Sage," he deadpans. "The guy's fucking obsessed with you. He isn't going to-"

"Obsessed?" Ellison says the word like it disgusts him. "I'm not obse-"

"Pipe down, Adrian 2.0," Dallas glares at him.

"Yeah," I snap as I round on him. "This is an AB conversation, so why don't you C yourself out of-"

"Okay, we really need to work on your threatening aura, Sage," Dallas sighs again, and then he runs his hands through his hair. "Look, he's obsessed with you, but he's got a tell. He fucking licks his lips when he's about to lie. Could've spotted that a mile away. Not to mention he does that thing with his hands. He isn't going to kill you. We're going to weaponize him."

"What?" I rasp, confused about how things have flipped over again since Dallas walked in the door. I feel like I'm trying to balance on little toy blocks and they keep getting knocked over time and time again.

"We'll discuss it tomorrow," he turns to reach for the door.

"But where are you going?" I call out again, and he doesn't bother turning back around.

"I'm going to the bar," he throws over his shoulder.

"The bar?" Ellison says it at the same time as me, and Dallas and I both ignore him.

"It's four in the morning, Sage," he lets out the most drawn-out, exasperated sigh in existence. "You're going to send me into cardiac arrest and I'm not even thirty-five. I'm going to drink myself into oblivion and you're going to stay in this house today."

"Dallas! Wait! Dall-"

He slams the door in my face, and I have to really force myself not to grab the nearest vase and storm outside to slam it down over his head.

Patience.

I have to learn it.

Chapter 2

Sage

We don't speak for a long time after Dallas leaves.

The house feels too large around us. Too full of everything left unsaid.

I avoid him entirely while I get ready for my day, and he leaves me be.

The day passes by just like that, with both of us silent and avoiding each other. Until dinner arrives.

I sit at the dining room table with my laptop open in front of me, fingers resting on the keys without typing. The cursor blinks, unbothered and uninterested in anything I might will it to do.

And I just stare.

Ellison moves around the kitchen with quiet efficiency. No wasted motions or noise that doesn't need to exist.

He's quiet, like a ghost haunting my very halls, both the ones in my home and my head.

He cooks like he belongs here. Like he built this kitchen with his own two bare hands and knows how every granite countertop was cut.

And for the first time, I realize that Adrian never knew how to move quietly. He filled space. He wanted to be seen and heard and all attention to be on him at all times. From the way he breathed to the way he threw his words around, Adrian was always loud.

Ellison is the opposite. He takes up room without asking for any of it.

I watch him from behind the screen of my laptop even though I pretend not to. His shoulders are broader than I thought before. His stance straighter, the lines of his back firm, the way someone stands when they're a rigid weapon. He stands like Dallas. Military disciplined. Like he's been trained to do it.

We eat across from each other without speaking.

The silence is thick and weighted with everything we don't yet know how to say.

But I notice the exact second he senses me studying him. His fork pauses halfway to his mouth, and he lifts his eyes to mine slowly, like he's bracing for impact.

"What?" He finally asks, voice low and rough with exhaustion.

"You're still lying," I whisper around the tightness in my throat.

"What?"

"You're still playing him," I hope my voice sounds as steady as I need it to sound, but all it sounds like to me is hurt.

His eyes narrow just a fraction, not defensive, but I know he's not about to lie to me. He cuts straight to the truth. "If I stop being Adrian or slip up in front of anybody then all of this falls apart, Sage. You know that."

"If it's just us here, I don't want you to play a role. If you're my husband, then be my husband." The order sounds more like a plea than anything.

The hurt is clear in my voice. The anger. The disappointment.

The longing.

"That's a dangerous game to play, baby," he says, and his voice is quieter than before, something raw bleeding into it. "I can't just separate what I am and what I've done. You might not want me to play a role, but I have no choice."

I want to melt at the way he calls me baby. And he says it so confidently, like he knew it would get to me. I hate it.

I hate it.

And I love it.

But I don't love the look in his eyes. The one that seems like it pains him to have to hide from me.

"If it's just us..." I whisper, softer now. "I want you to just be you. I want to know who you actually are. You can't separate it, but I'm telling you that you have to. I never wanted Adrian before, and I don't want Adrian now. If you want me to do this," my voice breaks and Ellison looks like the sound physically pains him. "Then you do what I say. There's no going backwards."

"I'm not asking to go back, Sage. I'm just asking you-"

"And I'm telling you no!" I slam my hands down on the table and he doesn't even flinch, but his chest rises and falls quickly just like mine. "I'm telling you no," I repeat firmly.

He stares at me for a long time, quiet and assessing. The same way Dallas does. The way a predator does.

But he nods, slowly and barely noticeable, like a man acknowledging his next steps are going to damn him.

And I watch him let Adrian go.

Not at all at once.

Not dramatically.

Slowly, like he's shifting skin. Like he's shedding a veil.

Like someone pulled the ribbon on the back of his mask.

His spine straightens, not stiffly, but enough to show the tension bleed out of him. His shoulders drop a fraction, less cocky and confident and more subdued. And his eyes... the light in his eyes darkens. Not with something cruel, but with something right. These eyes are cloudy with emotion. With proof that he also has things he wants to say.

"Better?"

God, even that word sounds different.

His voice is lower. More real and less practiced. It's sure, not lazy like Adrian's. And there's a slight accent that I can't place just yet. I remember it from before, when he slipped up on the phone when we first started speaking.

"Yes," I swallow and reach for my glass.

The wine burns on the way down.

It feels like the air between us changes temperature.

He huffs out a small breath that's almost a laugh, but not quite. It sounds disbelieving in a way that's finally unguarded.

I want to scream.

I look at him again and he drags his eyes away, like the vulnerability of being seen is something he isn't used to.

This little cat-and-mouse tug-of-war game might be my undoing long before Andrew Hart.

Dinner ends quietly, and he clears the plates without me so much as lifting a finger.

I mean to. I do.

But I'm too distracted by the fact that he even walks like a different person now.

When I head to the bedroom, he follows me slowly, hesitantly, like he's not sure he's allowed.

He doesn't move to touch me. He doesn't try to follow me when I mutter that I'm going to shower.

He simply meets my eyes with something aching. Something longing. And I can't help but stare at him like I'm trying to learn a language I once knew and somehow forgot.

"You can lock the bathroom door if it makes you feel safer," he finally murmurs, and my lips part around something ragged.

I want to yell at him. I want to tell him to fuck off. That everything was perfect until he had to go and fuck it all up and this is just-

"Do you want to join me?" The words leave my mouth before I can second guess them.

Damn it all, Sage! That's not what you were supposed to say!

His expression changes but I can tell he's trying to hide it.

I see something ripple in his eyes, a fault line cracking the grey stone irises.

"Are you sure?" He asks, and it's not a challenge. It's not meant to undermine my decision.

"Yes."

He said yes.

Fuck, Sage, he said yes.

Now I have to pretend like I'm not going to combust the second I start undressing.

The bathroom fills with steam fast, clinging to the walls and fogging up the shower glass, softening the world into something blurred like my mind.

It should be comforting, the warmth, the humidity, the steady echo of water hitting tile. But it feels like standing still after an explosion, waiting for the ground to fracture.

I step under the spray first. The water is hot enough to sting, but I let it. Heat has never bothered me any, and I already felt it before I even stepped foot in the water.

I tip my head back and close my eyes, letting the water drag my hair down my spine like ink bleeding down paper.

I feel him before I look at him.

He stands just inside the shower space, letting the dual spray from his side hit his broad shoulders. Not crowding or touching, just simply there, existing in the space with me. And suddenly, I realize that I want him to.

I want him to exist in the space with me.

The thought is brutal as it settles in the back of my mind.

The way he holds himself is different. Not Adrian's practiced toleration, not the performative softness that I thought I loved.

He's still being himself, and that is what I need right now more than anything else.

His shoulder brushes mine as he steps closer to wet his hair beneath the spray. The contact is accidental, barely there, but it jolts something in me.

Like nerve endings waking after being numb for far too long.

His eyes are closed, but there's no way he doesn't feel me studying him.

I watch the water slide down his chest, the rise and fall of his breath, the way he moves without thinking, without tension. The water drips down his jaw, softening his harsh lines, but not enough to wash him away.

Ellison.

This is Ellison.

Not who he thinks Adrian is supposed to be.

Not someone cosplaying as my husband.

Ellison.

His voice is low when it comes, close enough that I feel the warmth of it on my skin.

"I love your tattoo," he says, almost quietly, a careful bridge of conversation. I don't even know why my throat tightens. "What's it mean?"

"It means that time will realign all of the wrongs I've been dealt," I softly murmur as I turn away. I feel his eyes licking up every inch of my spine, following the words that have long been etched in my skin.

I jolt when his fingertips brush my spine, but I can't bring myself to pull away. Not when I've already memorized his touch. His fingers are warm where they skim up my spine, tracing the ink upward as though he hopes it'll fuse into his own skin. The contact is careful and gentle. Asking.

Coaxing.

When he reaches my nape, I flinch. Not away from him, but just from memory, and I hear his subtle intake of breath.

I wonder if he knows I had the fleeting fear that he might close his hand around my throat.

But instead, his fingers slip into my hair, gathering it softly into his hands and brushing the water downwards.

"You have beautiful hair, Sage," his voice is so low and soft, nothing like the voice he's been forcing me to think was his. "It suits you."

It suits me?

I close my eyes as his hands work through the long strands, so careful and tender, purposely ensuring they don't tangle.

Adrian hated my hair. I heard the words slip when he spoke to his father one night. He always did prefer blondes. Blondes with short, choppy boring bobs with no color. Hair that wouldn't get in the way.

"He didn't like that it was long," my voice trembles as I say the words, but he doesn't stop brushing over the strands. "Or dark like this. Adrian used to hate it."

His response is quiet, but it feels like he's struck a match against my heart and used my blood as an accelerant.

"I'm not Adrian, baby."

I could sob, honestly. I really could.

Just because he's acknowledging it.

The truth.

Exactly what I wanted from him.

I can't help but turn around to look up at him, and God, it makes my heart throb.

"Can I wash your hair?"

I can barely meet his eyes. Eyes that are stormy and grey. Eyes that are so patient.

"Why?" My breath shudders out of my chest.

"Because you're my wife," he says with a softness that feels dangerous to my health. "And you're tense after everything that's happened in the past twenty-four hours, and it's my job to take care of you."

I'm not his wife.

Not really.

Not legally.

But his ring is on my finger.

We've christened our marital bed, and he knows me in the ways only a husband should.

He's not really my husband, and yet... he looks at me like he truly believes he is.

So, I nod my head and turn back around.

I stay patient and melt into his touch as he works his fingers into my hair, the pressure firm enough to soothe but gentle enough that I can move away if I need to.

But I don't.

I don't need to.

I have never felt the comfort of a man like this. To let one soothe me. To let one take care of me.

Never have I felt safe enough to do it, and yet the man who has perhaps lied to me most... the one who's tricked and manipulated me... somehow that's the man I feel safest with.

So, my body goes pliant while his thumbs work small circles at my scalp, down behind my ears and along the base of my neck.

The touch is intimate but not sexual, pleading but not demanding.

He's not asking of me. He's just simply there, holding all the pieces of me in his palms while I decide what to do with them.

When he guides me under the spray to rinse, he steps out of the water to wash his own hair. His movements are quick and efficient, those of a man who has lived in a barracks, or out in the woods where routine is all you know.

He finishes before I even notice, and he doesn't hesitate to put his attention back on me.

I should yell at him.

I should.

He doesn't deserve to even touch me.

He doesn't deserve to see me like this.

I melt under his steady hands as he washes my body, careful with the lingering tender spots that show evidence of me fighting him last night.

His hands move along my arms, my shoulders, my back. Everywhere that I'll allow. And he doesn't push it. Instead, he hands me the cloth when he's finished, letting me take care of the more intimate areas. At least he's somewhat respectful of my boundaries.

When we're finally out of the shower, he wraps a towel around me immediately, smoothing it over my skin before he starts patting my hair dry.

He doesn't even care that he himself is dripping all over the floor.

He tends to me first, bringing me one of his soft, oversized shirts, worn already by him so many times that his scent clings to it.

When he's done, I tell him I need to blow-dry my hair, but really, I just need a moment to breathe.

He hesitates for a moment as he looks at me, his lips thin, but understanding, and then he leans in and presses a soft, lingering kiss to my forehead. One that knocks the breath out of me more than anything else tonight.

And in the bathroom, when I'm finally alone, I feel the lingering warmth where his lips had met my skin, and I hate it.

I hate it so much.

I hate it because I don't hate it at all.

No matter how bad I want to.

When I return to the bedroom, he's lying on his side of the bed, not touching my pillow or taking up space that isn't his.

He doesn't look up when I slide under the covers, but the moment I settle, he hesitantly moves, wrapping his arm around my waist, letting me decide if I want to fall into him.

And I do.

I rest my cheek against his chest, and his hand moves slowly up and down my spine, warm and steadying until my breath finally starts to slow.

He's warm.

Warm enough to remind me that he's real, that this is real, that I am lying beside a man I shouldn't trust but still reach for every single time anyway.

His palm moves steadily in absent strokes, the kind someone does without thinking, like it's as easy as breathing.

I close my eyes and pretend it's just comforting to me.

Pretend that nothing has changed.

Pretend that I didn't learn yesterday that my life is the complete opposite of what I thought it was.

Pretend that I am still myself.

I've had years of keeping quiet, and I hate more than anything that he's able to unravel me with just his presence.

He knows that I'm awake, even after lying there still for nearly an hour.

It's in the way his chest rises a little deeper under my cheek.

The way his hand stills for just a moment and then resumes its careful path.

The way the silence feels empty instead of settling.

But his voice breaks the stillness eventually, low and unhurried, the words cautious but full of something like sadness.

"Don't pretend with me either, baby."

"Why the fuck would you say that?" I nearly choke on the words, all of them coming out strained and ragged. But it's too late. I can feel the gate break loose.

He waits.

He waits and waits.

He always waits.

So fucking patient.

And the waiting is what undoes me.

The tears don't come all at once. They never do.

They gather slowly at first, heavy behind my sternum, pressing right against my windpipe, tight and aching. I try to swallow them down, to hold my breath steady, to keep my body from shaking even just a little bit.

But I fail.

My breath trembles. A hitch so small that most people would miss it.

But Ellison doesn't.

His hand stills completely, then starts again, slower now, more intentional, moving down my spine in long, quiet passes.

I try to breathe around the tightness in my chest, but it feels like my ribs are splintering into my lungs, and I can't. My hand tightens into the fabric of his shirt, the cotton turning damp where my cheek rests. And my eyes sting, the traitors.

I press my face harder into him, like I can hide the fact that I'm falling apart.

I don't want him to hear me breaking down over him.

I don't want him to know how much I need him.

I don't want him to see that I'm choosing him, even now, when it's his fault that I'm like this in the first place.

But my breath stutters out of me, sharp and shaking, impossible for me to swallow down.

And then the tears really come.

Silent at first, but then like a tsunami.

My body shakes, small and uncontrollable, like I'm trying to keep the crying buried in my bones and it's slipping through all of the newborn cracks. My breath goes ragged, and I try to hide from him. I try to turn my face away, ashamed at how I'm falling apart.

Ellison doesn't let me.

His arms tighten, just enough to tell me that I don't have to go anywhere. His hand moves up to the back of my head, fingers sliding through my hair to hold me steady.

He presses his face to my temple, his breath warm against my skin.

He doesn't shush me.

He doesn't say it's okay.

He doesn't try to fix it.

The sound I make when the sob finally breaks free is small and painful, the kind of sound that only comes out when a person has been holding themselves together too tightly for far too long.

I clutch at his shirt like he might disappear, like I'm afraid I'll disappear with him if I don't hold on.

His voice comes out eventually, low, barely above a whisper, and wrecking me even further.

"I've got you, Sage."

My tears come harder at the reassurance.

He shifts to give me more space to fall apart against him, his arms wrapping around me fully now, enveloping me in a sense of safety that feels unbearable.

I cry until my limbs feel heavy and worn out, my breaths softening into shivering inhales, until my body stops shaking and sinks into exhaustion. His hands keep that same path down my back, holding me steady in the dark.

I don't remember falling asleep.

But when I do, he's still holding me.

And I know he's not going to let go.

Chapter 3

Sage

I wake up alone.

For one second suspended in time, I think maybe it was all a dream.

Maybe I invented the weight of his arms, the warmth of his chest, the rough tenderness in his hands when he held me together last night so I didn't fall all to pieces.

The sheets are cool where his body should be. The space beside me long since empty, the pillow an unmarked grave where his head should still be lying.

My heart trips when I realize... I'm completely alone.

It settles heavier than it should.

Alone has never been peaceful for me. It always meant that things were happening behind closed doors. Things that would later slam down on me like freezing cold water.

I jerk upright, my lungs seizing before my mind can catch up. The room is too quiet and too still, like it usually is before something happens. A calm before the storm. The curtains are still closed, a thin stream of light leaking in cautiously, like it's not sure it's allowed.

He's gone.

For one wild heartbeat, every worst-case scenario crashes into me at once.

The last thing I remember is crying myself to sleep in Ellison's arms, my fingers tangled in his shirt like he was the only thing I had left in the world. Now the sheets are flat, the impression of his body long faded, and my mind spirals toward the conclusion that it was trained to expect.

He left me.

He finished the job.

He went to Andrew.

He told him everything.

Men leaving without explanation has always been a constant in my life.

It's never brought me any peace with their absence, only reining terror trickling down from their decisions.

I swing my legs over the side of the bed and stand far too quickly, the room tilting for a second as blood rushes into my brain. My heartbeat is so loud it feels like it could set off the house alarms all on its own.

The bathroom door is open, and the room is empty.

The hallway is empty.

The foyer is empty.

Every empty space feels more like he is betraying me.

He's just like everyone else. He's just like everyone else.

My brain screams it at me even though my heart holds onto a thin shred of hope that he wouldn't do that.

I rush down the staircase with my phone tight in my hand. I don't even bother trying to rationalize what I'm doing. My survival has never been controlled by logic. Only cold understandings and the fight-or-flight phone calls to get me somewhere safe.

The marble floors are freezing against the soles of my feet, and the cold inches up my spine like dread. The house feels like it's holding its breath with me.

If he really left me, if he went to Andrew... there's nothing I can do now. I'll have to flee. I'll have to flee like I always do. If I don't, I'll be dead come nightfall.

The thought does nothing to stop the nausea that threatens to pour out my mouth.

Every step I take feels louder than it should, like the house is trying to save me from the reveal that's coming.

Every room is empty.

For a second, it really does feel like I woke up in a crime scene where all of the evidence has already been wiped clean.

And then I turn the corner into the kitchen and my breath halts.

He's right there.

Alone, shirtless, and barefoot at the stove.

Ellison stands with his back to me, his broad shoulders lit by the weak morning light streaming through the windows in the open dining room. There's a faint line of steam rising from the pan in front of him, accompanied by a subtle sizzling that feels almost domestic, which feels absurd considering the state of my life right now.

The coffee maker is a slow drip on the counter, already half-full, and my favorite coffee cup is waiting beside it, right along with the sugar canister and my favorite hazelnut creamer on standby.

The knot in my chest grows and refuses to weaken its hold.

I stand there for a moment in complete silence, wondering if the anger simmering under my skin has any valid belonging in this kitchen. I don't trust my instincts enough to act on them immediately. I can't do that. It's how I always get myself into trouble.

His shoulders move as he shifts the pan with smooth movements, just like he did days ago. He knows this kitchen and all of its ins and outs. Like he's been here longer than he has any right to be.

There's a faint scar on his shoulder blade, darker and raised, one that I never saw before on Adrian. But of course I didn't. I never really looked at Adrian.

Or, well, I did, but only to think about strangling the life from him at every chance.

With Ellison... it's hard *not* to look at him. My eyes keep returning to him without my permission.

Now that the truth has been laid bare in this very kitchen just days ago, the differences are impossible to ignore.

His posture is a glaring difference.

Ellison stands relaxed, but alert. He doesn't slouch or lean on every surface like he's physically incapable of supporting his own weight.

And his hair. I didn't notice before, or maybe I didn't want to, but Ellison's hair is a few shades darker.

Not to mention his eyes, but I don't focus on that too long or I'll spend hours waxing poetic about them and forget I'm supposed to be mad right now.

Sometimes it's easy to accept lies when you're looking into a person's eyes, and eyes like these... I won't do it to myself.

The urge to turn around and go back upstairs kicks in, childish and simmering, but I force myself to hold my ground.

I have every right to be angry. I have more than enough of a justification to never even speak to him again.

I want to tell him to fuck off. To get out of my house and leave me alone and never come anywhere near me again.

The urge builds in me so strong that I almost do.

And then I remember that I'm trying to be patient. Calm, and patient. Level-headed. Understanding.

"What are you doing?"

My mouth betrays me like it always does.

He goes still for a fraction of a second before he relaxes and glances over his shoulder at me. And the way that his eyes travel over me from the floor up makes my mouth nearly betray me again, but I bite down on my back teeth.

He looks at my bare feet, then my sleep shirt hanging off of one shoulder, then my face, and then my lips, like he's trying to gauge if the thin set of my lips is an indication that I'm upset.

But it's almost more than that.

It's almost assessing, like he's making sure I'm upright and breathing, and all in one piece. Like his first priority of the day was making my coffee and breakfast, and the second was my vital signs.

"Good morning to you too, baby."

Baby slides over my senses and I force it into one ear and out of the other. It annoys me more than anything that my stomach flips before my brain has time to veto it.

I am *not* going to do this with him today. I mean business. How at ease he is alone irritates me enough to snap.

"You weren't there when I woke up," I force the words out, and they come out more irritated than I want them to. "You could have at least said something." I cross my arms, and his eyes track the movement. *That's right, baby. I'm angry, and this is all your fault.*

"I could have," he agrees calmly as he turns back to the stove. "You were restless last night, so I didn't want to risk waking you up if I moved the wrong way. Thought I'd let you have a few hours of peace without me."

By restless, he's probably referring to how I fell asleep sobbing and slobbering and dripping snot all over his shirt, so I'll let that slide this one time.

"Why would you expect me to feel safe when I wake up and you are nowhere to be found? After everything that's happened the past few days, do you really think that was the best decision to make?" My voice trembles despite my best efforts.

"Sage."

God, why does he have to call me by my name when I'm angry?

Ellison clicks the stove off and turns around. He braces both hands flat on the countertop and tilts his head slightly. That dark shadow thing going on with his eyes is ridiculous. Who does he think he is?

"Baby," he says a little too softly. I bite my tongue again.

"I expect you to feel whatever you feel, and you have every right to be angry and frustrated and sad and any other emotion." He pauses, and I'm sensing a *but* to follow. "But..."

Ah, there it is.

"I'd like to get one thing straight between you and me."

"What?" My throat is incredibly tight with trying to brace myself for whatever he's going to say next.

"The safest place that you could be is under the same roof as me," he looks me right in the eyes as he says it, and I want to yell that he's lying, that he is the most dangerous thing to my health, but the look in his eyes tells me that he believes exactly what he's saying.

"That's not true," I snap, but it comes out strained and shaking.

"Do you really think that?" He asks, and why does it sound so wounded?

I don't.

I don't really think that.

"Why would I think any different?" My voice shakes again, and he's watching me carefully. "Of course, I believe that."

Something clouds over his eyes, almost like guilt.

But then it slips into something a little cocky as he looks at me.

He studies me like he's about to call my bluff.

Like he thinks I'm full of shit.

"Liar."

The word is clean and precise. There's no misunderstanding in it.

My vision goes red.

What the fuck did he just say?

"I said," Ellison cocks his head to the side again, and I want to knock his knowing smirk right off of his face.

And oh, God, did I say that out loud?

His lips twitch in amusement like he's enjoying this, maddeningly calm despite my flaring temper.

"That you, Sage, are a *liar.*"

I'll fucking kill him.

Ellison clicks his tongue, and I know I've truly screwed this all up. My mouth always betrays me.

Why does it always betray me?

Somehow, I know this is all my father's fault.

I have *got* to stop saying my inside thoughts out loud.

"I know you hated your husband, baby, but you can't hate both the first and the second one. Let's pick one and settle on it, okay?"

"I'll fucking kill you," I seethe, this time purposefully out loud, and my jaw hurts from how tightly I'm grinding my teeth.

"So do it then, baby," Ellison gently soothes, lowering his voice down to something achingly sweet and conspiratorial.

"Here," he backs up and opens the cabinet in front of him. I know I'm screwed. Damn Dallas straight to hell, where all men belong.

Ellison leans down, never breaking eye contact with me. I hear the click and squeeze my eyes shut as he retrieves one of the guns that Dallas stashed away for me.

Of course, Ellison would know it's there.

When I open my eyes again, he's right in front of me, reaching for my hand to put the gun there.

The metal is cool against my fingers, and it feels almost threatening, though I'm not sure if it's toward me or him. He even clicks the safety off and raises my hand toward him, tugging it until the muzzle is pressed against his chest.

I want to scream. I want to scream. I want to scream.

But not as much as I want to throw up when I see a gun, any gun, even the one in my own hand, pointed at him.

My hands only shake for a second before Ellison's taking the gun back from me. He clicks the safety back on and he leans forward, hovering over me before he presses a soft, fleeting kiss to my temple.

I can feel the restraint in the brief contact of his lips against my skin.

Knowing that he can hold back and I can't... the thought feels like poison in my head.

"You can say anything that you want to me, Sage," Ellison softly tells me. He reaches up to brush his thumb over my cheek as he cradles the left side of my face with his palm.

Nothing feels as dangerous or as right as his touch against my skin.

"I'll accept whatever you want to say since this is all my fault. But if you truly felt unsafe with me, neither you nor I would be here, and we wouldn't be tip-toeing around each other. So let's not lie, baby. Hmm? Let's keep being honest with each other. Okay?"

I wish I could tell him to leave. I wish I could.

I hate him.

And I hate what he's done and how he's done it.

But if he leaves, I'd hate him even more.

"Okay," I whisper.

His hand lingers on my cheek for one dangerous second longer before he steps away.

The gun remains on the counter between us.

He slides my coffee toward me.

I could cry when I take the first sip. Because it's made just right, with six spoons of sugar, and one big pour of hazelnut creamer.

"That's not even coffee at this point," he mutters under his breath as he spoons eggs onto two plates.

It feels like a bridge he's steadily building between us.

I don't know why I want to blow it all up.

I don't know why I want to trust it won't collapse under my feet.

"Shut up," I whisper back, not feeling very brave like I felt when I first walked down here.

"Yes, Ma'am," he snickers over his shoulder.

I have to fight the urge to smile.

And, of course, my mouth betrays me again.

I plan to still be petty by not eating my food.

But my stomach is growling, reminding me I didn't eat much yesterday besides a few bites here and there. He hears it. Of course he does. His eyes soften just a fraction, and I choose to ignore that.

"Sit," he points to my chair with one finger. "You can yell at me while you eat. I'll even pretend to be upset so it feels more satisfying for you."

He's just as petty as I am.

"I didn't even yell," I petulantly mumble as I pull out the chair and sit.

"Sure," he softly says, and then he's shoving bacon in his mouth while I glare at him.

The tension between his side of the table and mine is so thick, I don't even know how to break it. All while he sits there eating like he doesn't even notice me trying to cope with it.

"How do you want to handle today, Sage?" He asks after a few quiet minutes of us both finally eating. His gaze doesn't leave my face, and he must sense the confusion there.

"Aren't we supposed to sit down with Dallas? Make plans? Or, well, re-plan whatever you had planned before I popped back up to play rich-people house?" He gestures a lot with his hands as he talks.

"That's not funny," I deadpan, because I'm not going to admit that it was a little bit funny.

"Come on," he snickers at me, and I didn't notice before how his eyes seem to lighten when he smiles. "It was a little funny."

It was.

"No, it wasn't," I mutter, but I push my plate away and reach for my coffee, letting it warm my hands. "I guess we all need to sit down and talk. Your arrival wasn't exactly part of our plans, so, yeah, we'll have to shift some things around to make it work."

"Alright, what time?" He asks, this time without any sarcasm or teasing.

"I'll just call Dallas," I huff and reach for the phone.

Dallas answers on the second ring like always. "Still alive, or do I need to start shooting on sight when I arrive?"

"Good morning," I ignore him and tap the side of my coffee cup with my fingers, trying to pretend I don't feel Ellison's eyes trained on me. "We need to talk today."

"Define we," Dallas sighs, as if he didn't know this was the plan today.

"Listen here," I roll my eyes, and when I look up, Ellison's hands are folded in front of his face, hiding his mouth. I swear on my mother's grave that I will kill him if he thinks this is funny.

"I've already been dealing with one sarcastic asshole this morning, so I'm gonna need you to tone it down. Just come here."

"The sun is barely up, Sage," he sighs again. I hear a door slam in the background anyway. "You have no respect for the dead."

"You aren't dead yet," I mutter back. "But you will be if you don't hurry up."

"I'm already on the freeway."

The line goes dead, and I stare at Dallas' contact card with a scowl before Ellison's chair scraping against the marble floor draws my attention back.

"Guess that means he'll be here in less than ten minutes," he says as he collects our plates and heads toward the sink.

I nearly trip over the leg of my chair as I move to follow him.

"And how would you know that?" I ask, accusing and not friendly in the slightest. It's almost essential for him to admit to me that it was him spying on me all along, not Andrew.

"We both know I know more about you than your first husband ever did, baby," he steps around me and starts heading upstairs to get ready, and I might use that gun anyway just to put an end to my longstanding suffering.

"Do you think it would hurt if I shot you? Like... with a gun? In a very tender spot?" I trail up the stairs after him, and I have to pause when he laughs, genuine and intrigued by my audacity.

I'm starting to wonder if maybe the reason I didn't want Dallas to shoot him was so that I could do it myself.

"Been there, done that, sweetheart, and it wasn't nearly as shitty as it looked on TV, so find another way to get back at me," he teases.

"Don't give me any ideas," I cross my arms and lean against the doorway.

He seems so secure here, so confident and at home. Which, I guess this is his home, at least for now. But he just got here weeks ago, and he acts like he's lived here forever.

I watch him as he takes his shirt off to pull another one on and then trades his sweatpants for jeans.

"Where are you from?" I don't know why I ask. He probably won't even tell—

"Texas," he answers immediately.

"What?" I whisper, kicking off of the doorframe.

"Texas," he says again, raising his brows when he turns to look at me. "Why are you acting so surprised?"

"I just—well, I just—" I frown as I look at him. "Sometimes you have a little bit of an accent, but it didn't, I mean it doesn't *exactly* sound like a southern accent," I point out, this time not accusing, but genuinely confused.

"I've been in the military for fourteen years, baby," he says as he puts a belt through his belt loops. It's said gently, like he thought it would hurt my feelings. "I've been in the Middle East almost as long as I've lived in America. I made a career out of it. I don't think there's any part of Texas left in me, and there's not any part of me left in Texas either."

"But," I murmur, and he seems to soften at the downturned lines forming on my lips. "Don't you have any family?" I ask, and he only stares at me for a moment, like he doesn't have the heart to admit it out loud just yet. The look on his face makes my chest ache.

This time not with anger, but with understanding.

Having only yourself is a heavy burden to carry.

"Nope," he shrugs. The usual playfulness is all gone from his voice, and I hate that more than when he's being cocky.

"None at all?" I whisper, and he turns away from me to reach into his side of the closet for his jacket.

Or maybe it's so I can't see the look on his face.

"Just you, baby," he answers after a moment.

That stings.

That actually *really* fucking hurts to hear.

Are we both just all alone and fumbling for something to hold on to? A life to cling to? Someone to love?

I don't even know what I would respond with.

Even if he'd give me the chance to.

"I'll let Dallas in," he turns on his heel just like he always does, sure of where he's going. Except he bypasses me altogether, stepping around me entirely.

Just like always, he leaves my head reeling with no time to process the bombs that are dropping all around me.

Just like everyone else in my life always has.

And I hate that I don't know whether I want to run away or reach for him.

Chapter 4

Ellison

By the time Dallas pulls up, I already know two things with absolute certainty.

He didn't sleep, and he still doesn't trust me.

Sage is upstairs still. I can hear her rummaging around trying to finish getting ready. Wouldn't matter anyways. She'll still look better than anyone within a billion-mile radius.

I almost hope she's late coming downstairs.

It would satisfy me more than anything to see Dallas have to wait after she snapped at him on the phone. It's even more satisfying because she only got angry at him because I pissed her off first.

That's what he gets for holding that gun in my face.

I recognize the look on his face immediately when I open the door. There's tension pulled across his shoulders and shadows beneath his eyes, deep enough to suggest his head never once touched a pillow.

He doesn't acknowledge me when he enters, but he does shoulder-check me hard enough that I consider whether or not I should accept pissing Sage off more by making a scene.

The thought dead ends when Sage shuffles down the staircase.

One thing I can respect about Dallas is that his attention turns straight to Sage instead, and the message is clear enough that I can't be mad about the shoulder thing.

Sage is his priority just like she's mine.

I noticed it before I arrived a few weeks ago, and I was almost worried that she'd fall for him. He's certainly not charming in my eyes since he's a complete prick, but standing next to Adrian, he probably seemed like a God taking care of her in my absence.

Sage stayed strong though. Strong and loyal to her husband. To *me*.

I don't bother with niceties as I follow Sage to the vehicle outside. But I do keep my eyes moving while I make sure nobody is loitering around or watching her. They're all on Sage's payroll, but I wouldn't trust them on their best days. Not when their greedy hands are probably double-dipping on Hart's payroll.

I slide into the back seat, noticing how Sage heads straight to the front.

I'd like to have her next to me, but if sitting in the back keeps Dallas from shooting me, and Sage from getting any more upset, then it's the safest place I can be.

I'd almost rather be shot than see her upset, anyway.

I'm only here because she matters more than my pride.

She's the only thing that matters.

And perhaps that will be our fatal flaw.

The drive stretches on in heavy silence, thick enough that even looking out of the window doesn't make it any easier. It's hard not to notice Dallas' eyes meeting mine in the rearview mirror every few seconds, calculating, like he's measuring me.

I know it's not my fucking looks that's got him focused on me.

No. He doesn't trust me. Not one bit. Even if he does trust that I'd keep Sage safe.

He's watching me like my teeth are sharper this morning. Like I might go feral if he looks away too long. Like I might rip his neck out at the next red light.

Sage stares out of the window with her arms crossed tight against her chest, jaw set in a way I recognize now as a brace for impact.

I watch her face in the reflection because I know better than to crowd her when she's holding herself together by sheer force alone.

I did this.

I know I did.

I'm a dick for it.

It probably would be better if I left. At least for her.

If I weren't here, she'd still be living in her oblivious world, right in the middle of the Hart and Ledger family war, clutching onto hope that she won't go down with them.

She'd be mopping her floors and humming her songs and stealing things she probably shouldn't be touching.

And I'd be miserable.

Undoubtedly, I'd be thinking of all the ways I could get her back. How I could mend it. How I could stitch it back together.

That's not who I am. I know that. I'm not a healer.

I only know how to break things. My hands are meant for tearing things apart and slapping bandages over bullet holes until I can drag myself to safety. My hands are meant for carnage.

And yet I only want to touch her with them.

It's an aching urge. A constant one. Something I can't shake.

And if Sage wants me to go, then I'll go. But I know deep down that no amount of distance placed between us could alter the way that I want her.

My sights were set long ago, and Sage has been the target since the beginning.

Now I have to figure out how to fucking fix this.

And how not to destroy what Sage has already built.

The warehouse is a surprise to me.

I'll be honest, I was watching her as much as I could. But my reconnaissance could only reach so far when I was stuck in the unit.

I knew she was plotting and scheming behind Andrew's back, but I had no idea my sweet little angel was over here striking matches and burning things down.

The building is unmistakably hers.

Everything in it screams Sage, just like the house. It's clean and efficient, built for appearance and harboring secrets in its thick walls. Sage walks through it like she owns the place, because she does.

Everyone acknowledges her as she enters and passes, and they look at me like she's about to eat me alive.

I'd let her, of course, but it makes me wonder what's been said in my absence, and how much effort I'll have to double down on to reinstate my worth in this business.

Something warm and dangerous settles in my chest as I take it in piece by piece. The layout makes sense operationally, the redundancies layered just enough to suggest someone who plans for visitors and refuses to be caught unprepared when it happens.

I find myself slowing as I walk through it, absorbing the choices she made while everyone around her was underestimating her intelligence and her resolve.

She built this quietly, patiently, while being treated like a pawn by the men in her life, and the realization makes my hands tighten into fists.

I don't dare say a word, but I take a mental note of everything, the places I'd reinforce, the routes I'd reroute if she needed to get out of here, the ways she's already anticipated threats that men like Andrew Hart would utilize against her.

Pride creeps in before I can stop it. I shouldn't be surprised by her capability, and I'm not. Not really. I know she's more than capable. But no one else does. And maybe it's pride because she's successfully showing them. Maybe it's pride because I knew she could, and everyone else doubted her.

When we finally sit down in a conference room, it feels all too familiar.

I've sat at tables just like this one, countless times, with my thoughts straying straight to Sage. Now she sits across from me this time.

I listen to her speak. I can tell that it's not time for me to have an opinion here, as much as I'd like to.

But while I keep my tongue in check, I slowly start to realize that Sage isn't just methodical in her planning, but she's absolutely diabolical. A menace in every sense of the word.

She isn't just poking at Andrew. She's fucking him up on all fronts. Doubling down on making him sweat. Taking what he thinks belongs to him and pointing fingers at others.

She lays it all out on the table.

The Hart family business, the shipments, the drugs, the docks, the storage warehouses, the entirety of her plan. Sage has been slowly wedging herself in between the fingers of Andrew's grip, dismantling enough to knock him off of his pedestal without collapsing everything around him, and I can picture in vivid detail how this will all play out.

Dallas meets my eyes from his spot on Sage's left, and I can tell. Right away, I can tell... he is thinking the exact same things that I am.

There is no reward without risk. No capture of the queen without wading through the pawns... unless we stop thinking like soldiers and start thinking like strategists. One careful move at a time. Everything has to be planned and executed without Sage ever being touched. Every move has to be one that Andrew won't account for.

"Sage can't be in the middle of this," I say finally, and Dallas nods his head just once.

All eyes turn to me, and I meet them without flinching.

"You can't be in the middle of it," I tell her when she meets my eyes. "You can make all the plans you want, but do it from the back, not the front line."

I can tell she doesn't like it.

The audacity I have, I know. I can see she wants to yell at me. She's gripping her pen so tight I fear for her delicate hands.

"I'm not leaving you exposed," I continue, glancing at her only once more before turning my attention back to Dallas. "If I'm helping dismantle Andrew, then I'm staying close enough to make sure you keeps breathing while it happens."

Dallas studies me for a long moment, long enough I feel a little stripped bare, and I let him, because I have nothing to hide.

When he finally nods, it's not reluctant in the slightest. It's decisive and in agreement.

At least I know we have one common thought: Sage is the priority.

"I also think we need to relocate you. I know you love the house, and we can find a new one and make it whatever you'd like it to be, but Andrew has eyes on you at this house. He's got people on his payroll who are desperate for money and to keep their lives. We need to move you somewhere more secure."

I know it's going to explode before the words even leave my mouth. And I let Sage react first, let her anger burn hot and bright because I know I'm making her angry. I know it's all my fault. I try to keep my tone even, even though I know she's going to bring hers like a dagger to the heart.

"No."

That's fewer words than I was expecting.

"That house was bought by Andrew," I say calmly. "The people were bought by Andrew. The cameras were compromised before you even had the passcode set up for the system, baby. Loving it doesn't make it a safe place for you, no matter how much you want it to."

Her eyes flash with that white-hot anger, even though I can see she's trying to fight it. She knows what I'm saying is true. She's a smart woman, smarter than most, but I've already wounded her, and it guts me in a way I can't show right now. If I do, she'll try to take me down.

"You don't get—" Sage starts.

"I agree," Dallas cuts her off.

The room feels like it drops twenty degrees, and Sage's blue eyes go frosty with it.

"You don't get to either," she clicks her pen once. "Did the two of you have a heart-to-heart before I came downstairs? Or have you both lost it? I'm in charge here," she reaffirms, and oh boy, I know she is. She will always be in charge. But I'm not budging.

"You're in charge, yes, but your own security team agrees with me. There can't be a *plan* if the *planner* is taken out," I tell her, and I can see she wants to push back. She wears her emotions so clearly on her face. *We'll have to work on that.*

"I won't be taken out. I can stay close to the—"

"No, you can't," I cut her off, shaking my head. Her mouth drops open in surprise and her hands start shaking.

I fucking hate that I'm the one that makes her react that way.

"I will not let you be anywhere near your operations when they're going down, Sage," I tell her in the calmest, softest voice I can manage without sounding condescending. "You will stay away, just like you did the first time, where we can ensure that you are safe and away from Andr—"

I see the very second the switch flips.

My sweet Sage loses her humanity, and I know her words are about to burn a little.

"You don't get to make decisions here!" She snaps, slamming her hands down on the table. She's hurt that I ever even opened my mouth, and it feels like that's all I do is hurt her.

"Or did you fucking forget that it's *you* that flipped my entire life upside down again! Why would you think I'd listen to a *single* thing you have to say? You're a stranger who forced his way into my life and tore down everything that I've worked so hard to start building! You're a liar, and a thief and a fucking coward for pretending to be somebody you're not! And you made me fall for it! You made me fucking fall for the lie! You don't get to have a say in what I do with my past, present, or future! You don't get a say in anything!"

Her chest is heaving by the time she finishes handing my ass to me, and I'll admit that mine is burning a little after the third-degree from her words.

But I get it.

Really, I do.

And I'm not trying to make things worse. I don't want to make anything worse.

But I need her to get it through her thick, stubborn skull.

And apparently, Dallas agrees.

He tells us that he and Anderson will give us some privacy while we discuss it further, and I don't necessarily know if it'll be a discussion, but I foresee some hatred in my future.

"This is my home!" Sage flies off the handle again as soon as we're alone. "You're fucking up *everything* I've worked so hard on! Months of work, months of plans and secrecy, and—and you have no right to—"

"Sage." She abruptly cuts her words short when I say her name. She always does that. Like it resets her anger back to the starting point every single time I say it. I lean forward, bracing my elbows on the table to meet her fire head-on.

"Baby," I say, soft but controlled. "Do you really think I give a single *fuck* about your marble countertops?"

Maybe I could have been a little sweeter, because I worry for a second that she might cry.

The problem with Sage is that no one understands her.

No one except me.

Sage isn't stupid. She isn't naive or childish or unaware of the circumstances she's found herself in. She has things figured out.

Except she also doesn't.

She thinks she is doing everything alone. That no one gets it. That no one sees. That no one understands.

But I do.

She isn't lashing out because she wants to fight. She's lashing out because she thinks she's losing her control.

"I only care that you're alive," I continue softly. "That you're breathing, that you're still sitting in front of me with enough fire left to burn me to the ground. And if you're putting your hands in places they shouldn't be, then they're bound to get cut off, baby."

She looks away from me when I finish, and I have to take a very quiet, subtle, deep breath or I'll cave solely because of the look on her face.

"I know you can do this. I *know* you can. I trust you and your judgment and all of your plans. Don't think I don't," I tell her, but she still won't look at me. "I am so proud of everything you've accomplished, and everything you've been doing alone. I only worry that I'll turn around for ten minutes and come back to find you lying on the floor bleeding out."

She makes a sound when I say that. Something like a gasp mixed with frustration and fear.

"That is what happens when men like Andrew Hart think they have the upper hand, baby. You haven't been shot, but I'll go ahead and tell you that I have, and it hurts, and it's not pleasant, but taking you out of the hot seat makes it a little harder for somebody to get a hit on you."

Sage still won't look at me. I almost worry that it's beyond saving face.

Almost.

"Is it so bad that I want to see you alive and well? That I want to actually have you in my life for longer than a few weeks?"

She's quiet for a while, but her body language isn't.

Everything about Sage is loud. Her expressions, her voice, even her eyes.

But right now, she's quiet.

Except her hands are shaking, and her chest looks like she's trying hard to keep it still, and she won't look at me.

She's screaming internally and nobody is listening except for me.

"I almost liked you better when you were pretending to be Adrian," she mumbles under her breath finally, and the laugh forces its way out of me before I can stop it, unfiltered, because the irony is almost painful.

"That wasn't meant to be funny," she insists, and she's still squeezing her hands together, and she still won't look at me.

All of this anger is just a defense mechanism, and I know I'll have to push past it, but I want her to know that as much as she yells at me, I'm not going anywhere.

"It was, baby," I toss back, smiling despite myself, because I know something she'd never admit. "You'd never want me to be him."

"Why are you so confident in yourself?" She throws back at me, and this time, she looks at me. I feel a tinge of satisfaction when I see she's willing to fight me on it. "How can you be so sure I didn't like him more?"

"Well, sweetheart," I lean back in my seat and cock my head to the side. "Where do I start? My devilishly good looks?" She snorts at that, rolling her eyes before I even finish talking.

I shouldn't tease her, especially not when she is still so worked up, but seeing the blush rise on her face tells me I'm not totally doomed, just skimming the surface.

"Or maybe that I succeed in every area that he failed?" She snorts again. "No? Neither of those things?" I tap my chin and take a deep breath. "Maybe it's because I can actually please you in bed."

"Shut up," she whisper-yells immediately, sitting up straighter in her chair. Her face flushes so fast that it travels down her neck and dips out of sight beneath her shirt. She looks around quickly, like it's possible someone could overhear.

"These walls are soundproof, baby," I shoot back smugly, fighting the urge to grin. "You're the only one that knows about that last fact."

"Shut up," she says again, shooting up from her chair.

I don't have to ask to realize the conversation is over.

I simply follow after her.

When she opens the door, she doesn't even look at Dallas.

"Put together a list of suitable homes and bring them to me," she orders, and then she holds her hand out. "Give me the keys. Have Anderson take you home. We have errands to run."

I expect Dallas' smartass response, but he dips his head in acceptance and hands the keys over.

When Sage takes off down the hallway, the look that Dallas and I share tells me this is normal.

And I'll simply have to adapt or drown.

Chapter 5

Ellison

I thought when Sage said we had errands to run, it would be related to her super-secret plans.

I was not expecting her to drive us to the grocery store.

By the time we pull into the parking lot, Sage hasn't said a single word to me, and I know better than to try to fill the silence just to hear my own voice.

Partially because I know she's still tense.

Partially because I noticed she keeps glancing at me when she thinks I'm not looking, and that look... it's loaded and I'm not sure with what yet.

The silence feels tight and volatile, like a live wire stretched between us, and I'm being careful not to touch it unless she invites me to.

Anderson and Dallas linger where I can see them through the glass, close enough to intervene, far enough not to intrude.

I clock Anderson automatically, noting the exits and angles from the parking lot, the reflections, the way people move around Sage without realizing just how dangerous proximity to her really is. It's second nature to be on guard and also exhausting.

Somehow watching for threats to Sage feels more explosive than being active duty in the field.

At least there I knew what the bad guys looked like.

Sage doesn't look back at me when she starts toward the entrance, so I stay half a step behind her, close enough that my presence registers without crowding her. The doors slide open and the air inside is cool, fluorescent, and ordinary in a way that feels almost obscene after the morning we've had.

She grabs a shopping cart, and I take it from her without asking, but at least she doesn't fight me on it.

That alone tells me everything I need to know about how far her anger has cooled.

We move through the aisles with practiced efficiency, and I can tell this is a routine she's used to doing alone. She knows where everything is. She doesn't hesitate to grab it, like she has a mental checklist. She does it all quickly and quietly, like if she keeps herself busy enough then she won't have to look at me.

It doesn't work.

I catch eyes on her everywhere we go. Women, mostly. Some subtle, some bold, and some outright unapologetic. I probably should be jealous, but I know that Sage sleeps in my bed every single night, and they can all fuck right off.

The problem comes when I realize that it's not Sage they're always looking at.

Their gazes start to track me as I move, lingering in ways that would've amused me on any other day. I'm used to being under surveillance. I don't even notice it most of the time, and I only have eyes for Sage, so it never occurred to me that Sage might notice *them* watching *me*.

But she does.

I see it in the way her jaw tightens just a fraction, in the way her grip on the cart handle tightens, knuckles paling as she stares straight ahead like it would ruin her day to give them any sort of reaction.

Jealousy looks different on her than it does on most people.

It doesn't explode like her other emotions. No, jealousy on her is quiet and simmering, neat beneath that carefully controlled exterior.

It's iron tight under lock and key, hidden from sight, and incredibly hot.

Sage is somehow gorgeous even when she's getting ready to bite the heads off of any woman within a fifty-yard radius of me.

I step closer.

Not to provoke her.

But just close enough for my hand to brush the small of her back as I reach past her for that nasty-ass coffee creamer that she drinks.

My fingers skim her waist like it's natural. She stiffens under my touch, of course she does. But then she exhales just a little, like she's relieved by my touch even though her mind is still arguing.

"Baby," I murmur, low enough that it's just for her.

She shoots me a look that's half a warning, half something else entirely, something a little poisonous and predatory, and I know I shouldn't smile, but I do anyway, because I like when she looks at me like that. Like she wants to fight and kiss me in equal measure and hasn't decided which would hurt less.

I'd take either if it meant she'd touch me.

I keep it gentle after that. I don't crowd her, but I reach for everything she eyes in the store. I let her drift closer on her own, almost like she can't help it now that she's gotten a taste of my touch again.

Every time another pair of eyes linger too long, I lean in and murmur something mundane, and every time, she relaxes just a notch.

It relaxes me, too.

Or maybe I'm just imagining it. Maybe I'm just seeing what I want to see.

Maybe it's all in my head, and she still hates me, and this is going nowhere.

By the time we leave, the shopping cart is full, and the tension is thicker, and I can't tell if it's her or if it's me, but there's something simmering there under the surface, and I'm trying to let Sage be the one to address it. I can't be the one to dive in, and I don't think we can. Not after the explosion we had at the warehouse. We need to talk. To figure things out. To try to...

I forget every single prior thought when we make it home and start cooking.

Sage sits at the kitchen island, elbows on the counter, chin in her hand, watching me like she's trying to solve a puzzle, but some pieces are missing.

She still doesn't talk to me.

I set her bowl in front of her, and she eats, methodically at first, and then slower, like she's losing focus, her thoughts entirely somewhere else.

I keep my mouth shut and let her unravel at her own pace.

That's what I do best.

When dinner is finally over, I wash and dry the dishes, and when I turn around, she's standing right inside the entryway, just watching me.

The conflict is so clearly written all over her face. Anger worn thin by exhaustion and want and something she doesn't seem to know how to ask for yet.

I don't move.

I won't.

If she wants to close the distance, then she'll have to do it.

I've made my position clear all day, and I won't take what she doesn't freely offer.

She doesn't move from the doorway even when I turn to face her, but her arms stay firmly crossed over her chest, a defense I know is as thin as the cotton her shirt is made of.

I reach out for a dish towel to dry my hands and she doesn't stop looking at my face.

If anything, her eyes seem to get a little more unfocused, like she's imagining something she most certainly shouldn't be at the moment.

And okay, maybe I'll bite a little. I don't count it as giving in.

"What exactly is it that you want from me, baby?"

Sage doesn't waste her time with words.

"Can you please just—" she stops and lets out a frustrated sigh, and yeah, that's a good enough request, right?

"Can I what?" I ask, and I slowly step around the counter, like I'm the predator this time, and Sage is looking a little too delectable to be standing in my kitchen barefoot when I'm wearing running shoes.

"Can you just—" she starts again, but her voice is trembling a little as she sizes me up.

I'll be honest.

Maybe it shouldn't.

But a little thrill shivers down my spine when she looks me over, like I've got the answers to her questions even though she hasn't even asked them yet.

"Can I what?" I ask again, and this time, I stop just shy of her feet. She has to tip her head back to look at me. That gives a little thrill, too. Sage may be a sweet little angel, but I'm not.

I can admit I've got devious intentions when she looks up at me like that. Like a demon about to steal her virtue.

But I don't have to steal.

She wants to give it to me.

"Can I what, baby?"

"Please."

It's a single word.

But it's the white flag that I've been waiting for. A surrender on all accounts. At least for right now. The same flag I've been too stubborn to wave myself.

The last of my resistance.

Sage tastes like bliss.

Something you need to savor.

I want to devour everything in my wake. To strike a match and watch it spread, rapid and uncontrolled, eating up everything in its path.

But Sage can't be devoured.

Sage is meant to savor.

Her mouth is warm and pliant under my own, finally soothed that it's found me again.

She sighs into my hold, her tension somehow relaxing and tightening at the same time.

My hands move of their own accord, sliding up to cradle her face in my palms, to stroke her jawline with my thumbs, to keep her where I want her. The kiss is soft, achingly so, all things considered. It's a conversation that should have already happened, one neither of us seemed to be able to have with words.

I mean to keep it gentle.

Really, I do.

After everything that's happened today, I intend to keep it gentle.

But then her tongue traces the seam of my lips, a tentative, scorching touch, and something breaks open a little. Or maybe that was just my lips parting.

When they do, it's no longer just comfort. It's a rediscovery.

She isn't kissing Adrian this time.

She's fucking kissing *me,* and she *loves* it.

I can tell she does.

Every little slide of my tongue against hers makes a soft little sound escape her, something a little helpless and dizzying.

I pick her up and set her on the counter, tugging her against me, and everything feels like it's on fire.

To have her in my hands like this. To feel her against me like this. I know that I don't deserve it, but it's mine.

The way her heartbeat flutters away under my fingertips, the way she leans into me, the way she can't stay still, her hands starting to roam against my chest and stomach, and lower, lower until they're brushing over my jeans, that all belongs to me.

Sage belongs to me.

And I belong to her.

Her hips press into me, and she moans into my mouth when my cock presses against her lower stomach, separated only by a few thin layers of clothes. She can fight me all she wants, but she can't fight this. Not the way she wants me.

Her hands slide from my waist to my back, pressing into my shoulders, pulling me closer. She pushes her hips against mine like she just can't help it, a frantic, seeking motion that makes my vision tip a little sideways.

"Sage, sweetheart, let's slow down," I whisper against her lips, and she doesn't listen. Not my stubborn girl. I'm already gasping for air and all she's done is fucking kissed me.

I try to slow her hips, to keep her still, but even my hands on her hips don't make her any calmer. "I'm not going anywhere, baby, slow down," I breathe out.

But she's shaking a little in my hold, a full-body trembling that's full of frustration.

"Okay," I whisper. "Okay, baby," I relent, and the words get lost against her lips.

I don't waste any time after that. I lift her from the counter and pull her close so she can wrap her legs around my waist. Her arms tighten around my neck as I carry her out of the kitchen, through the dim living room and up the stairs.

Even with my trying very hard not to drop her in our darkened house, she doesn't care. She still tries to get closer, restless in a way that's driving me a little crazy. Her hands fumble with the hem of my shirt, tugging it despite it being stuck between us. All of her movements are uncoordinated from urgency.

I shoulder the bedroom door open and carry her straight to bed, and even then, she immediately moves to sit back up, to reach for me, to take back the little space between us.

But I reach out and gently push her back until she's lying back down, huffing like I'm making her life miserable and torturous.

"Patience, baby," I click my tongue, but I'm already planning my next moves.

Sage settles back onto the pillows; her eyes stuck on my face like she can read what I'll do next.

I climb over her, one knee on either side of her hips, and for a moment, all I can do is drink her in.

Her messy dark hair like ink on our bedsheets, her eyes focused on me, her parted lips, the rapid rise and fall of her breasts under her thin shirt.

I don't think I've ever wanted to be ruined more in my life.

This time, when I kiss her, it's slow and messy, a kiss that has her whimpering into my mouth. And fuck, it almost has me whimpering, too. Every little sound and adjustment feels like drowning.

I trail my lips over her mouth, her jaw, that sensitive spot just below her ear that has her gasping. And then lower, down the column of her throat, just to breathe her in. Over her collarbone, just to skim my fingertips over her breast.

Her hands come up to thread through my hair, holding me steady, right where she wants me, but she's not in charge this time.

She can give the control over to me for just a little bit.

My hands slide up her sides, over her ribs, my thumbs brushing the underside of her breasts. Her pulse is hammering against my hands, frantic like mine is.

It's not the first time I've touched her like this, but it's the first time she's known it's me. It's the first time since we've decided to stop playing that same old game of deceit.

Now we're both stripped bare, and there's no lies between us.

She moans when my hand drifts lower, skimming over her stomach, down to the waistband of her pants. I trace the line of it with a single finger, feeling her clench her stomach with a little arch off of the bed, a plea for me to do something.

"Please," she whispers again, the word ragged and pitiful. The last sound of her patience dissolving. "Please."

I stare down at her spread out underneath me, and God, do I wish for nothing else.

Sage is beautiful. So beautiful. Her eyes are glistening, cheeks flushed. Even her desperation is pretty.

I could never deny her. Not when she looks like this.

Not when I'm the only one in the world that gets to look at her like this.

I hook my fingers into her waistband and in one slow, smooth motion, drag both them and her panties down her legs. And then I help remove her shirt, all while she claws at my clothes to get them off.

Patience is not a virtue that my wife has practiced.

But when we're both finally bare, and I'm crawling back over her, feeling the damp warmth between her thighs, I understand the same restlessness she feels.

When I cover her with my body, lacing her lips with mine, pressing my hips down against her, she lets out a choked whimper that my mind will cling to for all of eternity.

Her head falls back, and my lips and tongue cling to that, too, working until I'm certain a mark will blossom, and she can scream at me for it later. I'll probably want her more when she does it.

But for now, I focus on the way she goes breathless when I slide my hands down her legs until I'm holding her thighs. I push them toward her chest, and she doesn't resist in the slightest.

This position is intimate, vulnerable... trusting. But she lets me do it anyway.

"Look at me, baby," I whisper, and her eyes meet mine.

There's trust there.

There is. I can see it even though it's a little thin.

But it is there.

It's the only reason I'm giving in.

The world narrows to the point where I'm not sure where I end and Sage begins.

To her, it probably just feels like pleasure.

To me, it feels like Heaven.

I could never express how blessed it feels to be inside of her. She doesn't even know how much I desire to have her. Let alone to have her like this. To feel her so intimately, to experience her just as she is, without any of the anger or fear or worry.

Just to feel her, to touch her, to know that she trusts me enough to do it.

Her eyes go wide as I push into her, lips parting on a soundless gasp. Her hands that were tight in the sheets find my back, pulling me closer like she thinks I'll leave at any moment. But I've no plans to go anywhere.

I try to give her a little grace to adjust to me.

Try being the keyword.

But it's a sweet, almost unbearable ache with how tight Sage is gripping me. It almost feels like being held hostage, except I'm right where I want to be.

"Oh... G—god, I'm—I can't—" she finally breathes out, the words trembling and ragged.

"Just breathe, baby," I whisper through clenched teeth, trying to keep my voice soothing. And it only takes her an agonizing minute to let the tension in her thighs ease, let that initial shock melt into a throbbing warmth. "There you go, Sage, just like that."

My patience spreads thin and I don't bother trying to get it back.

I withdraw, just an inch, and Sage lets out a sharp, needy sound. But then I'm pressing forward again, a little deeper this time, making her arch into me. Her fingernails dig into my back and my mouth drops open at the sharp bite of them.

Even the pain she brings me is pleasurable.

"More," she begs, tilting her hips up to meet mine. "Ellison, please, more."

Fuck it all.

Hearing her call me by my name while I'm inside of her... I'll dream about it for ages. It'll be the last thing I see when my seven seconds of life flashes in my mind during death.

I can't help but kiss her again, swallowing her please. "Slow down," I whisper against her lips, but I push deeper, grinding a little faster.

Even that can't satiate the creature clinging to me.

She still tries to take over, her hips seeking a rhythm I'm intentionally trying to withhold from her until she's ready.

I try to keep my pace, to focus, to keep my thrusts a little merciful, but her whimpers turn into full-blown moans, and her hands slide down to clutch my hips, trying to bring me deeper, closer, faster.

"I can't—I need," she chokes off her words, tears of frustration and something overwhelming making its way in.

And I don't fucking like that.

I still my hips, still buried inside of her, and suddenly it clicks.

She really is all about control.

And mine is splintering.

I take in her flushed face, her swollen, kiss-bitten lips, beautiful blue eyes glazed with a desperate look.

My cock is throbbing painfully, and still, I can stop and see what she needs.

Is that not what love is? Putting your wife's needs before your own?

My Sage needs control.

Not just the connection, not just the pleasure. She needs proof that I can match her fire.

It's about the surrender.

"Okay," I whisper, brushing the tears forming at the corner of her eyes. "Okay, baby. Take what you need from me."

In a quick, fluid motion, I roll us both over. The world spins, and suddenly Sage is the one on top, and I slip in even deeper than before.

Sage lets out a gasp, one that I'm not sure is from pain or pleasure. Her hands go flat on my chest. And my fucking eyes roll into the back of my head for a second.

I can give up control.

Absolutely.

When I open my eyes, Sage is looking down at me, her hair falling over her shoulders, like a vision, all intensity, and all overwhelmed. But I've never felt more proud in my life. My hands come up to rest on her thighs, and Sage is trembling.

"I—I don't—" she whispers, and this is something I haven't seen from her. A shy hesitation making her freeze up.

"You do," I whisper back, calm and certain. She can do this. I can help her. My hands slide up to her hips, grip firm and guiding.

"Just move with me, baby. We'll make you feel good together." My hands help lift her slightly, and then bring her back down, a slow, deep roll of my own hips helping guide me in deeper.

"Like that, baby. Just... fuck, yeah, just like that," I rasp. I sound more wrecked that she does, but I don't have it in me to feel embarrassed.

Sage follows my lead, letting me take care of her while letting her have a semblance of control. She gives a few hesitant rocks that quickly turn into something more instinctive.

Like this, the friction is different, the angle even better, a grinding pressure that was exactly what my girl needed.

And a broken little sound escapes her. *"Oh..."*

"That's it," I softly encourage, reaching up to brush my thumb over one of her nipples. Her lips part around a soft, needy noise, and I feel that same urge to devour her. But I can't. Because Sage is in charge right now.

So I keep one hand on her hip, a steadying, directional presence. "Use me, baby. Take what you need." Guiding her into a rhythm is nothing at all. She doesn't waste time once she realizes what she likes, and I'm honored she's even letting me inside of her.

"You feel... fuck, Sage, you feel so good."

I can tell that my praise is what she wants to hear. She moves in earnest after that, guiding herself while letting me keep my grip on her hips. Her head falls back, a moan tearing from her throat as she rides my cock.

The sound... God, the sound will haunt me. I can see the strain building in her thighs, the dark heat in her eyes as she falls apart on top of me.

Her movements start growing erratic with her waning strength, and I can tell she's getting frustrated again.

"I—I can't—" she pants, rhythm faltering.

Now, it's my turn.

"You can," I tell her, but I shift again, strength effortlessly taking over. I roll us both once more, and pin her beneath me, never slipping out.

Sage can act like she doesn't like me all she wants, but she falls apart the second I manhandle her, so we'll be exploring that later.

But right now, I thread my fingers through hers and press our intertwined hands into the mattress on both sides of her head.

This time when I move, it's different. It's not her frantic pace, and it's not my controlled one. This time it's deep and purposeful, for one goal only: to make us both come.

This time, I kiss her while I fuck her, and we both turn desperate for a release. There's no gentleness in this kiss, just lips and tongue and nothing but hot desire.

"This," I gasp against her lips, each breath one of her own. "This is what it's supposed to feel like," I slip my hand down between us to press on Sage's lower belly and her moans choke into high-pitched whimpering. "This is what it feels like—" my vision starts going white while my hips start turning unsteady. "—when it's *real*, Sage."

The words are both of our undoing.

Sage arches against me, a raw, aching cry pouring from her lips as she clenches around me in a relentless rhythm. I hope she isn't aware of my own choked out groan, or of the hot, sudden come filling her.

If she does, she's too nice to say anything about it.

But her nails dig into my shoulder blades, and her lips find mine, and I don't give a fuck how embarrassing I sound.

I don't dare stop grinding my hips as I kiss her, even as I do start to slow them.

But eventually, she starts whimpering because it's *too much* this time.

When I do finally pull out, it's with a calm reluctance.

Both of us are breathing heavily, but I've still got a job to do.

I pull Sage against my chest, wrapping my arms around her, and bury my hand into her hair to pull her into another kiss.

This one is slow and steady, everything I want to feel every time she kisses me.

I brush her hair from her face and tuck it behind her, and she clings to me like she's afraid I'll leave again. She's still trembling in my hold, but calmer now, tears she probably didn't remember letting out still sticking to her cheeks.

Even like this, wrecked and exhausted, she is still the most beautiful person I've ever laid eyes on.

And she's mine.

She will always be mine.

"Sage," I whisper, and her eyes tiredly open again to meet my gaze. I can feel her heartbeat pounding against mine, working to slow itself.

"You can still be angry at me tomorrow," I assure her, and she holds my eyes even though it takes all of her effort. "But I need you to know that I was being honest before," I brush my hand over her hair, and she relaxes a little more against me. "You are my priority," I whisper. "Now, and forever. And I'm not going anywhere no matter how much you push back."

Sage's eyes tear up, and I know she doesn't want me to see it.

She squeezes her eyes closed and burrows further into my hold, and I brush my hands over her hair as she takes a deep breath against my chest.

I can clean her up later when she's finally asleep. But for now, I just hold her, and I feel her trust deepening even in this moment.

Sage might not fully believe it right now, but with time, she'll see it... that I'm the only one that truly loves her as she is, that I'm the only one who sees her.

That's all it takes to fix this.

That's always all it was ever going to take.

Chapter 6

Sage

The first thought that runs through my mind when Dallas hands his certified list of potential houses over is that I want to light it on fire. It feels like a betrayal even though I know, realistically, it makes the most sense to relocate.

As frustrating as it is, Ellison is right.

I'm a moving target, and as much as I want to have a hand in every jar, I know I can't.

The folder he hands me is unassuming. Plain, with no dramatic flair. Just addresses and information I don't want to look at, and all of Dallas' notes scribbled in his sharp handwriting.

I had shoved it right off to Ellison and he had shoved it right back into my palms.

I'm not sure if that's better or worse, but we have a timeline to stay on, so I flip the first page and hope for the best.

I don't know what I expected the list of houses to look like. Something ridiculous and high class maybe. All glass and steel and grand staircases meant to impress people. Something that feels like a threat designed as luxury.

But the first house is quaint.

Something sitting in the middle of an open field, surrounded by forests and long gravel drives and places I don't want to be.

"It's too exposed," I say immediately, shoving the paper away. I wait for the pushback, but it surprisingly doesn't come.

"I figured you'd say that," Dallas hums like he was expecting it.

Ellison doesn't argue either. He leans in, reading over my shoulder, his warmth wrapping around me, and I hate that my body reacts to it before my brain does. "Too many sightlines," he shakes his head, and Dallas scribbles a big fat NO over the address.

"So you don't like it either?" I ask, and my cheek brushes against his shirt when I turn my head to look up at him. He always looks like he's seconds away from confessing his undying love to me, and I wonder when he'll finally let go of his restraint and do it.

Sometimes I think he's close, but then he tears his eyes away from me, and I see him force it back down.

It's not the right time. I know that. We're in the middle of a family war and worried about me getting sniped on a busy street in broad daylight, and I'm wondering why he won't tell me he loves me when I see it in his eyes.

Not to mention I don't know what I'd say if he did tell me.

Half of me still hates what he's done, and the other half... the other half has too much hope for something that could collapse at any second.

It's a slippery slope to be on.

And despite my best efforts, I've found it difficult not to give in at every turn.

"It's not about what I like, baby," he murmurs over my shoulder. "I like you alive, and this one doesn't help with that."

"We still have to go look at it," I mumble back, and he says okay so softly that I know he hates the idea before we even leave the house.

The car ride is loaded in a way that's been following us everywhere lately, like we're all holding our breath, waiting to see who cracks first.

Dallas drives, and Anderson follows closely behind us.

We're supposed to be making appearances today, but it's difficult for me to stay focused when I know that there's things happening behind the scenes.

Peter and Trevor are somewhere they shouldn't be, putting hands on things they shouldn't... all because I ordered them to.

My hands have been shaking all morning, knowing that they're doing something that could cost them their lives, and I'm playing house with my husband who isn't actually my husband.

My stomach has been turning with nausea, and I pray that Samuel is playing Dallas' role like he should be. Dallas said he could handle it. He promised me he could. But I know that Trevor is sometimes too careful, and Peter is sometimes too trigger-happy.

The only reason I know that things are progressing smoothly is because Dallas is as calm as usual, and he's the one with the communication feeding into his earpiece.

Ellison is calm beside me. Of course he is. He did this for a living.

He's close enough that our knees brush whenever the road curves, and when my hands start shaking too fiercely, he reaches out and brushes the back of my hand with his thumb.

It's reassuring. It should be reassuring.

And yet my hands shake all the same.

If all goes as planned today, Andrew Hart will be losing approximately two hundred pounds of coke from his port warehouse.

He's been sloppy. Somehow even more sloppy than my father. Easy access and limited security.

He's been too comfortable. Too complicit. Too stupid to see me moving things right in front of his face.

Today, he will face the first major loss in his business.

The realtor keeps talking as she shows us a house that I will never accept.

Something about square footage, about how the foundation of the house is solid, about how it's rare to find something like this so close to the water and the woods provide privacy you can't often find in the city. I nod in all the right places, smile when expected, ask about schools I have no intention of sending any future children to.

Meanwhile, two men are cutting through Andrew Hart's port operation like a scalpel through soft tissue. It was never about the money. It was about the chaos. The fall. The control, and the loss of it.

It's about cutting out the infection that is the Hart family.

Dallas' jaw tightens just slightly. Anyone else would miss it. But I don't.

His fingers flex at his sides, then settle.

That's the first tell.

Ellison feels it too. I know he does. His thumb pauses against my skin for half a second longer than necessary, a silent question he doesn't voice aloud because this isn't his war to command.

The warehouse should be quiet right now.

Midday shipments lull, just a skeleton crew and guards who are so complacent that they hardly pay attention.

Trevor is already inside by the time the realtor offers me tea that Ellison declines for us. He's wearing someone else's badge, walking like he belongs there, because that's what Trevor does. His confidence is louder than any gun could be.

Peter won't bother with that part. He'll be watching the perimeter, cataloging exits, memorizing faces, deciding who gets to live by the end of it. And if someone stumbles where they shouldn't, he'll make a choice, and he'll enjoy it just enough that I'll have to force myself not to think about it before I go to sleep tonight.

The house is beautiful, but it isn't safe. Too many tall windows. A gate that can be walked right around. All pale stone and too many open entry points.

Ellison watches me walk through each and every room, so tense I almost forget I'm supposed to be playing a role here.

He doesn't watch me like my father does. He watches me like he's trying to understand the way my mind works. Like he's trying to figure out if I have the same thoughts about each room that he does.

"We could make this work," I murmur to him while the realtor runs to the bathroom. "With enough changes."

"Do you want to make it work?" Ellison doesn't look around. He only looks at me.

"I—" I stop and swallow as I glance around the living space again. "I don't know."

"Then it's not the one," he murmurs back.

"You sure you want to encourage her level of pickiness?" Dallas raises an eyebrow.

"It's her fucking house, Dallas; she gets to be picky."

"How 'bout you suck my—"

"These large windows are truly so lovely," my voice rings out as soon as Angela briskly walks back down the hallway. "Aren't they lovely, baby?"

"You could sit right here and drink your morning coffee," he agrees in a voice that sounds nothing like him. "You know, Angela, you came with such high recommendations, we knew you'd be the perfect person to help us find our next home. And Sage really loved the options you sent us."

"Oh, gosh, Mr. Hart, thank you so much. And you, Mrs. Hart, truly, it's an honor to finally meet you. I've heard such lovely things, but we rarely get to see you out in the community."

"We will certainly have to change that," Ellison laughs in that old-money way that grates my nerves. I save that thought for later because I saw him practicing it in the mirror just yesterday, and somehow between then and now, he's perfected it.

"Yes, we would love to be more involved in the community," I cut in, nodding along eagerly, cringing over the fact that this house still smells like fresh paint. "I know our family isn't exactly welcome in some places, but we would love to change that. Our marriage has only brought us closer together, and we would love to show how we're trying to change things for our community."

"Oh, no, Mrs. Hart—"

"Please, Angela," I reach out and touch her forearm in fake solidarity. "Call me Sage."

"Sage," she blushes at the attention. It's not every day that a member of the mafia invites you to be on a first name basis. "You could always come to the gala this Friday."

"A gala?" I ask, tilting my head in contemplation. It's the first time I've heard of it.

"Of course! Didn't your fathers extend an invitation?"

"You know how they are," Ellison laughs it off. If both of our fathers will be attending some gala and hid it from us, then it's because they didn't want us there. "I'm sure it slipped their mind."

"Yes, that's understandable!" Angela's shoes clack against the tile as she crosses the room to grab her phone from the countertop.

Dallas exhales slowly through his nose. That's my second tell.

I let my hand drop from Ellison's, because if I keep squeezing it so tight, I might give it away that something is wrong. Instead, I walk through the living room, crossing over to Angela to peer at her screen.

"It's a ball, see? A masquerade type thing," she waves her hand and slides over to the next screen. "Here's my mask. I loved it at the store and knew I had to get it!"

Behind my eyes, the warehouse doors are rolling open. Forklifts are moving pallets that won't be missed until they are catastrophically, irrevocably gone.

Ninety bricks. Already clean cut, wrapped, logged, and counted.

They'll be erased like they were never there.

Andrew Hart will stand in that warehouse later, surrounded by men who won't meet his eyes, staring at an empty space where his money used to live.

He will go quiet.

And then he will get angry.

And then heads will roll while he finds a name he's been holding in his mouth for months now, tasting the bitterness, waiting for an excuse.

I step back and look at Dallas over my shoulder. He's back in his relaxed posture and I take a breath before I smile at Angela.

"Angela, if you'll email us the details, we will certainly make an appearance, and we'll be certain to let everyone know how helpful you've been with this process."

I can already see the flames engulfing Andrew's product on my back patio, the dollar signs depleting as we watch it go up in flames.

It isn't theft.

It's chaos.

And Andrew Hart is about to learn what it feels like to lose something he never imagined anyone would ever dare to take.

"Shall we go see the second house?" Angela claps her hands and I pull out of my thoughts again, nodding with matching excitement.

"Yes, please, lead the way and we'll follow."

It doesn't take long for us to finish the second tour. I hate it immediately. It's safer, yes, but it feels like a bunker pretending to be a home.

It almost makes me wonder if Angela sees a ticking clock over my head that's slowly running out of time.

I don't say that out loud, but Ellison seems to read it anyway.

He steps closer and lowers his voice and Angela drones on about the upgraded features. "I know I said it was your choice," his breath against my neck makes me shiver. "But I fucking hate this house."

"I do, too," I whisper and then tell Angela I'd love to see the third one.

The third is the last one on our list for today.

It doesn't take long to get there, and the house isn't even on the main road. Trees wrap around it like it's meant to be a secret. The gate is old and solid, lining not just the entrance but the entire property. It's the kind of place you don't stumble onto by accident.

I walk inside and can feel it before I can explain it.

"This one," I say softly, not bothering to explain myself.

Angela seems thrilled, and Ellison exhales beside me, reaching for my hand again. "Yeah," he agrees. "This one seems like a perfect fit for us."

Dallas watches us like he's seeing something settle into place, something he won't comment on yet. "You want to walk it again. Just to be sure?"

I do.

And I can see it perfectly.

I imagine the walls changing colors. The furniture in the exact position I want it. Lights changed out.

I imagine mornings here. Arguments and laughter and silence that doesn't feel threatening for once.

And I imagine me, right here in this room, existing with a family that I made myself.

Ellison trails behind me with his hands in his pockets, letting me lead through each room as I take it all in. He doesn't bother or question me.

He just lets me process it all on my own terms.

We end up in the back room where the windows look out over the trees instead of the road, where the light comes in soft and filtered, not like the glaring city lights that feel like a spotlight on all my mistakes.

I stand there, staring out at the property line, and I realize my shoulders don't feel as tight anymore.

Ellison steps up behind me, close enough that I can feel the heat of him at my back, close enough that it would be easy to lean into him if I wanted to.

Things have been... different lately.

Not different, but muddled.

Like I'm wading through so many emotions and can't decide which one to stick with.

I want him close, and yet I keep him at arm's length so I don't become dependent on him, and then I get angry because he's giving me the space that I need.

And still, he doesn't push me. He lets me go at my pace, and feel what I feel, and he doesn't demand I get over it.

I crave his touch, and when I have it, it's everything I ever wanted to feel, but I look at him sometimes, and I see the man that lied and deceived me.

Still, I know that how he has handled me is not how any other man would handle me.

Any other would put me back in my rightful place.

They wouldn't put me on a pedestal.

Not like Ellison.

Not like him.

He reaches out slowly, like he's giving me time to pull away if I need it, and he brushes my hair back behind my ear. The touch is gentle, careful, nothing like the violence I know men like him are capable of.

His fingers linger there for just a second longer than necessary, knuckles warm against my skin and I tilt my head without thinking, lifting my gaze to find his.

I've seen this look before.

Not directed at me.

But in my parents.

My father used to look at my mother like this. Like she was the object of all of his desires.

That was before the money and power went to his head. Before he forgot that I was more than a steppingstone. Before the rage settled in and he got my mother killed.

I thought it was love I was seeing, and now, I'm not so sure.

Now, I wonder if it was ever love before.

Because the light never shone quite as bright in my father's eyes as it does in Ellison's when he looks at me.

It never looked like this. Like he craves my eyes on him. Like he'd kill for it.

"Are you sure," he asks quietly, voice stripped of every performance he's worn all day, "that this is the house you want?"

I look around again, at all of the walls and the windows and the potential. It doesn't feel like a prison, or like a performance, just an empty house waiting to be filled and lived in.

"I want it," I whisper up at him, and he only nods, brushing my cheek once with his thumb.

"Then you'll have it," he tells me.

We hold each other's gaze for a moment that stretches a little too long to be appropriate, a little too intimate to still have lingering doubts about where our loyalties lie, and I wonder briefly if anyone could see us right now and if they'd understand how much is being said without either of us admitting it out loud.

Dallas clears his throat from the doorway, and I step back immediately, putting space between us even though it takes effort, and I turn to nod my head.

"We'll take this one!" I beam at Angela. "Please, if you could send the paperwork over, we'd be delighted to get started."

Angela squeals like this is the highlight of her career.

And Dallas looks at me like he knows I'm way too in over my head.

The car ride home lacks the stress from when we drove out here.

Dallas waits until we're back on the main road before he speaks, telling us that the guys were successful, that the product is secure at the warehouse.

"Good," I reply, and Ellison's hand brushes mine softly. Not holding, just touching.

"What do you want to do with it?" Dallas asks.

"Burn it."

Dallas turns his head just slightly, surprise breaking through his composure. "You sure about that, Sage?"

Ellison glances over at me, but he doesn't say a word.

"We could flip it," Dallas carefully suggests. "Recoup some of the loss. That much product isn't small money."

"Too many families have been ruined at the hands of the Hart family," I evenly respond, glancing out of the window. "We aren't here to make it worse."

I meet his eyes in the rearview mirror.

"Burn it all."

Dallas nods once, and he doesn't fight me on it because he understands. "I'll handle it personally."

"The gala," Ellison speaks up after a moment.

"I don't think it's a good idea," Dallas grimaces, turning the wheel to pull into the driveway.

"It probably isn't," I agree. "Which is exactly why we need to go. Both of our fathers will be there, angry and humiliated, expecting neither of us to be there. We were invited by Angela. Not by them. And the people there need to see how close we are. They need to see unity."

"It will probably shake Andrew and your father both to see us there. They expect us to stay hidden. Stepping out isn't something they're anticipating. But Peter, Trevor, and Samuel stay nearby."

"They will," Dallas says. "Already on it."

"Imagine it," I murmur.

"Imagine what?" Ellison tilts his head toward me.

"To see Andrew Hart's face," I say softly, "at a gala just days after he's taken a hit this big."

"I imagine it'll be full of hatred," Ellison huffs out a laugh.

"I hope it is," I reply. "I hope it hurts, and he feels what it's like to take a loss."

Ellison's hand wraps around mine, slow and careful. Our fingers intertwine, and I close my eyes and lean my head back against the seat.

I hope it hurts.

I hope it hurts everybody that ever sought to hurt me.

And while everything they love burns to the ground, I'll be there to watch it happen.

Chapter 7

Sage

The dresses are too ridiculous to feel real.

When Ellison suggested we find something to wear to the gala, I thought we'd be ordering something from one of the fancy places on the Hart payroll.

But Dallas and his traitorous new friend... my husband... teamed up on me, and now I've been dragged to every shop in town that has no ties to Andrew Hart or my father.

And finally, we broke down and called Angela, our new family friend apparently, for a favor.

We finally made it to the one she suggested, and I wonder if she's secretly in the Hart family pocket anyway, because the price tags on these dresses are absurd.

Everything in this boutique is curated to look effortless, like it simply exists this way, born immaculate and untouched by hands that had to work for it. The lighting is soft, flattering on my skin no matter what way I twist or turn, and the floors gleam so brightly that I'm half convinced they could reflect my guilt if I stood long enough.

I'm trying on frilly dresses and men died under my orders yesterday.

Dallas hid it from me until we were home, but Peter's trigger-happy fingers got the best of him once again, and two of Andrew Hart's underlings were fished out of the harbor with untraceable bullets that flew because I told them to.

Ellison looks like he belongs here.

It feels like just another distraction. And it is... distracting.

He moves through the boutique without hesitation, without that subtle stiffness people get when they're pretending to be someone they're not. He doesn't fidget or mess with the itchy fabrics or too tight shoes. He looks nothing like a man born of blood and dirt and bullets. Nothing like he spent half of his life in the military.

He looks like a Hart. Polished and primed. Calm and commanding.

And that does something sharp and unpleasant to my heart.

I won't admit it to anyone, but I prefer Ellison. I prefer him as Ellison. Not pretending to be something or someone he's not.

I want the unfiltered Ellison. The one who has that violent little look in his eyes when he's meeting Dallas' gaze. Like they're thinking alike, plotting alike, wanting to kill alike.

I drift through racks of fabric I don't intend to wear, touching silk and lace with fingers that feel too unsteady for this kind of place. I tell myself it's the stress, that the gala is looming in three days and Andrew's silence is louder than any threat he could be making toward me.

But then I catch my reflection in the mirror at the end of one aisle, and Ellison is standing behind me, close enough that we nearly overlap in the mirror.

He isn't touching me. These days I feel like he doesn't need to.

The way he watches me is intimate enough all on its own.

"Having trouble, baby?" His voice is quiet and sultry, just like the silk from the last dress I ran my fingers over. I have to swallow before

I speak because I know my voice will come out a little too affected if I don't, and I won't give him the satisfaction when he seems so effortlessly put together in a suit that looks like it was hand-made to fit his body like this.

"There's nothing here that I like," I murmur, looking him in the eyes through the mirror.

Ellison's gaze slides over my reflection once more, slow and assessing, before he steps closer. Closer enough that the air between us changes. Close enough that I stop breathing without even realizing it.

His hand settles at my hip.

Not gripping but resting in a way that somehow feels worse.

The contact almost feels scolding, like I've done something wrong without knowing what it is, and my body reacts before my mind can catch up. My breath halts, my shoulders going tense as if I should be pulling away.

But I don't.

I never do.

I lean back instead, the back of my head brushing his shoulder as my eyes stay locked on his in the mirror. I can see the faint tightening of his jaw, the way his posture shifts like he's restraining something that wants out.

It's been like this all day. Him, watching me. And me, watching back.

My hands tremble faintly at my sides.

His hand moves, gliding from my hip upward, tracing a line that makes my pulse trip over itself. It skims upwards along my jaw until his fingers gently turn my face in the reflection.

"What about that one?" He asks quietly.

His eyes drop towards a dress just out of reach on a rack I haven't gotten to yet. It's satin and midnight blue. The fabric looks like liquid even on the hanger, clinging to curves it hasn't even touched yet.

I just know it would look so good on me.

The attendant doesn't wait for me to respond. She plucks it from the rack, eyes skimming over me as she guesses my size and brings it over.

It makes my face burn as Ellison takes it from her hands.

The satin brushes my waist as he holds it up against me, the contact feeling loaded even though it was barely anything, and my breath catches again. He leans in, close enough to my ear that I feel the warmth of his words more than I hear them.

"What do you think of it?" He asks.

"I like the color," I admit, my fingers sliding over the smooth material. "I like it a lot."

"It looks good on your skin," he nods at my reflection.

"Do you like it?" I ask.

"I like you."

I swallow at his choice of wording, suddenly feeling like my mouth is incredibly dry. "Don't you mean the dress?"

He doesn't hesitate with his answer. "No. I meant you."

My gaze drops for half a second before I force myself to look back up at him in the mirror.

"It would look even better with your hair down."

"It's a masquerade gala," I remind him. "Most people will have their hair up for their mask. And a dress like this doesn't exactly fit the theme."

Ellison's mouth twitches at the edges and I just know he's about to say something stupid. "We aren't most people, baby." His eyes meet mine again in the mirror and he tilts his head to the side. "And I don't give a fuck what anyone else is wearing or not wearing. Just you." The words make my stomach flip a little, knowing he's probably considering what I'm wearing and not wearing now.

"Do you want to try it on?" He softens his voice a little, losing some of the teasing from his tone.

I look at myself in the mirror again. At my very obvious flushed cheeks. The tension in my body. The way I look like I'm about to step off of a cliff to my death.

I slowly nod my head.

And then I watch Ellison confidently tell her I'd like to try it on. Moments later, we're being ushered toward a private room.

When she gestures for me to enter alone, Ellison steps in after me without missing a beat, and the attendant's cheeks turn pink just like mine do when I see him wink at her.

When the door closes behind him, it feels like sealing my fate. The room is quiet and feels far too small for both of our presence.

"Go on," he murmurs at me. "Take your time."

Take my time?

I might seriously be sick if he keeps looking at me like this. Fuck.

I hesitate at the soft-spoken order. The heat creeps up my neck as I turn my back to him, and I feel like fleeing.

But I can't do that. God, I'd look so pathetic if I fled the man who is supposed to be my husband. I mean, he's seen me naked for Christ's sake.

He doesn't rush me at all.

But he does sit down in one of the chairs, spreading his hands over the armrests like he's settling in for a show, waiting just for me.

My heart is pounding so loud I'm convinced he can hear it in this quiet room. I just know the attendant has her ear plastered to the door, wondering if we're doing something disgusting in her very fine dressing room.

Come on, Sage. He's just your husband. Come on. Don't be a sissy.

My hands are slow to slide up to my shirt, but I finally start to undress, feeling ridiculous and exposed. The second the fabric slips from my shoulders, he shifts in his chair, jaw tightening like he's the one under pressure, fingers digging into the armrest hard enough that his knuckles start to whiten.

He doesn't look away for one second. Not while I undress or while I pull the dress on.

Finally, it slips over my head, and it feels just as good as I knew it would.

I turn back toward the mirror, adjusting the material with hands that just won't steady, and suddenly, Ellison is behind me again before I even realize he's moved.

He reaches for the zipper, eyes meeting mine in the reflection as he slowly pulls it up, his fingers brushing up my spine, over the tattoo that I know he's crazy over. The contact sends a shiver through me that I can't suppress.

"There," he murmurs, taking a very small step back. It's barely enough room to do anything, but he still adds, "Give me a little turn."

I tilt my head at him, looking at him like he's finally lost it. "Aren't you getting a bit too much satisfaction out of this?"

His lips are already forming into a smirk before I finish talking. "You're my wife. All I want to do is look at you all day. Let me live, Sage."

A quiet laugh slips through my lips, breathless despite myself.

I give him the little twirl he wants, turning slowly, the satin clinging exactly where it's meant to, and stop once I'm facing him. "Well. What do you think?"

Ellison inhales deeply, like he truly needs the extra oxygen. "I think I'd like to be the one taking that dress off of you after the gala," he says calmly, like he didn't just send my heart rate skyrocketing. "If you'd be so kind and willing."

My voice drops to a strained whisper. "You're being a bit bold today."

"I can't help it," he replies in a lower tone to match mine. "Not when you look like this."

"Are you saying I don't look beautiful when I'm not all dressed up?"

He steps forward again, crowding my space this time. His hands settle on my hips before he gently turns me back toward the mirror, pulling me flush against his chest.

I really need to get out of this dress and this dressing room or we're going to have a serious problem.

For now, I simply squeeze my thighs together to get rid of the heated feeling traveling down my body.

He lifts a hand, brushing my cheek with his thumb as he looks at us together.

"I wasn't talking about what you're wearing, baby," he says quietly. "But seeing you flushed and nervous is a good look for you."

"Shut up," I whisper, pulling away from his hold.

He only laughs at me.

"Fucking unzip me," I swat my hand toward him, and he reaches out before I can yell at him any further.

"We'll get this one," I straighten the dress out once I put it back on the hanger.

"I was hoping you'd say that."

I turn away before he sees what that does to me.

The attendant is still blushing when we step out and tell her we'll be purchasing both my dress and his suit.

The masks come next.

The one I pick out is intricate, dark and edged in silver that brings out my eyes. And he instantly picks up one to match.

I immediately don't like it.

He slips it off of his face when he sees my lips turning downward into a frown.

"You don't like it?"

I hesitate to answer, but he waits for me. He always seems to be waiting for me.

"I prefer you as yourself," I quietly tell him, watching as the attendant wraps up our garments and tallies up the thousands of dollars we're about to spend.

"I'm only myself with you, baby," he murmurs in my ear.

I have to remind myself to breathe while Ellison pays, but it doesn't matter once we're back in the car.

The silence settles in immediately, thick and suffocating, pressing in on me from the second the door slams shut.

I try to focus on the city as it passes by, blurring lights and movement that I don't pay the slightest attention to.

Ellison's hand lands on mine.

Not in an asking way or a tentative way.

That dress must have really done it for him because he never acts first. He's always waiting for me to make the first move. For me to take the action.

But now, his fingers lace through mine and hold on. I don't look at him. If I do, I'm not sure I'll be able to keep pretending that nothing has shifted.

Ever since I figured out who he really is... ever since he promised not to hide anything from me, it feels like things have started spiraling deeper and deeper. I keep telling myself it's him. That he's doing this. That something is wrong and I shouldn't.

And yet I know it's all me.

I know it's me. These are my feelings and my emotions and my spiraling.

He didn't have to do a thing.

I was already fucked the day he promised me, back when he was still playing Adrian. I was already in too deep then, when I knew he wasn't my husband but still wanted to believe he meant what he said... that he wanted to be a good husband to me and make things work.

I was never going to be able to take it back.

Now, it's only getting worse. Or maybe better. I haven't decided which one yet.

I can still feel the satin from the dress against my skin, and his hands, hot and heavy on my waist. I can still feel his eyes on me. Still hear how low his voice was as it brushed against my ear.

I try to focus on the hum of the engine. The sound of passing cars.

But every red light feels like an interruption, and every green light feels like permission to barrel headfirst into whatever is building between us.

I'm hyperaware of everything. The heat of his hand against mine, the steadiness of his breathing, the way his grip tightens every time the car starts slowing.

And by the time we pull into the driveway, my nerves are stretched so thin they feel like they'll snap.

The car rolls to a stop, and no one moves.

Dallas pulls in behind us, and he's quick to get out and come to the driver's side window.

"Anderson said everything's clear-"

"Great, Dallas, that's so wonderful," Ellison cuts him off, and Dallas furrows his brows at him, like he's not sure what the hell he's doing. "I'm about to do some inappropriate things to my wife so if you would, could you please go literally anywhere fucking else?"

"Ellison!" I exclaim, my breath catching both in shock and disbelief.

I hear Dallas' confused and disgusted voice starting up.

But Ellison's already rolling up the window, and I pray to God this window tint is as dark as I think it is, because I'm already climbing over the center console when he starts moving the seat back.

His stormy blue eyes are already on mine when he helps me climb over the console, and his hands are moving underneath me to undo his belt and his zipper.

I'd like to say I'm stronger, that I don't need any man and they're all beneath me, but... he's already beneath me, and God, he just feels so good when he's inside of me.

And this is the first time he's not waiting for me to give it to him. This is the first time he's deciding to take what he wants.

I settle into his lap, and I can already feel how hard he is through his jeans, and I swear I don't mean to make the sound that slips through my lips.

"That's it," he murmurs, hands coming up to my hips to help me. "So fucking sexy today, Sage. Doesn't matter what you do, could watch you all day."

Oh God, I'm going to pass out.

He leans in, and his lips collide with mine in a way that isn't slow or calm or longing. This kiss is hot and heavy against my lips, a continuation of a conversation we'd been silently having all day long. Just tasting him, after all this tension, makes me moan into his mouth. His tongue slips against mine, devouring and tracing like it already memorized just how I love to be kissed and taken apart.

My hands fumble for his shirt, pulling it up. I need touch. I need to feel him and to touch him like he wants to touch me. He breaks the kiss long enough to help, his breathing a quiet rasp against my lips as he pulls the fabric over his head and drops it in the passenger seat. My palms slide over his chest, over his hot skin and all of the scars and bruises that make him mine.

"You're so beautiful like this," he rasps, the words breathing against the shell of my ear. "Desperate for me just like I am for you. In our fucking driveway where anybody could see. My wife rutting against my lap."

I swear I'm not an exhibitionist, and I know the window tint means not a soul can see into this car, but the words make heat spread over my skin, and I flush from head to toe at how filthy it sounds.

His hands slide under my shirt, palms lingering over the sensitive skin just below my ribs, and then higher, finding the lace of my bra, tracing the straps before he's unhooking it with practiced ease.

And then his hands are on my breasts, the cool air of the car a sharp contrast to how searing his touch feels. His thumbs circle over my nipples, already tight and aching for touch, and my head falls back, eyes closing at the pressure of his hands.

"I know," he soothes, even though I haven't said a word. But his touch isn't soothing. It's scorching, like lava burning through everything in its path. He lowers his head and takes one of my nipples into his mouth, and I know we aren't making it out of this car until we've both gotten exactly what we want.

The wet heat of his tongue, the gentle sucking, his hands on my body, I can't take it. I grind down against him, the rough texture of his jeans providing a delicious, frustrating friction that only serves to make me more desperate. I can feel the dampness seeping through my panties, and his voice against my ear, whispering sweet nothings, is only making it worse.

But he doesn't care. He switches to my other breast, lavishing it with the same attention, his teeth grazing just enough to make my entire body jolt.

"Please, Ellison," I hear myself whisper, the word ragged and desperate sounding.

He pulls back, his eyes dark and wild looking just like I feel. With one hand, he reaches down to push his pants and boxers just low enough to free his cock, and I swear my mouth starts watering when it pushes full and thick and flushed against his stomach.

"These," he whispers against my mouth, his fingers hooking into my waistband. "Have got to fucking go." He pushes my pants and panties down in one rough shove, and then he's guiding himself to my entrance, the broad head pushing against me soft and dizzying.

My hands grip at his shoulders, my nails biting into his skin, and still, he grips my chin and pulls me forward into a filthy, sinful kiss.

I don't think I've ever been kissed like this. Like he won't live if he can't taste me. Like my lips are a gateway blocking the entrance to Heaven. That's how he kisses me.

"Look at me, baby," he commands, his voice low against my lips.

I force my eyes open, my icy blues surely drowning in the storm of his. He holds my gaze, a deep, possessive connection that I can't force myself to break, and then he's guiding my hips a little closer.

And then he's filling me.

One slow, delicious inch. Then another. A stretching, burning fullness that felt like pure perfection. A choked cry tears from my throat as I take him all in, an overwhelming fullness that felt right.

Perfect. It feels so right. So right, no matter how wrong anyone ever tries to tell me it should be.

I won't believe it.

Because nothing wrong could ever feel like this.

"Fuuuuuuck, Sage," he groans, his forehead dropping onto my collarbone. "So good, baby. So—"

"Perfect," I rasp, finishing the sentence for him. He lets me adjust only for the next two heartbeats, and then his hands tighten on my hips.

"Take what you want, baby. Come on. Use me."

God, I love when he says that.

I begin to move, tentative at first, a shallow testing rise and fall. But the angle is intense, each descent driving him impossibly deep. And then a rhythm finds us, urgent and so good. The only sounds are our ragged breathing and the sound of our bodies meeting, the creak of the car taking our weight.

And the entire time, he watches me, his eyes devouring every semblance of pleasure on my face.

"Just like that. There you go, baby, just like that. You're so perfect, Sage. So perfect. So—fuck—so fucking good. You deserve everything you desire, baby. I'm going to give it to you—"

His words are like gasoline hitting fire. I move faster, riding him like my life depends on it. And my body coils tighter and tighter. His grip on my hips turns directive, helping me lift and fall, controlling the pace, the depth. He's orchestrating my pleasure and finding his own just by making me feel it.

"I'm... Ellison, I'm gonna..."

"Do it. Come on my cock, baby."

It's the permission I didn't know I needed.

The world shatters into a frantic explosion. My back arches, my whole body shaking as I clench around him in hard little pulses. The pleasure feels intoxicating, a tidal wave pulling me further into him.

And through the haze of it all, I feel his control slip with me. A groan pours from his lips as he fucks up into me a few more desperate times before I feel the hot, sudden rush of his release inside me.

It feels like ages as we sit there together, tangled and sweaty and breathless. I keep my face buried in his neck, breathing him in, clinging to his body.

And finally, he shifts and leans me back so he can lean over and reach into the glove compartment, pulling out a packet of tissues.

With a tenderness that contrasts violently with the frantic passion from just a few seconds before, he cleans between my legs, dabbing gently to clean the mess up from my inner thighs.

Our clothes are a wreck, and I almost laugh at it.

We just spent thousands of dollars on two outfits, and yet, ruin the ones we already had before we even get home.

"Okay," he whispers, lips brushing against my temple. "Okay, love."

He's never called me that. Even though I feel it when he touches me.

"I'll clean us up better when we get inside," he murmurs. He helps me back over the console, a little wobbly and more than exhausted. I barely notice as he fixes his own clothes, and then he gets out and comes around to open my door.

He lifts me into his arms as if I weigh nothing, cradling me against his chest. He carries me up the paved drive, through the front door of our massive house.

I barely hear Dallas' exasperated, "Finally!" as Ellison carries me up the staircase and into our bedroom.

The bathroom is warm before I even register how we got there.

The mirrors are already fogging over, softening it and making it comfortable.

Ellison sets me down on the edge of the tub like I'm fragile, like he might break me if he's not careful, and I don't have the energy to argue with him about it.

Nor do I want to, since he just fucked me literally into contented silence.

My limbs all feel heavy, loose in a way that comes from too much adrenaline burning off all at once. I let him undress me without comment, his hands slow and sweet, brushing my skin carefully like he's trying his best to keep me pliant without bothering me.

This isn't about taking anything from me like before.

It's about keeping me.

When he helps me into the bath, the heat sinks into my bones immediately, easing my entire body. I sigh before I can stop myself, sinking down further until the water laps at my chin.

Ellison steps in behind me a moment later, until he's fully settled with his long legs bracketing my hips, solid and immovable at my back.

Safe.

That word keeps circling my thoughts whether I want it to or not.

I don't remember a time I ever felt truly safe in the presence of a man. Not one that's known me intimately.

I've always been a pawn. A means to an end. A distraction.

Never has a man made me feel safe or wanted. Never has a man made me feel like he was here just for me.

Never anyone before Ellison.

He reaches for the shampoo, working it between his palms, and then his hands are in my hair, massaging gently at my scalp as he works the day out of me strand by strand. I close my eyes without thinking, my head tipping back just enough to rest against his shoulder.

"You don't have to be so tense," he murmurs against my temple.

"I don't know how not to be," I admit quietly.

His fingers pause for half a second, then continue their steady path over my skin. "I know, baby."

He rinses my hair with a small cup I keep on the edge of the tub, careful not to let water splash into my eyes, his palm firm at my forehead. When he's done, he presses a soft kiss to my head.

His hands move to my shoulders next, thumbs rubbing at muscles I didn't even know were screaming until it starts to give under his touch. I feel myself leaning my full weight back, settling fully against his chest.

"You've been carrying too much alone," he says finally.

I let out a humorless huff. "That's kind of my thing."

"I know," his voice is gentle, but there's something frustrated underneath it. "I don't like it, though."

"Then you know what you have to do," I say it partly as a joke, but the underlying fear that he will up and leave me still sits just under my skin.

"Stick around to annoy you for the rest of our existence?" He teases back, voice full of mirth all of a sudden.

"So, you do know then?" I laugh quietly, shaking against him.

"Of course, baby. Not like I had any other plans anyway," he brushes his lips over my temple and leaves them there, and we both breathe together for a few minutes, just relishing in the quiet comfort of holding each other.

"I don't trust Andrew," I say eventually, leaning back against him to rest my head against his chin. "Not after what we did. I feel like he'll be on guard at the gala."

"I don't either," Ellison admits. "That's why I want you to stay close. I don't want him to get any ideas. Even if he does point fingers at your father, he might target you in revenge."

"How close do you want me?" I murmur, tilting my head just enough to look at him.

"Where I can see you," he tells me, looking down at me with nothing but affection in his eyes. "Where I can touch you. Where no one gets near you without going through me first."

"That sounds ambitious," I whisper, and his lips twitch at the corners in the hint of a smile.

"Ambition's my middle name, sweetheart," he deadpans.

"Wait a minute," I mutter. "What actually is your middle name? You never told me," I point out.

"It's stupid," he mutters back, and I tilt to really look at him, squinting.

"Is it Carl?" He snorts and tips his head back against the edge of the tub. "Oh, God, is it something redneck like Buck or Rifle?"

"Give me a break, baby," he laughs, and his eyes light up with something that looks dangerously close to love.

"I mean, you are from Texas, so it's like... not that far-fetched to think," I defend myself, but I laugh too. "I can see it now. Ellison Buckshot Gray."

"Jesus," he laughs, leaning back up to kiss me like it's so silly that he has no choice but to. "It's Grant," he finally tells me. And oh, that's not so bad.

"Not so bad?" He chuckles.

"Oops," I sheepishly smile at him. "I didn't mean to say that out loud. Ellison Grant Gray," I murmur it out loud, testing the words on my tongue. "I think I like it."

"You think?" He smiles at me. "It's not as pretty as your name, but it'll do."

"My middle name is-"

"Selene," he cuts me off, and I can only look at him in surprise. It should probably freak me out that he knows undeniably more about me than I do about him, but for some reason it doesn't. "Sage Selene Ledger," he continues. "I know, baby."

It should feel suffocating.

But it doesn't.

Instead, I lean back against him and rest my weight against his chest again. My fingers wrap around his forearm where it rests against my stomach.

"I like your last name better. If it matters," I whisper.

The words feel like a confession. I'm not sure if he takes them that way, but perhaps that's the way I mean them.

At least here, in his arms where I feel safe, I can say it. I can admit it. Even if I say it with words that don't name what I feel.

He exhales against my hair, and I know he feels what I feel.

"Everything you feel matters," he quietly says. "It may not have been my name you took at the altar, but maybe we can renew our vows on our anniversary," he softly suggests. "Do it the way we would have wanted."

"I would love that," I whisper back.

The bathwater laps quietly at the sides of the tub as he holds me there, warm and safe, until the tension in my chest finally, mercifully loosens.

For the first time since everything started moving too fast to keep up with, since the day my father told me he was putting me in a position I could never escape from, I let myself breathe.

Maybe this fate that was chosen for me will be the one that settles my heart.

And maybe one day, I will be able to say the words I really mean.

And maybe Ellison will say it back.

Chapter 8

Ellison

The mask is the easiest part.

It's a simple thing, light in my hand, expensive in a way that is evident from the material alone. When I lift it to my face, I can almost pretend this is what I was built for. Adrian Hart. The heir. The sloppy one. The one who belongs in rooms like this, where it smells like alcohol, perfume, money, and sins that people pretend are respectable.

I could play this role in my sleep.

That's the problem, isn't it?

Because the second Sage steps out of the bedroom and I see her in that midnight satin, I forget every single plan I practiced in my head, every line I intended to deliver, every angle I meant to cover, every smile I meant to weaponize, and my brain does something primitive and useless.

It goes quiet, it goes hot, and it goes feral.

If I were the real Adrian Hart, I could probably look right past her. Past all the glitz and glamor. Past her dazzling, addictive blue crystal gaze, and her long dark hair. Past her hips and the pissed off way she still glares at me.

I could probably do it.

But I'm Ellison fucking Gray, and nothing in me can look past this woman.

She looks like something that shouldn't exist in the same world as Adrian Hart.

A sin someone would kill for. And the worst part is that I know they will. The same way I know how to disassemble a gun in the dark, the way I know how fast a throat will bleed when it's cut right.

I could kill for her.

I would.

I know I will.

It's only a matter of time.

I stand in front of the mirror in my new fancy suit and mask, and try to be the man they expect to see, but my eyes keep sliding over to her reflection instead, to the way the satin clings to her hips like it was made with her body in mind, to the way the silver at the edge of her mask pulls the coldest blue out of her eyes and turns it into something sharp enough to draw blood.

I fucking love it when she looks at me like that. The thrill I get from it is indescribable.

Sage looks at herself like she is assessing a weapon.

And I look at her because I already know she is one.

"You ready?" I ask, and my voice is steady, a manufactured calm because my hands want to touch her so badly it borders on pain.

She shifts her gaze to me through the mirror and the corner of her mouth twitches, not quite into a smile, but a sort of twisted satisfaction.

She knows how bad I want it.

Just two days ago, I had her dripping all over me in the front seat of the car. It was delicious and messy, and so fucking good.

And it was also worth the smug satisfaction I felt when I jingled the keys in front of Dallas' face and told him to take the car to get it detailed.

"You look like you belong in a museum. But for like... rich people to dazzle at."

"Is that an insult?" I snort, stepping closer, slow and careful, because Sage is still Sage even after everything. She can be soft with me in private and still razor sharp with her words.

As much as they sometimes cut me, I don't want her to withhold it from me.

I ache for it, the authentic version of her. The one that doesn't pull her punches and shows me just how hurt she still is, no matter how tightly she tries to keep it contained.

"It's an observation," she points out, and then, like she can't help herself, she looks me over from head to toe and adds, "You sure do look more like him when you dress like this. It's a little unnerving," she shudders.

I let out a quiet huff of laughter and slide my hand to the small of her back, palm warm against the bare skin there. "I might look like him, but we both know I'm nothing like him, baby."

Her posture stills for just a second, like it always does when I point out that I'm not Adrian. But then she exhales, and I feel it in the way her shoulders relax against me.

I feel it in the way she leans back slightly, propping her weight against me, knowing I'm immovable.

Sometimes I wonder if she's testing me, to see if I'll hold solid while she uses me in whatever way she needs to.

Sometimes I wonder if she even realizes that she's doing it.

She might notice, but I do.

I notice everything about her. And this is one of those things that makes me understand her just a little bit more.

Sage is independent because she had no choice to be. She's angry because everyone who has looked her in the eyes and told her they'd support her was a liar. She's scared, because she expects me to let her fall just like everyone else, to abandon her when she needs me most.

And I'll never do that.

I skim my hand over her stomach and Sage tilts her head slightly, letting her long dark hair cascade over her shoulder.

She's beautiful. Ethereal. Alluring in so many ways.

I just wish she could see herself the same way that I do.

For a moment, I simply hold her like this. A solid presence against her back, not moving or pushing or coaxing her in any way. Just letting her feel me beside her, knowing I've no plans to move or falter.

Dallas finally appears in the doorway like a bad omen, dressed in black, an earpiece already in. His expression is dull in a way that tells me he's already thinking twelve moves ahead and about to overwhelm Sage with all of them. Anderson, Sage's shadow, follows behind him. I still don't know how I feel about him just yet, but at least Dallas is tolerable.

He glances between us once, and something almost like satisfaction flickers over his eyes before he strangles it. "Car's ready."

Sage doesn't look at either of them. She keeps her gaze on me in the mirror.

"Ready?" I ask softly, and she nods once. "Remember the plan?"

"Angela first," she nods sharply.

"Angela first," I echo. "We're not seeking them out. We aren't hunting them down. If they find us, they find us, but we stick to our plan."

Her lips part like she wants to argue that she is the one calling the shots, and then she seems to remember that she already did decide that.

"Right," she murmurs.

I keep my hand on her back all the way down the stairs. Not because she needs help walking, not because she's fragile, not because I'm trying to put on a show, though it will read that way to every pair of eyes that sees us tonight.

I keep my hand there because I do not trust a single person in this city.

Not Andrew Hart.

Not Ian Ledger.

Not the allies they parade around like loyal dogs.

Not the staff.

Not even the fucking valet parkers.

I could trust enemy soldiers more than I could trust these people. At least in war, we have some sense of understanding of each other.

Here, there are no morals. They kill because they're snakes. All they know is how to feed until there's nothing left to bite on.

My paranoia isn't a personality trait. It's a survival mechanism from being in the field.

And tonight, I'm going to listen to it.

The drive to the gala is short and loaded.

Sage stares out the window like she's memorizing the route for future escape.

Dallas' gaze keeps catching mine in the rearview mirror, a constant silent understanding.

Sage is the priority here.

Anderson follows close behind, another vehicle, another set of eyes, another line of defense on top of the others that I already know are waiting at the venue to keep her safe.

We pull up and it looks like something out of a television show meant to distract people from the fact that all of these people are monsters and leeches.

A private estate dressed in lights and flowers and soft music, a line of luxury cars, men in suits that cost more than most people's houses, women glittering like expensive bait.

The second the door opens, the noise hits.

The loud obnoxious laughter, the clinking glasses, the sound of power changing hands, unbeknownst to everyone twirling around dancing.

And underneath it all, the thing that always lives in the background of events like these.

Predation.

I step out first, because that's what Adrian would do, because that's what a husband does when he knows his wife is being watched, and because I want to be between Sage and the world the moment she steps out of this car.

I offer my hand, and Sage takes it without hesitation.

Her gloved fingers lace through mine, and her grip is firm and confident, like she is reminding anyone who might be watching that she is not some silly little girl playing dress up.

Sage is a grown woman who commands presence.

Angela spots us near the entrance and nearly trips over her own heels rushing over, face alight with the kind of excitement people get when they think they've brushed shoulders with danger and lived to tell the story.

"Sage," she breathes like she can't believe we actually showed up, and then her eyes land on me and she does that little blink people do when they realize the man they pictured in their head is not the one standing in front of them. "Mr. Hart! You clean up so well!"

Sage laughs it off, but what Angela really means is that I don't look like the demon she expected to show their face at this kind of event.

"Angela," I greet her smoothly, warmth coming easy and effortless. I keep my voice pitched just like Adrian's, because if there's one thing I can do, it's turn charm into a weapon. I hold my hand out to grasp hers, and she flushes when she takes it. "I believe you promised us introductions. Should we take some pictures for the benefit?"

"Yes," Sage smiles easily, reaching out to pat Angela's arm. "We were so happy to get your email with the invitations and thank you so much for extending extra for our security. We would love to take some photographs with you."

Angela laughs, flustered and delighted at Sage's enthusiasm. "Yes! Yes, of course! I told everyone you'd come. They didn't believe me!"

Sage leans into my side, just enough to be felt, and I take that cue to play it. I let my fingers brush the back of her hand, stroking slow and possessive over her knuckles, and I watch Angela's eyes flick to it, and then rapidly away, like she just realized she's intruding on something intimate.

"Oh, and Angela," Sage leans in like it's a private conversation. "We had no idea you were heading the event until we received your invitations! I hope you don't mind, but Adrian and I wanted to support you since you were just so helpful with the house hunting. We prepared a donation for your event."

"Oh!" Angela exclaims, and a few people turn their heads to see what the excitement is. "Oh, Mrs. Hart!"

"Please, call me Sage," Sage reminds her, and Angela flushes again.

I knew Sage was more than capable of making it through this event but seeing her in action is truly astonishing. She's a natural, fitting in so effortlessly that it's hard to remember she grew up in this lifestyle, surrounded by these monsters.

"Sage!" Angela beams at her. "Oh, please, you didn't have to!"

"We wanted to support our new friend, Angela, and we hope this is the beginning of a long term partnership between us."

"Of course, Sage," Angela sputters. "I'd love that. Oh, please, let me have the honor of introducing you guys to the floor! I have a speech at the end, but I'd love to showcase your donation and generosity during my speech if you'd allow it."

Sage's eyes cut to mine for a quick, panicked second, and I nod my head just once, giving a silent agreement.

This isn't part of the plan at all, but it'll be a slap in the face to both Andrew and Ian to see Sage thriving like this.

I know Dallas is listening in, and I scan the room in search of him.

When our eyes finally meet, he dips his head once, too, in agreement with our decision. He glances to his right, and I cut my eyes in that direction, seeing what must be one of his men leaning against a pillar with an untouched glass of wine in his hands.

"We'd love to, Angela. It would be our honor."

We walk with Angela through the crowd, and I can feel eyes tracking us immediately, like we just tossed a lit match into a room full of gasoline.

People look at Sage like she is a myth they finally get to see in person. And people look at me like they can't believe there isn't a glass of alcohol in my hand and a slur in my speech.

Their faces say it before their mouths do.

This is not the Adrian Hart that Andrew described.

The first couple that Angela brings us to are older, the kind of wealthy that has calcified into something entitled and permanent. The man's handshake is too tight, like he's testing me, and I take it in stride, keeping mine just as firm. The woman's eyes flutter over Sage like she's not quite believing what she's seeing.

"Sage Ledger Hart," the woman says, voice dripping with admiration that feels like envy in disguise. "My goodness. You're stunning just like your mother."

I can tell the mention of Sage's mother trips her up slightly, and I see the tremor in her hand that she shakes out just inches before her hand lands against the woman's own. She smiles, polite and razor-edged. "Thank you so much. My mother was beautiful."

"And you, dear! And you!" She reaffirms, and Sage smiles through it all, lips full and sweet and poisonous with every word.

I don't wait for the next compliment. I step in like it's instinct, like it's the truth because it is.

"Yes, Sage is the most beautiful woman in every room." The woman laughs, and her eyebrows lift like she's a little astonished like I'm not crediting her as well.

Sage's fingers tighten around mine, and I know she's smiling over at me, trying not to let it show that my compliment affected her. But I feel it anyway. I feel the tension in her. I feel the heat that flares underneath her composure.

"That's very sweet of you," the woman says. "You two are quite the cute couple," she points out, and my anger flares a little.

"Thank you," I give a practiced smile. "My wife dresses me in these fancy clothes, but I know I'm not on her level," I chuckle. "What can a man do?" I turn my head toward Sage like I can't help myself, like I'm doomed to her, like she's gravity and I've been falling since the second I saw her.

Sage's eyes brighten behind her mask, and she looks away with a breathless little laugh.

"Forgive me, but wasn't your marriage an arrangement between your fathers?" The man finally speaks up again, and I can see him questioning us. He must know one of our fathers.

"Well, yes," Sage laughs. I'm surprised she's answering, because I was about to lay it on extra thick. "We had a bit of a rocky start, but it's nothing a bottle of wine and a good screaming match couldn't fix," she teases, reaching up to brush my shoulder with her hand, leaning her face against me for a moment.

"One of my last bottles," I laugh, too. "She just had to put me on the straight and narrow."

"Oh?" The woman exclaims. "You don't drink?"

"Oh, no," I wave it off with a laugh. "I enjoy a glass of wine with Sage every once in a while, but only at home."

"That's right," the man points out, and his tone tells me he's about to try to undermine me. I can tell he thinks he's about to try to drag me down. "I believe your father mentioned you had a bit of a substance problem."

"Mr. Crenshaw!" Angela's voice is ten different shades of scandalized.

"Ah, no it's okay, Angela," I wave her off good-naturedly. "My father likes to exaggerate every once in a while," I chuckle. "I did have a little party phase in my early twenties, but what college boy doesn't?"

"And have you put all of that behind you?" Mr. Crenshaw points a cigar at me, reaching into his inner coat pocket to retrieve a lighter.

"I have," I assure him. "I think you'll find I've become a bit of a homebody."

"Not working then?" He throws a cheap shot.

I laugh, but Sage does, too. "Wherever would you get that idea?" She asks, rubbing my shoulder like it's truly humorous. "I guess that's our fault since we've been so private since the wedding."

"Well, when my wife looks like this it's only a given that I'd like to stay home to enjoy her company," I smile at her, ignoring the others in our circle.

"Stop, baby," she blushes on cue, and it's so natural, even I believe it. I can only smile as I turn my attention back to them.

"Sage and I wanted to venture into our own sector of business along side the... family business," I delicately say.

"Business? Of what kind?" This seems to genuinely surprise the man, and he gives us his full attention now, genuinely curious.

"We're in private security," Sage effortlessly slides in, and I move my hand to her lower back, skimming my fingers to encourage her. "We provide security for dozens of businesses and families in the community, as well as personal bodyguards for events and meetings. We specialize in military grade protection details and are contracted with many different local businesses."

"Local?" He echoes absently, glancing over at his wife. "We were not aware that the Hart family was involved in the community."

"Oh no," I thin my lips, dropping my voice slightly. "This is a personal business decision that my wife and I are involved in. We made the joint decision to get involved with our community."

"Does your father know of this business?"

"I'm not sure, sir." The prick seems impressed that I address him as sir, like he's earned the respect. "I like to keep my business affairs separate from our families. To help further our own success. You understand, of course. Angela mentioned you and Mrs. Crenshaw built your business from the ground up, and now you're one of the most influential tech companies in the United States. Sage and I are starting at the bottom, but men and women like you are proof it's possible."

Sage smirks slightly beside me, and I know she's thinking the exact same thing that I am.

Mr. Crenshaw likes praise just as much as my wife does.

He's practically eating it out of my hand.

I watch him dig into his coat pocket and flip open a metal case. He fishes a business card out and slides it over to me between two fingers. I pluck it from his grasp and pull my own designer wallet out, slipping it between the folds.

"It's not often you see young entrepreneurs making business decisions apart from their family's support. Perhaps we should set up a meeting," he suggests, finally lighting his cigar. "Send me an email. We can discuss potential partnerships in the future, so long as your family is... separate from your business."

"I assure you, Mr. Crenshaw," I hold my hand out to shake his in another firm grasp. "My wife is the brains behind the operation," I glance at Sage. "But we have very strong beliefs and have no plans to involve either family in our business. I'd love to hear about potential partnerships, and I look forward to your response to my email."

Mr. Crenshaw steps away after giving us one more parting goodbye, and Angela turns to gush about how Mr. Crenshaw is impossible to get meetings with, and how everyone was watching us.

I hear Dallas crack a low dig in my earpiece about me being cornier than the real Adrian, and I use my middle finger to brush my hair slightly, hearing him laugh in my ear.

Angela moves us through countless introductions.

All of them go similarly to the first. Sage and I both collect so many business cards that my wallet starts to overfill, and then we're having to stack them in Sage's clutch.

Every single time we meet someone new, the comments border on the same.

How different I seem. How I'm not what they expected. How my 'father' tells everyone I'm still recovering... and he doesn't mean from my military injury.

He's painted Adrian to be a shitfaced alcoholic, incapable of even speaking properly from this liquor eroding his brain.

And well, he isn't necessarily entirely wrong, but his own fucking son? That's harsh.

I laugh along with every little dig, like my father's lies are harmless and amusing. Like it doesn't make me want to put my fist through a wall.

It'll take careful relationships to undo the bullshit Andrew's crafted.

"My father has an iron grip on the family," I say with a grin that reads playful to anyone who doesn't understand what disrespect sounds like when delivered politely. "He doesn't like competition, so it's only natural I'm the bad guy."

Their eyes all glitter.

I'm competition. His own son. His flesh and blood.

A few of them chuckle like it's a solid joke.

A few of them glance subtly towards the edges of the room, where Andrew Hart is likely watching. I know they hear the insult under the humor.

Sage has been glancing around often, and I know she feels uncomfortable.

She's wondering just like I am why this all seems so easy.

We're both wondering why we haven't been approached yet. We haven't so much as seen Andrew or Ian since we arrived, but we know they're here.

One man leans in as if we're old friends and claps me on the shoulder. "So, tell me, Adrian. Are you interested in stepping into the family business?"

I feel it, the instant calculation, the tension, the question of whether I will overplay my hand and give away secrets.

I don't.

"I'm interested in understanding it," I say, keeping my answer clean. "I'm interested in getting my hands on it personally. I don't like being out of the loop or relying on secondhand information."

"That's refreshing," the man nods like he's impressed.

"It's practical," I shrug. "Sage and I are enjoying our own business right now, learning the ropes and keeping it close to the chest. Protection is a good business to be in. Plus, I have my own family to protect, as well. Family is most important, isn't it?"

I slide my hand to Sage's waist and draw her closer, and she leans into me, smiling up at me like a lovesick young girl seeing first love for the first time. I watch the man's gaze shift to my hand and then back to my eyes. His expression shifts subtly to respect and understanding.

This relationship is not about ownership.

It's about unity.

The most dangerous thing in the room is a man willing to do whatever it takes to protect his family.

It only takes a second, but the man pulls a card from his pocket. "Here. Call me some time this week. I'd like to talk business."

He doesn't offer it to anyone else standing around. He offers it to me.

I take it without hesitation and hand it over to my wife. She looks it over quickly before she tucks it into her clutch, teasing about how it's becoming heavy to carry.

Suddenly, Angela checks her watch, her excitement bubbling over in a way that borders on frantic.

"Oh," she says, clapping her hands together. "That's my cue! I have to go up on stage."

She glances between Sage and me and straightens out her clothes. "Stay right here!"

Before either of us can respond, she's already weaving through the crowd, heels clicking with purpose as she ascends the short set of steps up to the stage.

The soft music fades, replaced by the polite hush that ripples through the room as people turn their attention forward.

My hand tightens at Sage's waist, just slightly to remind her that I'm here.

Angela grips the microphone, beaming as the spotlight catches her mask. "Good evening, everyone," she begins warmly. "Thank you all so much for coming out tonight and for your continued support of our community."

Applause follows, practiced and polite, and I feel Sage lean into my hold.

"This fundraiser means more than I can express," she continues. "Every dollar raised tonight will go directly toward supporting local businesses in our district. The shops, services, and families that make this place what it is."

She encourages more applause, and then she glances over at us.

"And before we continue," Angela adds, her smile growing wider, "I'd like to recognize a very special contribution."

My spine straightens instinctively, and I feel it before it happens. Sage straightens too, and suddenly Angela is gesturing over to us.

"There are some people in this room who exemplify exactly what this event is about," she says. "Generosity. Growth. Community. And I would like to invite Adrian and Sage Hart to join me on stage."

The room turns toward us all at once. Sage's breath catches and I feel it against my chest. We knew it was coming, but still, it's nerve-wracking to have all eyes in the room on us.

I lean in just enough for her to hear me. "I've got you," I murmur. "Look at me."

She nods, and I take her hand to lead us to the stage.

The walk to the stage feels longer than it should, every step measured, every eye burning into us like a spotlight of its own. I help Sage up the steps, my hand firm at her back, acutely aware of how exposed she must feel right now.

Angela practically vibrates when we reach her.

"Everyone," she says, gesturing to us proudly, "Adrian and Sage have made an incredibly generous donation of one hundred thousand dollars to tonight's fundraiser."

The applause is immediate and surprised, echoing throughout the room and accompanied by whispers.

I keep my expression warm and appreciative, even as a dark, private satisfaction builds.

If only they knew.

"These two," Angela gushes, "are newly married, building their life together, and already making such a meaningful impact on our community. Supporting small businesses. Investing locally. Striving to bring people together."

She turns to Sage with shining eyes. "You are both an inspiration."

I step forward, taking the microphone with a practiced smile.

"Thank you," I begin, letting my voice carry. "Truly. Supporting Angela and this fundraiser was an easy decision for us."

I glance at Sage, letting the affection show. "Angela recently helped us find our ideal home. We're preparing to move into it now, and having someone local, someone who understands the heart of this community, made all the difference."

Murmurs ripple through the crowd. I can only imagine Andrew's face right now, wondering how the hell we managed to get into something as big as house buying without being on his radar.

"That kind of dedication," I continue, "should be the standard." I shift slightly, angling myself toward Sage. "And I couldn't have done any of this without my gorgeous wife. My better half. My solid ground."

Sage's eyes meet mine, bright and relieved to have me next to her during this time. I can see it, how she feels more at ease with me here.

"She's my heart," I say simply. "And without her, none of this would be possible."

The applause swells again, warmer this time. Sage steps forward smoothly, accepting the microphone with a poised smile.

"When my husband was in the military," she says, voice steady, "I spent a lot of time feeling lonely. Searching for comfort. For belonging."

The room quiets, leaning in, hanging off of her every word just like I do. We didn't plan for this speech, so every word is new to me, too.

"There's nothing more comforting," she continues, "than knowing you can lean on your community. That you're making a positive impact where it matters."

She turns slightly toward Angela. "Angela has been so gracious, a lifesaver, and the best realtor we've spoken to. Supporting her was the easiest decision we could have made."

Angela looks like she might cry. A flare for the dramatics, that one. But at least she's been the most genuine person we've spoken to tonight.

"We found our perfect home because of her," Sage says, "and we hope that one day, our family, our future children, will feel the same sense of belonging that we feel here tonight."

The mention of future children makes my heart burn a little bit, knowing that could very well eventually be a possibility, if Sage lets me stick around for that long.

I never thought children would be in my future.

I always thought I'd meet my death in some barren desert far from here, with bullets flying overhead, wondering when the dirt started feeling cold.

But Sage makes me hope for things I shouldn't.

The applause after she finishes speaking is immediate and over-whelming.

Sage reaches for my hand and I take it, bowing my head slightly as the noise washes over us. She brushes Angela's shoulder in quiet thanks before handing back the microphone.

We step off the stage together.

The moment we disappear back into the crowd, the air shifts.

The warmth fades.

The noise dulls.

And that bad omen we thought of earlier arrives like the plague.

Andrew Hart stands in front of us, his smile tight and unreadable, eyes burning beneath his mask.

And just behind him, Ian Ledger watches, patient and calculating.

The hunt is over.

Now the real game begins.

Chapter 9

Ellison

A ndrew Hart steps up, close enough that I can smell the cologne and alcohol in equal measure. "Adrian," he says warmly, like we're one big happy family. "Sage."

"Father," I greet, just as polite, perfectly controlled.

He glances around like everyone else in the room is an inconvenience, then back to us. "I don't recall extending an invite."

Sage's fingers tighten around mine, and I feel her anger rising like it's my own.

I step half a pace forward, not to block her, but positioning myself in a way that forces Andrew's attention on me. "Just because you didn't invite us doesn't mean we weren't invited," I smile at him. "Angela was kind enough to extend an invitation."

"You must be mistaken," Andrew says, still smiling, but the threat underneath it is thick. "These events are... selective."

"Any yet," I reply lightly, "here we are."

Sage steps forward, right beside me, standing on equal footing. "We won't take much of your time," she says, tone sweet enough that I can taste the poison on it. "We're just making rounds. Being involved in our community."

Andrew's eyes narrow slightly behind his mask. "Of course you are," he grits out between clenched teeth. "You and your little projects," his voice drops lower.

I glance around and notice the small crowd, but Andrew doesn't see it. He doesn't realize people can see how unhinged he looks, threatening the woman who just gave such a kind donation and sweet speech.

Andrew leans forward, like he means to say something in Sage's face, and I step to the side, directly in front of her.

"Father," I clear my throat. "Perhaps you've had too much to drink," I say, and I hear a few gasps from the crowd around us.

It does exactly what it needs to do.

It paints Andrew as the drunkard, and me, as the man protecting my wife from my father's anger.

Andrew whirls around and storms up to Sage's father, drawing even more attention.

"You put that fucking daughter of yours on a leash! Do you understand me? Do it now or I'll put one on her and I'll do it my way!"

He knocks into Ian Ledger's shoulder, and many of the guests look appalled at his words.

I start to guide Sage away with my hand on her waist, my grip firm enough to reassure her and remind Andrew that he does not move us.

We walk, and my pulse is steady, but the anger inside me is a living thing, clawing at my chest. If I had my pistol and fewer witnesses, I'd blow his fucking brains out and make sure he bleeds out before the ambulance arrives.

How *dare* he.

How dare he act like he decides where Sage exists.

How dare he think he can put her on a leash.

And her father. That piece of shit stands here and says nothing.

Her turns toward us and stares for a second before he starts to approach.

That look isn't pride.

It's anger.

Sage doesn't flinch, at least not outwardly, but I feel the change in her. The way her spine goes rigid, the way her breath goes shallow, the way her hand tightens in mine like she's bracing for impact.

She's scared of this man. Of her own father.

Ian stops in front of us, eyes burning through his mask as if the thin layer of fabric isn't enough to hide the rage underneath.

"Sage," he addresses her, not me. "What are you doing?"

Sage's smile is beautiful but deadly, even though she's scared. I don't think I could be any more proud. "Attending a gala, Dad. Making rounds. Doing some good."

"Don't you play these goddamn games with me," Ian snaps quietly, but it's just loud enough for those nearby to hear. "You were not invited."

"Yes, I was," Sage says, and she tilts her head, eyes pointing toward Angela as if to remind him that she has allies in places he can't control. "You make friends when you're friendly. Funny how that works."

Ian's eyes narrow further, and he steps forward, his voice absolutely menacing. "You are humiliating your family, Blue."

I feel Sage stiffen this time, and the look on her face tells me she's genuinely upset at his little nickname. And the look on Ian's face tells me he used it on purpose.

"Which one?" Sage's expression goes cold. "The family that sold me? Or the family that bought me?"

A hush ripples around us.

People lean in without pretending not to.

This is prime entertainment for them.

This is blood in the water.

Ian's nostrils flare. "Watch your mouth!"

Sage's voice stays calm, but it's laced with something dangerous. I'll admit it's nice not to be on the receiving end of it.

"You're the one who told me to keep control, *Dad.* And I am. I'm in control of myself and my marriage, and you are only angry because you aren't."

Ian's face goes red, and he takes a step forward.

But I take a step forward with him.

The entire room goes silent.

Even the fucking music seems to dull.

I feel Sage's hand wrapping around my sleeve, and I'm not sure if it's a warning or comfort.

"Adrian," he says it like it hurts to say my name. "Is this what you want? A wife who disrespects her own father?"

I smile slightly, and I wonder if he can see the bloodlust in my eyes or if I just imagine the tinge of fear in his.

"What I want," I take another step forward. "Is my wife to be safe and respected. And if you can't manage that, then you should probably stop speaking."

"You forget yourself," Ian's jaw clenches so hard I can see his veins straining.

"No," I reply, voice soft and acidic. "Let me make myself quite clear." Sage grips tighter on my sleeve, but her other hand settles against the middle of my back.

"You and my father may have started this union, but Sage is my wife. Both on paper and in union. You made sure of that," I grit my teeth. "If you think I'll stand by while you try to intimidate that woman I love, then you are mistaken. I suggest, for the sake of what is left of your relationship with your daughter, that you learn how to mind your business and your tongue, lest someone cut it off entirely," I quietly tell him.

Ian is in quiet disbelief, his eyes glaring at me for a long moment before moving to Sage over my shoulder. "This is your fault," he hisses at her. "You're going to get yourself killed. You want to get in bed with a Hart, then you'll have to lie in it when it comes back to bite you."

"You're right, Dad," Sage's voice trembles just a little, but I know she can handle it. I know she can. She's strong enough to. "I have been in bed with a Hart. He is my husband," Sage squeezes my forearm. "And I love him. And I want you to stay away from our family."

Ian looks like he might lunge, but my heart is racing, and I might be sick, because Sage just said she loves me.

I'm not sure if it was just for show or not, but it doesn't matter. She said it, either way. And my brain will cling to it for all of eternity.

I lean in and let my tone drop into something intimate, meant only for him, even though those closest will hear.

"You try to put a leash on my wife, and I'll cut your fucking hands off," I murmur.

And then I take a solid step back, keeping my eyes on Ian as I reach for Sage's hand. "Let's go, baby."

A few people nearby inhale sharply, and the whispers start immediately.

Adrian Hart just threatened Ian Ledger.

And Adrian Hart just defended his wife publicly.

She moves behind me instantly, clinging to my hand as I lead her out of the crowded gala room and out toward the parking lot.

"You ungrateful little—"

"Careful," I call over my shoulder, and this time my smile is gone. "You're at a gala, Ian. There are rules tonight. Even for you."

Ian stares at me for a long, furious moment, then he turns sharply away like he can't stand to look at us anymore without doing something that would cost him.

He disappears back into the crowd, stiff-backed and humiliated.

Sage's breath shudders out behind me, and I squeeze her hand. She swallows and whispers that she's fine, and I don't believe her.

We make another round to bid our goodbyes, and we wish Angela well, promising to call her. We smile and charm all over again.

But the gala is over the moment Ian's rage flashes in my peripheral vision again.

It's over the moment Andrew's eyes find Sage from across the room and his stare holds too long.

It's over the moment my instincts start screaming that we have overstayed.

I lean down close to Sage's ear, my lips brushing the edge of her mask as I speak. "We're leaving."

Sage doesn't argue this time. She nods once, and the ease of her agreement tells me she's exhausted too, even if she won't admit it.

Dallas appears at our side as if summoned by my thought, eyes scanning, posture tight. "Car's ready."

"Good," I say. My hand finds Sage's lower back again, guiding her toward the car, and I keep my head on a swivel while still forcing my posture relaxed. The performance does not stop just because we stepped outside.

This is the most dangerous part.

The walk. The in-between.

The moment where a man can do something stupid and disappear into the dark before anyone can react.

Sage is halfway to the car when I see it.

A vehicle rolling too fast down the lane.

A little too controlled.

A little too straight.

Not a drunk driver. Not a mistake.

A decision.

My blood turns to ice.

"Sage," I snap, and I yank her back hard enough that her heels skid, hard enough that she stumbles into my chest.

The car swerves. Its bumper clips the space where her body was going to be.

A sick, violent whoosh of air follows, and Sage's sharp intake of breath tells me she's scared.

It's an attempted hit. A near miss.

Enough to get my blood boiling and for me to see red.

Dallas moves so fast it's almost unreal. His gun is already up, already aimed, and the crack of the shot splits the night.

The tire blows and the vehicle jerks.

The car fishtails and slams into the edge of the drive with a clash of metal that makes Sage gasp against my chest.

Anderson is there too, coming in from the side, weapon drawn, moving with that brutal efficiency that says he's done this before, and he will do it again.

Sage's hands clutch at my suit jacket, fingers shaking, and I can feel her heart pounding.

I can feel her fear.

And the rage that rises in me is so fast and so violent I can taste it.

I want to kill.

I want to tear.

I want to drag whoever is inside that vehicle out by their hair and make a point so loud the whole city hears it.

How dare they.

How dare they try to touch her.

I jerk forward, and Dallas catches my shoulder with a hard grip. "Adrian," he barks, and the authority in his voice is not a request, it's an order. "Get her in the car. Now."

"That piece of shit tried to hit her! He tried to–" My voice comes out low, shaking and out of control. I've never been so angry in my life. "He fucking tried to hit her."

"I know," Dallas snaps, eyes wild, weapon still trained on the wrecked vehicle. I've seen that look before. I've worn it. He's just as angry as I am. Just as shocked that they'd try this with so many people around. "And we need him alive."

Alive.

The word draws me up short.

Sage makes a small sound, the kind of sound that breaks my heart, and it's what pulls my focus back at her. Not Dallas' grip. Not Anderson's stance. Not the douchebag in the wrecked car.

Sage.

She's pale, and her eyes are wide. She is trying so hard not to fall apart in public, and I've got to keep it together for her sake.

I take her face into my palms, forcing her to look at me. "You're okay," I say, trying to keep my voice from shaking. "You're okay. You're breathing. Look at me, baby. You're okay."

Her lips part, but no words come out. I can see she wants to be brave, but can't find it fast enough.

I lean forward and press my forehead to hers, just for a moment, just to settle myself, and then I guide her toward our car with a hand on her back, steadying her like I'm holding a weapon that might go off, except the weapon is me.

Dallas and Anderson move in on the crashed vehicle, and shouting follows. A door yanks open, and I hear a sickening thud, the sound a body meeting pavement, and Dallas' voice is low and vicious.

I don't look back. I keep Sage moving.

Because if I look back, I won't stop myself.

I won't be the man who escorts his wife home.

I will be the man who makes an example in the driveway.

And Sage doesn't need me to be that man tonight.

We get into the car. Sage's hands are still shaking when I pull her seatbelt across her, my fingers fumbling once because my own hands are not steady either, not with the rage under my skin.

It only takes a few moments, but Dallas appears at the window, eyes angry, but his expression softens by a fraction when he looks at Sage.

"Anderson's taking him. Here," he hands the keys over, and then he's gone again.

I start the car, and my hand grips the wheel so tight it aches.

My other one holds Sage's like I'm a perfect angel trying not to taint her.

We're halfway home before she finally speaks.

"Did they just... did they just try to kill me?"

I should lie to her. I should.

But I promised I wouldn't.

"Yeah, baby. They did," I clench my teeth as I say it, and I feel her look over at me.

"How did you even—" her breath catches. "How did you even see them coming? I didn't—" she shakes her head, swallowing through the words clogging up her throat. "I didn't even see them coming," she whispers miserably.

"You're my priority, Sage," I tell her, and I know she knows I mean it.

"You looked like... you looked like you were going to kill someone," she whispers again.

"I was," I keep my eyes on the road when I say it.

I want to tell her that man will be dead in the morning. I want to tell her I'll burn the world down before I let her be hurt. I want to tell her I love her.

But I don't.

Not yet.

"I'm sorry," she whispers so quietly I barely catch it.

"No, baby," I shake my head no. "Don't apologize. You did so good tonight. So so good, and I'm so proud of you. You were perfect."

"But I made them angry," she whispers, and her hands come up to hold her face. "I should have just kept my mouth shut."

"That was the point, sweetheart. We were meant to shake things up a little bit. This just shows that they're more affected than we thought they were. Don't think about it, okay? You did nothing wrong. We can talk about it more tomorrow."

We get home and the house is too quiet. Too big. Too empty.

I force myself not to slam doors and to keep my steps light. I won't show Sage the same anger she saw from her father growing up.

I'm not like these fucking cowards who pay people to do their bidding.

And I don't take my anger out on the people I love.

So I lock the doors.

I check the cameras.

I move through rooms like I'm hunting something.

Sage trails behind me for a minute, then she sinks onto the edge of the couch and takes a deep breath. I kneel in front of her and take her hands, rubbing my thumbs over her knuckles until I feel the shaking start to fade.

"It's fine," I tell her, voice low and steady. "Everything is fine. We're home. You're safe."

Her eyes search mine, and I see so badly that she wants to trust me. "Are you sure?"

"Yeah, baby, I'm sure," I say, and the lie is clean because I need it to be.

Inside, I am anything but fine.

Inside, my rage is a living animal clawing at my ribs.

Inside, I am seeing her body under the headlights, the near impact, the sound of that car cutting through the dark.

Inside, I am already imagining what I would do to the man who tried it.

What I *will* do to the person who tried it and the person who ordered it.

Sage leans forward slowly and rests her forehead against my shoulder, just for a second, a quiet collapse she won't call one.

She leans on me, because she knows she can trust me. Because I'm the one who keeps her safe. Because I'm the one who loves her.

My hands move automatically, one sliding to the back of her head, the other wrapping around her waist, holding her like she might slip away if I don't.

"I'm okay," she whispers, but her voice says she's trying to convince herself.

"I know," I whisper back, and I press a kiss to her hair because I can't stop myself. "I know, baby."

She pulls back and forces a small smile like she's regaining control. "We should get ready for bed."

"Yes," I agree. I help her stand. I walk her upstairs. I close the bedroom door.

I tell her again, steady and calm, "Everything is fine."

And when she finally turns away, when she finally steps into the bathroom to wash the night off, I stand in the quiet and let the mask crack just enough for my anger to breathe.

Now it's my hands that are shaking.

I stare at the closed door and try to force myself to stay still.

I listen to the sound of running water, to the faint clink of glass as she moves things around on the counter, to the steady proof that she is alive and breathing and untouched.

Only then do I let myself move.

My hands tremble as I flex my fingers once, twice, forcing the adrenaline down, forcing my body to remember restraint. The mirror over the dresser reflects a man I recognize all too well.

I inhale slowly, then exhale long and even.

Because she needs me calm. She needs me steady. She needs the man who walked her out of that gala with his head high and his voice even, not the one who wants to tear the city apart brick by brick.

Someone tried to take her from me.

Someone looked at my wife and decided she was expendable.

My jaw tightens.

I don't pace. I don't rage. I don't break a single thing in this room.

I wait.

Because I can wait.

And whoever thought tonight was the end of this conversation is going to learn just how patient I can be.

Chapter 10

Sage

The first thing I notice when I wake up is silence.

Not the normal kind either. Not the kind that comes from early morning sun and a house that smells like breakfast and coffee. But the kind that feels suffocating and empty. Like the house is holding its breath.

Like something happened in the night and the walls decided not to tell me.

My hand reaches across the sheets before I'm even fully awake, fingers searching for warmth, for skin, for the solid weight that I always find waiting for me before I even open my eyes.

And there's nothing.

The bed is cold on his side, and my chest tightens so fast it almost makes me nauseous.

I sit up slowly, hair falling into my face, body still heavy with the exhaustion from last night, from the adrenaline, from the way I was shaking in his arms in the driveway while he told me I was safe, and everything was okay.

It was a lie.

Not a malicious one, maybe, but a lie all the same.

I can feel it now.

The house is too quiet.

I push the blanket off slowly and step onto the floor, my feet cold against the tile. For a moment I just stand there and listen, hoping and praying to hear Ellison cooking downstairs, for any evidence I should stay calm. To find the threat before it finds me. To read the silence screaming back at me.

There's nothing.

No running water. No drawers sliding. No footsteps up the stairs.

I pull one of Ellison's shirts over my head without thinking. Not because I need it, but because it smells like him and I need something to keep me calm before my mind spirals into places it shouldn't... just like the last time it did when I woke up alone.

I leave the bedroom and move down the hallway, eyes turning toward every corner and doorway out of habit, and when I reach the staircase, I expect to hear something, anything.

And there is something.

A low sound, muffled like a dull thud, distant enough I can pretend I'm imagining it if I want to.

My stomach twists as I make my way down the stairs. The entire first floor feels like it's been wiped clean, like someone pressed reset on the night and left me in the aftermath.

And then I see him.

Anderson is in my kitchen, like a fixture at my countertop. Like he belongs right there next to the salt and pepper shakers.

He's reading the newspaper, sipping coffee that wasn't made in my machine.

His posture is relaxed in that terrifying way men like him can be when they're armed and unbothered. He looks up when I step into the room, eyes sliding over me with quick, professional assessment.

He's dressed, clean, and calm, and not at my door where he's usually standing guard when he's not trailing me somewhere.

Like last night didn't happen.

Like I didn't almost die on a driveway under some idiot's headlights.

"Ma'am," he greets me.

I stop at the edge of the kitchen, staring at him like he's the only thing in the room that makes sense and also the only thing in the room that shouldn't be here.

"Where's my husband?" My voice comes out rough and wrecked by sleep and a kind of fear I've never felt before. "Where's Ellison?"

Anderson takes a slow sip of his coffee, and my heart constricts in my chest.

"He's downstairs, ma'am."

I have to blink a few times before I can open my mouth again, because that doesn't make any sense at all.

We don't have a downstairs. I've seen the drafts for this house. There's no basement on them.

"What do you mean downstairs?"

Anderson sets his coffee cup down carefully, like he's choosing his next words carefully.

"In the basement, ma'am."

"We don't have a basement," I whisper.

I stare at him, and I realize something that makes my blood run cold.

Andrew Hart picked this house out. He picked this house out and knows all of its secrets because he planned them. Of course, there's hidden spots that I haven't found.

I didn't know.

I didn't know my own house had a lower level.

Because he didn't want me to.

I didn't know there was an entire space beneath me that I have never stepped foot in, and the fact that I am only learning about it now, on a morning when the house is too quiet and Ellison is missing from my bed, makes something violent and furious rise up under my skin.

"Okay, so take me there," I order.

Anderson's gaze holds mine and he takes a breath like he's steadying himself. "I'm afraid I can't, ma'am."

The words are respectful, but they're a refusal, and I might shoot Anderson in my quiet kitchen.

"And why not?" My hands are shaking again.

"I was instructed not to."

A laugh pours out of me, humorless and close to hysterical.

"Instructed," I repeat, like it's the funniest thing I've ever heard. Like it isn't making my pulse pound behind my fucking eyelids. "And who instructed you to keep me out?"

Anderson's eyes don't waver. "Your husband, ma'am."

My vision narrows, and suddenly I can hear my heartbeat in my ears. The kitchen feels too bright. Too clean. Too sterile.

My... husband.

Not my father. Not Andrew. Not Dallas. Not some outside threat. My husband.

The man who has been in my bed, in my space, in my body, in my life, slowly inching closer every day like he's becoming something I can't cut out without bleeding to death.

He instructed my staff, my guard, my household... to hide something from me.

I take one slow step toward Anderson.

"You don't answer to my husband," I say, voice low and dangerous. "You answer to me."

Anderson's jaw tightens just slightly, and for the first time since I've known him, something like discomfort clouds his expression. "I understand, ma'am."

He doesn't move. He doesn't stand or act like my words are an order to get the hell up and take me to the basement.

"No," I say it sharper and even more pissed off. "I really don't think you do."

"I've been instructed to keep you here," he says instead.

Keep me here.

Like I'm a child.

Like I'm a liability.

Like I'm a thing to be placed somewhere safe while the men go and handle the ugly part.

My stomach turns, and suddenly that muffled sound I heard earlier crawls back into my head, and I know. I know exactly what they're doing down there without anyone having to tell me.

Because last night someone attempted to kill me. And Dallas said we need him alive.

I stare at Anderson and really try to keep my voice steady even though my chest feels too tight. "Take me to the basement."

Anderson stands slowly. "I can't do that," he repeats softly, and something in his tone shifts, like he doesn't want to fight me, but he will if I force it.

I take another step forward, close enough that the kitchen island is all that separates us, and I lean in, lowering my voice.

His eyes shift toward the hallway.

"Listen to me," I say, each word clipped and livid. "I do not get kept anywhere. Not by you. Not by Ellison. Not by anyone. If you want to remain employed by me, you will take me to the basement."

Anderson holds my gaze for a long minute, and then he simply sits back down, as if my words mean nothing.

A hot, ugly pang of betrayal hits my throat, and before Anderson can say another word, before the tears can build in my eyes, I leave the kitchen without looking back.

I act like I'm going back upstairs, but instead, I follow the line of the hallway, looking from floor to ceiling, like the doorway might jump out at me.

Until I finally reach the wall panel that looks like decoration and nothing more. The moment my fingers touch it, I feel the seam.

I push, and it gives.

The panel shifts, opening into a narrow stairwell that descends into darkness.

And somewhere below me, I hear something again.

Not words.

Not my husband.

But something that makes my stomach turn acidic. A low strained exhale. A chair scraping desperately against the ground.

Something heavy striking something else.

I freeze, because the part of me that is still human wants to go back upstairs and pretend I never found this.

But I've never been good at pretending.

Each step down feels colder than the last.

The air changes as I descend, damp and thick. And my heartbeat is pitter-pattering away in my chest.

The stairwell ends at a steel door.

Of course it does.

I push it open, and it's surprisingly light considering it's meant to keep people out.

The room is larger than I expected. All concrete flooring and walls. A drain is in the center like someone planned for a mess.

And in the middle of it all, is a man.

He's strapped to a chair, head slumped forward, face swollen so badly I couldn't tell you what he looked like before. His hands are bound, wrists raw and bleeding. He's breathing somehow, but it's labored and shaking.

We need him alive.

Dallas' words echo in the back of my mind. I turn my head and look at Dallas. He's standing off to the side, sleeves rolled up, his expression unreadable. There's blood on his hands, both old and new.

And Ellison is closer.

Too close.

He's crouched in front of the man, forearm resting on his knee, head tilted slightly as if he's having a casual conversation in a bar instead of interrogating someone in the basement that he's nearly beaten to death.

His suit is gone. He's in a plain black shirt, sleeves pushed up, forearms marked with faint smears that make my stomach roll.

He doesn't look at me immediately.

Not because he doesn't hear me.

Because he does.

I know he does. The second I stepped foot into the room, I knew he felt me.

He turns his head slowly, and the moment his eyes meet mine, something that looks awfully close to fear ghosts over his face.

Not of me.

But of what this could do to me.

"Sage," he says, voice low and strained. He looks like he hasn't slept for a single second, and I wonder how long my bed had been empty while I fitfully laid there alone.

Dallas straightens immediately, eyes narrowing before he turns to me, and for the first time since I've known him, he looks uncomfortable.

My gaze stays on Ellison.

I don't look at the man bleeding in the chair again.

I don't look at the metal supplies on the table.

I don't look at anything else.

I look at Ellison, because I'm about to lose my mind.

"What is this?" I whisper, because my voice will crack if I speak any louder.

Ellison stands slowly. Carefully. He takes one step toward me, palms open at his sides like he's trying to show me he's not a threat.

That almost makes me laugh.

"You shouldn't be down here," is all he says.

My hands shake, and I hate it. I hate that my body is doing it, that my nerves are frayed enough to betray me in front of him, in front of Dallas, in front of a stranger who tried to kill me.

"I shouldn't be down here," I repeat, voice rising. "I shouldn't."

Ellison's jaw tightens.

"Sage," he says again, this time softer.

"Do you even hear yourself?" I snap, the anger finally breaking through my shock. "Do you hear what the fuck you're saying? *You shouldn't be down here.* Like I'm a child! Like I'm something you put upstairs and keep in a pretty room while you do whatever the hell this is!"

Ellison takes another step toward me, and I take one back.

His eyes trail down, just briefly, to my bare feet, to his clothes clinging to my body, to the fact that I came down here in a state that makes me look more vulnerable than I ever let anyone else see me.

It makes his expression soften.

And that makes me even angrier.

"Don't!" I hiss, and he stops where he was trying to take another step closer.

"I'm not trying to control you, Sage," he says softly.

"You instructed my own protection detail," I yell, voice trembling. "You instructed Anderson to keep me upstairs. You instructed my staff like I'm not the one who owns them, like I'm not the one who pays them, like I'm not the one who decides what happens in my own house."

"Sage," he says again, and there's an edge to it now, more weight behind my name. "He did what I asked because I was trying to protect you."

Protect.

The word is a match to gasoline.

"Protect me?" I spit the words out. "From what, Ellison? From the truth? From what you are? From what this life is? You think I don't know? You think I haven't lived it for nearly thirty years?"

His eyes flash with guilt.

"I know you have," his voice is strained. "I know you can handle it." Dallas shifts slightly, like he's bracing for worse, but Ellison doesn't look at anyone but me. "But you do not need to see this," Ellison says. "You do not need to stand in this room and watch this go down."

I nearly can't even swallow with how tight my throat feels.

There it is. The line. The one he drew without asking me.

"You decided that for me," I whisper, and Ellison's face shifts to frustration.

"I decided it," he says, voice still calm, still trying, still holding the reins even though it's slipping, "because you were shaking in my arms last night. Because you could barely breathe. Because you were trying so hard not to fall apart, and I was trying to keep it together for the both of us."

"I didn't fall apart!" I hiss, tears burning behind my eyes. "I didn't break, and I wouldn't! I won't! I'm not weak!"

"I didn't say you were weak," his voice etches a little higher.

"You treated me like it," my voice cracks. "You treated me like I'm someone that needs to be protected from reality! Like I'm not living in it every single day."

Ellison inhales, slow and deep, like he's trying to keep himself steady.

"Sage," he says quietly. "I am not your father."

That makes me want to scream.

It makes my chest burn.

"I know you're not," I whisper, voice trembling. "But you're doing the same thing. You're making decisions and moving people and commanding my house. You're putting me in a place where I don't get to see, don't get to know, don't get to have my hands on it, all because you think you know better."

Ellison's jaw clenches. He looks at me like he wants to say a hundred things, and he's trying to choose the softest one.

"I was trying to spare you," he says.

I laugh, but it's broken and bitter.

"Spare me," I whisper. "From what? Your violence? From the fact that I'm married to a man who tortures people in my basement and leaves me alone in bed after someone tried to kill me last night?"

Ellison flinches at that.

Dallas clears his throat quietly from the side, like he's reminding us he exists, like he's trying to give Ellison a chance to step back and get himself under control.

But Ellison keeps his eyes locked on mine.

"I didn't want you to see it," he says, voice rougher now, "because it's not for you."

"And I didn't want you to decide that," I shoot back, louder now, anger ripping through me. "Do you understand what it feels like? To wake up alone. To come downstairs and find my house has parts I didn't know existed. To have my guard tell me he's been instructed to keep me upstairs!"

Ellison's nostrils flare.

"I know what it feels like to wake up and think somebody is after you," he says sharply. "I know what it feels like to realize you were one inch from dying, and I don't want you to deal with that."

"I *was* one inch from dying last night," I spit.

"And I watched it happen," he snaps back.

The room goes still.

Even the man in the chair seems to stop breathing for a second.

Ellison's chest rises and falls heavy.

He is trying so hard not to become something else in front of me.

I can see the restraint cracking.

And I can see the rage trying to keep contained.

"Ellison," I say, quieter now, because something in his expression warns me that the next thing he says might hurt.

He takes one step toward me, and this time I don't step back.

"You said you would not hide things from me, and yet you're doing it right now," I whisper. "You promised me you wouldn't, and you did it at the first chance you had."

"Sage," he says, and his voice is shaking now, the control fraying at the edges. "I have been calm, and I have been patient. I have let you lead and I let you bite and claw and push and pull and test me, and I have held steady because I know you need to know that I won't leave, but you—"

"No, you still lied to—"

Ellison's gaze flickers, pain flashing across it so fast it almost looks like anger.

And then he breaks.

"God damn it, Sage, don't you get that I'm in love with you?" He nearly yells it.

It almost feels like I've been shot.

For a second, I am nothing but shock and heat and something dangerously close to grief because everyone who has ever told me they loved me has left shortly thereafter.

Ellison's chest is heaving.

His eyes are wide, like he didn't mean to say it, like it slipped out of him and now he can't put it back.

He looks furious with himself.

He looks terrified.

He looks wrecked.

"I—" he starts, and his voice breaks. "I—damn it, Sage."

He drags a hand through his hair, breathing hard like he just ran a mile, like the admission weighed more than any fight he's ever been in.

"Don't you get it?" He asks again, quieter, broken with the words.

My throat feels so tight I can barely speak. I swallow, and it burns. My voice comes out strained. "Get what?" I whisper, and my eyes sting, and I hate that I'm this close to tears, hate that he can see it, hate that I can't stop it. "Get what, Ellison?"

"I love you," he whispers. "Sage, I am in love with you."

My chest aches so hard it feels like something inside me is splitting.

Ellison takes a step closer, careful again, like he's scared I'll run.

"I love you," he repeats, voice trembling just like mine. "And I'm trying to keep you alive. I'm trying to keep you safe. I'm not trying to step over you to do that."

He glances over his shoulder for half a second, toward the man in the chair, toward the reality of what he did this morning, and his jaw clenches.

"I spent my morning beating this man nearly to death, and I don't regret it. I could continue, and I wouldn't feel an ounce of shame if he died under my hands," he admits quietly. "And forgive me if I didn't want you to see it."

My stomach twists.

Ellison looks back at me, and there's no apology in his eyes for what he is.

"I'd do it again," he continues. "I'd do it again and again and again if it meant you stayed breathing. If it meant you stayed in my bed sleeping. If it meant I could still argue with you just like this."

My lips part, but no sound comes out.

I stand there like I'm frozen, like my body doesn't know what to do with the words, with the love, with the fact that he just confessed something I've been circling around.

Ellison takes another step closer, and I can't move.

His voice drops, gentler now, but still trembling.

"Baby, I'm not trying to cage you," he says. "I'm not trying to keep you in the dark, and I don't want to hide anything from you. But I don't want you to see this shit when you don't have to. I don't want you to get your hands dirty if you don't have to. I don't want you to hear things you don't have to. I want you to sleep upstairs, and I can tell you about it while you drink your coffee and eat your breakfast."

My eyes burn, and finally, a tear slips down my cheek before I can stop it.

I hate it.

I hate that I'm crying.

I hate that he's the one who can do this to me, who can crack me open.

Ellison's expression shifts, softening so fast it almost hurts to look at.

He reaches up slowly, like I'm the one who hurt his feelings, and he brushes the tears away with his thumb.

"Baby," he whispers, and my breath shudders. I shake my head once, not trusting myself to say anything.

"If it means that much to you, then I'll tell you exactly what I'm doing, and where I'm doing it, but I don't want you to see any of this," he tells me. "You're right. I lied, and I hid something from you, and for that, I'm sorry. I told you I'd be a good husband, and I meant it, and clearly I'm fucking it up right now, but I promise my intentions toward you were good."

"You can't just—you can't just say you love me and then treat me like I don't get a say and a choice," my voice shakes. "You can just *do* that. And you can't just l—leave me in bed and leave me wondering where you are and have f—fucking *Anderson* of all people to give me vague answers about where you are and why he can't tell me. You can't do that."

"I was wrong," he says softly, brushing more of my tears away. "I should have told you and I'm sorry. I just—" he exhales, long and frustrated.

"I saw you in front of that car, Sage," he whispers, and there's a tremor in his voice that makes my stomach ache. "And something in me wanted to do unspeakable things. I can't. Sage, I can't do that again.

I can't watch you almost die. I want you out of this bullshit. As much as you can be out of it, I want you out of it. And, yeah, I should have just—I should have just fucking talked to you and trusted you, but I just wanted to deal with it myself."

My hands shake, and I want to reach for him just as much as I still want to scream at him, and yet I can't do either.

"What did he say?" I whisper, glancing at the man in the chair without fully looking at him. "Did he say who sent him?"

Dallas shifts at the side, eyes sliding over to Ellison, and Ellison's jaw clenches tight.

Something dark shadows over his face, and I know.

I know before he says it.

Because the universe is cruel like that.

Because it's never the enemy you expect.

"He hasn't said it yet." He takes a deep breath. "Not exactly. But he indicated that it's your father."

I feel violently close to throwing up, but I shove it all down and nod my head.

"Anderson," I say suddenly, looking toward the door behind me as if Anderson might appear like a ghost again. "He was told to keep me upstairs."

Ellison's gaze holds mine. "Yes," he says quietly.

"By you," I whisper.

"Yes."

The anger flares again, but it's weaker now, tangled up with grief and that raw, impossible confession hanging in the air between us.

"You love me," I whisper, like I have to taste it again to believe it.

Ellison's eyes don't move. "Yes," he says. "I do."

My throat tightens and I press a hand to my chest like I can hold myself together physically.

"And you tortured a man this morning," I whisper.

Ellison's jaw clenches. "I did," he says.

"And you'd do it again," I say, voice shaking wildly. I don't know why I'm repeating it all back like a checklist, but I need to make sure I have it all down before my next decisions.

"Yes," he says, and the certainty in his voice is terrifying.

My eyes burn.

"Then stop lying to me about it," I whisper. "Stop deciding what I can handle. Stop keeping parts of my life behind locked doors and calling it protection."

Ellison nods again, slow this time. "I will," he says, voice rough. "I will. I swear I will, Sage."

My hands tremble and I nod along.

And then, because I'm me, because I don't know how to accept something soft without testing it, without biting it, without making sure it's real, I whisper the thing that has been clawing at me since I woke up alone.

"You left me," I say, because for some reason, that's the worst part of this entire thing. "You left me in bed."

Ellison's face shifts, pain flashing across it. "I didn't mean to," he says quickly. "I didn't. I just—" he exhales. "I couldn't sleep," he admits, voice quiet. "I couldn't close my eyes because every time I did, I saw the car. I saw you. I saw you and just—" he trails off.

"And Dallas," I whisper. Ellison's eyes flick briefly toward Dallas.

"He needed me," Ellison says. "We needed to figure out who did it. We needed to make sure it doesn't happen again."

"And you didn't think I needed you?" I whisper.

Ellison looks like I stabbed him.

"I did," he says hoarsely. "I did. I just thought—I thought if you woke up and I wasn't there, you'd be angry. But you'd be safe. And I can handle you angry at me, but I can't handle you dead."

My eyes burn.

I hate that he's trying to protect me.

I hate that I want it.

I hate that I want him.

I swallow hard and take one shaky step closer to him.

Ellison doesn't move.

He waits.

Like he always does.

I lift my hand and press it against his chest, right over his heart, because I need to feel if it's just like mine.

His heart is pounding.

Just like mine.

"I'm not weak," I whisper.

"I know," he says instantly.

"I'm not fragile," I whisper.

"I know," he repeats, and his voice breaks a little.

"And I don't want to be kept upstairs," I whisper, voice trembling. "Ever again."

Ellison nods once.

"You won't be," he says.

My breath shakes.

I blink hard, trying not to cry, trying to hold myself together, because I can't fall apart in a basement with a man bleeding in a chair behind my husband and a bodyguard upstairs taking orders like I'm not the one who signs his checks.

But then Ellison's thumb brushes the side of my face again, and his voice drops into something softer, something so intimate it almost hurts.

"I love you," he whispers again, like he can't stop himself. "I'm sorry I yelled it. I'm sorry it came out like that. But it's true. I didn't say it on the fly to keep you from getting angry. You can be as angry as you want, and I'm still not going anywhere."

My lips part but I don't know what to say.

Because half of me wants to spit venom and remind him of what he did to me, of the lie, of the role, of the deception, of the way my life has been a chessboard, and he walked in and made me believe I had control.

And the other half...

The other half wants to collapse into him and let him hold me until I stop shaking.

"I'm really upset with you," I whisper, and he nods his head rapidly, like he's expecting it. "And I won't forgive you if you lie to me again," he brushes his thumb over my cheek again. "And I won't forgive you if I wake up alone again," I whisper.

"I know, Sage," he whispers back.

"And I love you," my voice shakes violently as I say it, but he freezes altogether. His entire body goes rigid, and he looks at me like he's in disbelief, like I just told him the secret to immortal life or something else crazy that he can't digest.

"And if you ever instruct my staff not to listen to me again," I add, voice cracking, anger flaring weakly, "I will bury you in this house and no one will ever find you."

Dallas makes a faint sound that might be a laugh if anyone else did it.

I close my eyes for a moment.

Then I open them again and glance past him, toward the man in the chair.

"Is he going to talk?" I ask, and Ellison's expression hardens, just slightly, like the soldier in him is stepping forward again.

"He will," Ellison grits his teeth. "We'll make him talk," he assures me. "But for now, I'm going to take you upstairs to get some water, and we're going to sit down and breathe for a bit. And then I'll tell you everything we figured out this morning. No hiding."

He holds his hand out, bloody and bruised, and still, I take it.

I don't know what to do with any of this.

But I know one thing.

I'm not walking back upstairs alone.

Ellison holds my hand the entire time, and when we get back upstairs, he guides me to a barstool to sit down.

I watch him get a glass and fill it with ice water, but he doesn't hand it to me right away. He sets it on the counter beside me and steps forward, slow and careful, and then he settles both hands on my face.

He leans down, and presses possibly the softest kiss he's ever given me on my lips.

"I'm sorry," he whispers. "I should have been in that bed when you woke up."

My breath shudders out of me and I tip my head back to look up at him.

"I hate you," I whisper, and it's a lie, and we both know it.

Ellison exhales something that almost sounds like a laugh and almost sounds like he's in pain. "I know, baby," he whispers. "And I still love you, anyway."

Chapter 11

Sage

Morning doesn't crash into me with dread this time.

There's no jolt of panic, no sharp intake of breath like I need to brace for something to go wrong. Just light, pale and quiet, falling through the curtains to remind me that another day has come and gone.

Ellison is closer than usual.

His body is plastered to mine, limbs all wrapped together like we both couldn't stand the thought of the other leaving. His warmth bleeds into my skin, bringing with it a comfort that I didn't know I was craving.

For the first time since we've met, I'm awake before him. That's to be expected after knowing he didn't sleep the night before, but I still wonder if I should lie here and let him rest or wake him so we can get our day started.

I consider just lying there, but it almost feels unfair that I can't see him.

I don't know if I'm entitled to it after my blow up yesterday, but he took it all in stride and stayed with me for most of the day yesterday, even though I could tell his brain was scattered after everything that happened.

So, despite knowing it'll wake him, I shimmy out of his tight hold and turn in his arms.

He makes a small noise in the back of his throat, something soft and innocent, drastically different from the anger and frustration yesterday. His hands tighten around me instantly once I'm facing him, rubbing over my spine in haphazard patterns like he does it without a single thought. He leans his chin over my shoulder, tucking me into his chest, and I lie like that for a few minutes... until I start to overheat and can't get out of his grip.

"I seriously can't breathe," I huff against his collarbone, and I feel his chest shake with quiet laughter.

"Two more minutes," he mumbles back and I shake loose from his hold with a grumbled no.

"Your body heat is like a billion degrees, you big freaking furnace," I protest, and he laughs again, pushing me away until I fall over onto my back.

"So is your morning breath," he tosses back, and I lean back over just to smack him on the chest. But he catches my wrist and brings my hand up to kiss it. "Apologies, my lady. Forgive me for being so rude. Your breath is all I think about. I crave it. I yearnnnnn for it, Sage." He dramatically claims, and a laugh tumbles out of me whether I want it to or not.

It tapers off, and when I open my eyes again, Ellison is looking at me with something longing in his eyes. Something quiet but all-encompassing. Something that I would call love... if I was certain I knew what that looked like.

"Good morning, Sage," he murmurs, reaching up to tuck my hair behind my ear.

The discoloration on his knuckles is dark against his skin. He doesn't hide them from me or apologize, and I'm not sure I want him to. I wonder if they ache under the weight of what he did to try to keep me safe.

"Good morning," I whisper back, and I lean into his palm until he brushes my cheek with his thumb. "What are you and Dallas doing today?" I ask, and Ellison's eyes soften into nearly disappointment. Not in me. But in himself. I can see it plain as day.

"Dallas and I aren't doing anything," he softly answers. "You and I are."

"Are we?"

"Yeah, baby," he moves back so he can sit up, and I miss his warmth immediately. "I talked to Angela yesterday when you were in the shower."

"Angela?"

"Yeah," he gets up and makes his way into the bathroom, turning the shower on, and I clamor out of bed after him.

"What did she say?"

"She said we're signing papers today," he tugs his shirt off. It's very difficult for my eyes to stay on his face.

"Papers?" I exclaim, grabbing his arm to keep him from moving any further. "Like... the house papers? Are we signing the house papers?" Muted excitement rushes through my body, and Ellison leans forward to kiss me softly on the lips. It catches me off guard like it always does.

"Yeah, baby, we're signing house papers," he smiles at me, and then he's undressing and stepping into the spray of water, acting like he didn't just tip my morning over, this time in a good way.

I watch him for a moment. Watch how the water soaks through his hair, plastering it to his forehead. Watch how unhurriedly he reaches for a bottle of shampoo. My shampoo. The one I used to use alone but somehow started sharing when he came back as Adrian.

And I miss his warmth all over again.

I miss being close to him, and the way he touches me like he needs it. The way he looks at me. The way I want to feel everything that he feels when he's close to me.

I slowly remove my own clothes while he washes his hair, and I don't ask before I push the glass door open and slide in between him and the spray.

And he doesn't get annoyed with me.

He doesn't ask me what I'm doing.

He doesn't tell me to get out.

He doesn't question my sudden closeness.

He peeks his eyes open, wondering where the spray of water has gone even though he heard the door open and knows it's me hogging his water.

He looks down and he sees me instead.

He sees me taking all of the water, leaving him in the frigid air, and he smiles at me.

He smiles at me... like he's happy I'm taking the water. Like he's happy I'm in his space. Like he's happy I even bothered.

Instead of waiting for me to do anything, he reaches for the shampoo again. And he waits until my hair is soaked thoroughly before he reaches for me next.

I stand there under the running water, taking up the space and the warmth and his patience, while he lathers the shampoo and threads it through my hair. And I tip my head back and let him take care of me all over again.

Maybe it's stupid.

Maybe I don't deserve it after going off on him yesterday and caus-ing a scene and embarrassing myself, and maybe he'll get tired of my explosions and my shifting moods and my anger and everything my father taught me, and he'll leave.

But for right now, I let him hold me together, and I take what he'll give me, because I don't know what else to do. I don't know how to tell him that I'm scared he'll leave. That I'm scared he'll flee and I'll be sitting right here on a shelf, wondering why I wasn't good enough for him to look past everything else and choose me.

I'll sit here and wonder why he couldn't just choose to love me through all of my flaws, through all of the confusion, through all of the fear.

"Sage," he murmurs next to my ear, and I turn my head slightly to look at him over my shoulder.

"Yeah?"

"Would you like to spend the day together?"

For a moment, I just look at him, feeling both warmth and appre-ciation settle over me, and I slowly nod my head.

"Just us?" I ask, and he nods too.

"Just us," he assures me, brushing over my hair to keep rinsing the conditioner out. "I just figured... after everything yesterday, maybe we need a quiet day. If you're okay with that," he softly suggests.

I have to turn away from him again so he won't see my eyes starting to tear up. After yesterday, everything feels raw, even if it is muted now. I'm still hurt over the decisions he made without me.

"I'd like that," I rasp, and he hums at my response.

It's mostly quiet after that.

We finish showering and move downstairs where the house isn't as quiet as I expect.

Dallas is there, standing impatiently by the coffee maker, watching the torturous slow drip move like it's mocking him.

And Anderson... who I don't even want to look at, is standing next to the kitchen island instead of his usual place at the door.

It's not normal for both him and Dallas to be here first thing in the morning. Usually, they're out walking the property or handling things at the warehouse. It makes me wonder if I should be bracing for something.

And maybe I should have, because the second I sit down at the counter, Anderson is approaching me.

I nearly tell him to leave me alone, like a child.

But I don't. I can't.

Because I'm supposed to be in charge here.

I look up at him and hold his gaze until he lowers his eyes. For a second, there's a quiet discomfort in the kitchen, with everyone waiting to see what will happen.

Finally, Anderson lowers his head in a short show of respect, and when he lifts it again, he looks me in the eyes.

"I apologize for yesterday, Mrs. Hart."

It's almost comical. Really. Having someone on my payroll ignore my direct orders just because my husband told him to, turn around and apologize to me in front of said husband.

"I've been instructed only to follow your orders henceforth, regardless of who else instructs me."

"Did Dallas force you to apologize to me?" I mutter under my breath, slightly petulant.

"No, I did," Ellison slides my coffee over to me, freshly made and just like I like it. My eyes rise to meet his and he crosses his arms and leans back against the counter.

"I overstepped yesterday," he continues, and my mouth parts to say something, but no words come out. "I instructed Anderson without consulting you, and we spoke yesterday afternoon about it. Moving forward, if any orders I give him are in conflict with what you tell him, he will follow your orders instead of mine, unless your life is directly in jeopardy. I won't interfere with what instructions you give him."

"But that's—" I struggle with the right words.

That's what I wanted, isn't it? For me to be the one in charge. For me to be the one who gives the orders. For Ellison not to hide things from me.

Isn't it?

"That... isn't fair to you," I practically whisper, feeling shame and confusion and upset all at once, and Ellison looks just as confused as I do.

I lean forward to put my elbows on the counter, and run my hands over my face, taking a deep breath.

"I—" I know these words are about to sting. "I apologize, too," I murmur, and my lips turn downward on their own accord. "I was upset yesterday, and I wasn't thinking rationally. I just—I just didn't want to feel like the three of you were conspiring or excluding me from something. I was—" I swallow around the thickness in my throat. "I was upset, and I shouldn't have tried to threaten your job over it," I turn my attention to Anderson. "I apologize for that."

"You don't have to apologize—"

"Yes, I do," I cut Anderson off, keeping my voice level. "I do. I don't want to be some kind of tyrant that won't let anyone else have a say, and I don't want to... I just don't want to turn into my father," I admit, voice tapering off with shame. "I rely on you guys for a lot of things, and half the time I have no clue what I'm doing. I don't—I don't think

I ever tell any of you, but I truly could not do any of this without you, and it's just—it's just a lot."

"Sage, we don't expect you to have all of the answers," Dallas quietly cuts in, and I can barely lift my eyes to look at him. "Sometimes we make decisions and take immediate action because it's all we know. This thing," he gestures around the kitchen, and then points down the hall toward the basement door. "That thing in there... it's nothing to us. It's just another day at the office. We weren't trying to undermine you or hide it. But sometimes, you have to understand, that we do things without telling you because it's stuff you aren't used to seeing and we just thought to spare you."

"But I am used to it," I whisper, and my eyes start burning all over again. I don't know why my emotions are all over the place; I just can't stop it. And the tears rise faster than I want them to, sitting right there for everyone to see.

Ellison takes a deep breath like his own eyes are burning just from seeing me fight my own, and I can't bear to look at him right now.

"Not like that, kid," Dallas shakes his head. "I'm sure you've seen terrible things in that house of yours, and Lord knows you experienced worse growing up at times, but you haven't seen us like that, and quite frankly, Sage, I don't really want you to."

I have to force myself to lift my eyes to look at Dallas, and I think it's the most emotion I've ever seen from him swirling in his eyes.

"I can't speak for them, but I personally don't want you seeing me like that. I'm here to protect you. We all are. And I've no doubt you think me capable of it. I don't doubt my abilities either. But there are... particular things about me that I don't want you to see. And the violence is one of them."

Dallas stands up a little straighter and his lips purse into something contemplative. He looks like he's carefully measuring his next words.

"You aren't stupid, Sage. You know I'm capable of it. But it's what I'm trained to do. It's what I'm best at. And I don't want you to see me raging and torturing a man in the basement when you could be up here, knowing we're getting results without having to see how bloody I have to get. It's not about hiding the truth from you. But violence is a means to an end," he murmurs and takes a slow sip of his coffee before he looks at me again.

"I don't want you to see how violent I can get and worry there will be a time when I might turn it on you. So, I hope that you can forgive that I wanted to shelter you from that. And I hope you won't be too hard on Ellison, knowing that he had the same sentiment that I had, only stronger."

I have to reach up to hastily wipe the tears from my cheeks.

I know he's right.

I know he is.

And it feels so childish that I'm still angry over it, knowing that he had every right to want to keep me away from the violence.

I just wanted to know.

"You have every right to still be upset and angry, Sage," Ellison speaks up softly, like he knew the exact route my brain was spiraling down. "It's okay, and nobody faults you for it. We trust you and know you're more than capable of handling things, regardless of how brutal they get. But some things, you don't have to see to know. From now on, we'll be transparent, and we'll keep you informed of everything that's being discussed before we make any moves."

"Thank you," I whisper, strained and a little wet sounding. That's all I wanted. To be aware, to know what's going on in my own house, with my own husband.

Anderson clears his throat and announces he'll be outside walking the perimeter, and then Dallas slides the keys across the counter.

"You're not very good at driving, but here's the keys," he glares at Ellison as he passes me the keys. "Last time I gave him the keys, I had to take that shit in for a detail," he shudders, and I let out a wet laugh. "Actually, now that I think about it, that was more your fault than his," he mutters and snatches the keys back.

"I'll just follow when you leave the house later," he sighs, and he slams the keys into Ellison's chest as he passes.

I can't help but laugh softly as he leaves, watching after him, and I also can't help but feel a little emotional.

Just months ago, I didn't have Dallas. I didn't have anyone in my corner, and I didn't know anyone that would ever look me in the eyes and apologize for hurting me.

But Dallas did.

Dallas did, and I won't ever forget it.

I take a deep breath when Ellison walks around the kitchen island and turns my barstool so I'm facing him.

And then he pulls me against his chest and wraps his arms around me.

I think it's exactly what I needed, because I melt against him, and my breath shudders out of me like it's letting go of all of the bad feelings and leaving me with nothing but settled exhaustion.

Ellison's hand comes up to brush over the back of my head, and I make a low, embarrassing sound on contentments against his chest.

Safe.

That's what this feeling is.

Safety.

Knowing right here is exactly where I crave to be most.

Knowing right here is where I'm safest, even when I sometimes fight it. Even when it sometimes upsets me.

Right here is where I belong.

Chapter 12

Sage

The title agency smells like moth balls and dusty copy paper.

It's quiet and professional in a way that makes everything feel a little more important than it probably is.

Angela greets us outside when we arrive, gushing about how this is the right decision, and tells us she will go check to make sure everyone else has done their part.

I scuff my foot across the concrete sidewalk while Ellison tries to look like he's not doing full blown perimeter sweeps as he looks around.

"Angela's gonna talk nonstop," he mutters under his breath.

"She's good at that," I huff under my breath.

"You like her?" He asks, glancing around again quickly before he settles on me.

"She's not exactly my cup of tea, but... I'm grateful for her. She was the only one willing to work with us without talking to our fathers first."

I don't even notice the slip. *Our* fathers. As if Andrew really had any blood relation to Ellison.

"Best to keep her in our pocket, then," Ellison gives me a tired smile. "Might need her to keep a foot in the door." His smile builds and I squint at him, not understanding why he's so chipper all of a sudden. "Someone's coming out. Put your smile back on," he cocks his head to the side, showing me all of his teeth.

"You look like a serial killer when you do that," I whisper, but I whirl around and put on my best smile for the receptionist coming to collect us.

We're led to a large office full of people we have to play nice with for a little while.

Angela is already seated when we arrive, moving through some papers stacked neatly in front of her, pens lined up perfectly on the edge of the paper.

She is all smiles when we come in.

"There they are," she brightly announces, clapping her hands. "I'm so happy you decided to go with this house. I was scared you'd change your minds after the... push back, at the gala," she delicately says.

Ellison smiles politely, all calm composure and easy smooth laughter as he brushes it off. When I slide into the chair beside him and set my purse at my feet, he stays close. His knee brushes mine under the table and that eases me a little bit, like he knew just how heavy and exhausting the day will be.

"Not a chance," I tell her, and she laughs and starts pulling documents forward.

The process is smoother than I expected. I sign so many documents and write so many dates it's dizzying. My name flows across the page again and again until my hand starts to ache, a physical reminder that this is real, that we're doing it together, despite the fact that our families don't want us to.

Ellison signs Adrian's name right next to mine, steady and unhurried, like he does this every day.

Watching him perfectly craft Adrian's signature sends a pang of sadness through me.

Sadness that no matter how long we stick together, on paper, he will always be Adrian to everyone else.

When, to me, he's nobody but Ellison. The person who I care about most.

Knowing his name is lost under the weight of his decisions, it makes my heart ache, and I hope, that even though it has to stay something private within our household, me giving him his name back brings him peace that he's making the right decisions.

When it's finally all over, Angela slides the keys across the table, and they land between us with a finality that makes my heart skip beats.

"Congratulations!" She warmly rubs my arm, and I give her maybe the first genuine smile since we've met. "You're officially homeowners!"

Ellison reaches for them first, but he doesn't hold them hostage.

He brings them straight to my palm and presses them there, and then he wraps his fist around my hand, holding them with me.

Because we're in this together. We're doing this together.

I look at him for a moment, my heart beating frantically in my chest when he smiles at me, and then I turn to Angela again.

"Thank you," I say to her, meaning more than just the keys. "For everything. For the... the calls and the announcement at the gala, and the rushed showings, accommodating all of my requests. You made this somehow feel manageable when in my head, I thought it would be terrible."

"Oh, no! It has totally been my pleasure!" Angela responds in a chipper laugh. "I would love to help you in the future with anything you may need!"

"Of course," Ellison smiles at her. "You'd be our first call."

"Actually, Angela," I cut in, not really meaning to, but feeling that it may benefit us in the future. "We appreciate you so much for your help at the gala, but we would really love to get more involved in our community. If there's anything you ever need help with, we'd be more than glad to lend a hand."

Angela's eyes widen, and I almost feel guilty that she thought signing these papers would put an end to our relationship with her.

Then again, our families aren't the type to get involved with things like that.

"I—That's so generous of you, Mrs. Hart!" She stutters, squeezing her stack of paperwork toward her chest. "I do have an event coming up if you'd like to help. It's... maybe not something you'd be interested in, but we always need volunteers, and well," she clears her throat. "May I speak candidly?"

"Yes, of course," I encourage her, more than intrigued to find out why she seems to be uncomfortable all of a sudden.

"Forgive me if this sounds bad. I assure you I mean no offense!" She scrambles and looks around to make sure no one is nearby to hear her. "Mr. Hart..." she murmurs, sheepish as she looks at Ellison. "Well, you have a bit of a reputation. And there are... certain rumors about your... activities with women and partying."

Ellison actually flushes.

Like actually turns red, and I tilt my head at him.

He knows damn good and well he didn't do anything wrong. That it was all Adrian and his bad habits, but somehow he still seems embarrassed by it.

"There isn't much in the media or the... circles, about you, Mrs. Hart. Many people have contacted me wanting to know what you're like and how you... tamed your husband," she closes her eyes like it pains her to say it.

"I know that this was a legitimate business arrangement, but I also understand that it likely is part of a plan to correct past public opinions of Mr. Hart."

I cut my eyes to Ellison and he gives me a subtle nod.

"You're right, Angela," I take a deep breath and thin my lips out. "Adrian and I had a very difficult start to our marriage, and while we didn't pick each other, we have grown to care for each other deeply. Adrian was very... controlled by his family at the start of our marriage, as was I. But we have come together and decided to work on our relationship, and ourselves, while trying to repair some of the," I sigh. "Well, Angela, I know that you know what kind of business our families deal in. It's no secret."

"No, it isn't," Angela bites her lip and looks at Ellison again.

"I'd like to right my wrongs, Angela," he speaks up after a moment of silence. "I know that my image isn't particularly good for publicity, and I'll be the first to admit I've made plenty of mistakes, but I am learning from them. Having Sage by my side has made me look at things differently, and I'd like to bring a better image to the public. What my father does... is different than how we would like to be perceived as a family. Sage and I would like to stay independent from that. And yes, having you in our corner, someone honest that we can trust... that's hard to come by, Angela."

"Yes, it is," I agree, leaning into Ellison's chest a little. I look up at him, and he smiles at me like he's exhausted, though now I know how to tell when he's acting. Now I can see it.

"I'd like to get more involved, and I'd like to change my image. Both of those things are true. Whatever events you have, whether there's media there or not, we'd like to help. Our image is important, yes, but we would genuinely like to make an impact in the community."

Angela nods slowly, like she's comprehending what we've said and taking it into consideration. "There is one event coming up," she starts and looks at Ellison. "But it is a male only event," she grimaces. "I apologize, Mrs. Hart, as you probably won't like it."

"May I ask what it is?"

"There are... certain expectations that come with catering to elite clients. We have a sort of auction coming up."

"What kind of auction?" I ask again, and I feel Ellison's hand settle on my lower back.

"There were some properties that were seized years ago..." she lowers her voice. "From the Kim family."

Holy fucking shit.

Ellison stiffens behind me.

He has no idea. Oh, God, he has no idea.

"The Kim family?" I lower my voice and lean in. "Really?"

"Really," Angela rapidly nods. "They're holding the auction in one of our warehouses. It will be completely anonymous. Each auction buyer will be represented by an anonymous name. But what really interests the buyers is that... the properties are sold as is. Any personal belongings, any files, documents, money. All of it is still intact. As well as the," she shivers in discomfort, "—the crime scenes."

"And... you would be able to get Adrian into this auction?" I carefully ask.

"I can put him on the list," Angela assures me, glancing at him again. "The event... it is anonymous, but once the properties are bought, the paperwork is brought in and signed. The deal is sealed as soon as the money turns over."

"So once it's processed, the buyer's information will be public?" I probe.

"Not exactly," she fumbles with her bag to pull her phone out. It only takes a few seconds before she shows me the paperwork. "The buyer will still be anonymous, but the buyer will be listed under a sponsor. And... I would be Mr. Hart's sponsor, should he enter."

"Would that not put you in danger?" Ellison suddenly asks. "Forgive us, Angela, but as much as we'd love to be involved, we don't want to draw unwelcome attention your way."

"I appreciate that, Mr. Hart, and you're right. It will draw attention, but there are certain lines that are not often crossed. I'm a realtor, yes. But I'm also a liaison. Sponsoring someone who purchases anything in the auction will make my services appear more desirable."

"A liaison?" Ellison questions.

"She's off limits," I explain for him, crossing my arms. "She is considered the message man. Like in war," I respond, hoping he'll understand.

"So, it's a breach of etiquette but not necessarily an act that can prompt retaliation?" He clarifies.

"Yes," Angela admits. "I don't work for any one family or company. It doesn't matter who I do the favors for but harming me is seen as a sign of disrespect to all of the families."

"I see," Ellison clenches his jaw. "So, you would be safe if you sponsored me to enter the auction?"

"Yes," Angela nods. "That is, if Sage is on board with it, too. I must warn you that there are often alcohol and other substances present at these parties, and... I do believe both of your families will be there. The Kim family had a hand in many different pots. It's said that they had it in too many, but the proof is inside of those homes."

"We'd like in," I say immediately, and I hear Ellison's neck crack when he whirls around to look at me.

"Maybe we should talk about it," he says, and I look him in the eyes for a moment before his brows furrow softly. "But if my wife accepts it, then yes," he turns back to Angela. "We'd like in, please."

"Of course," Angela nods. "Shall I email you the paperwork?"

"Please," I nod. "And if you could, Angela, please think of anything else I could assist with. I'd love to help you with anything you might have in mind."

"Of course, Mrs. Hart," she says again, but then she checks her watch and frowns. "I will send everything over at once, but I must go. I have a meeting in thirty minutes across town. Please, let me know if you have any questions about the paperwork."

We both wave her goodbye before we make our way to the car, and once the doors shut, Ellison turns his whole body toward me.

"Who the fuck are the Kim family? And do we have money to be entering this auction? That's... Sage, that seems like a lot, and I don't know shit about this kind of thing."

"Just drive, and I'll try to explain," I breathe out.

Surprisingly, he listens.

I expect him to go home, but soon, he's taking the path to where I know our new house sits, empty and waiting for someone to make it a home.

After he turns onto the main road, I reach over to take his hand, just to feel the warmth, and he cuts his eyes over to me for a moment before he squeezes my hand.

"The Kim family," I start, and turn to look out the window. "Was the second largest mafia family in the Northwest before all of the smaller ones popped up."

"What happened to them?" Ellison murmurs as he turns the wheel to get off of the highway.

"They were massacred."

"What?" He rasps.

"They were killed. All of them. In one night," I explain. "The same night my mother was killed."

"Sage," Ellison cuts in, but I don't listen. "The Kim family used to work with a lot of the smaller families. Whether it was drugs or money or guns or—or whatever. They used to deal with too much. My father used to talk about it, but I think he was involved with them, too. If you need money, or a loan of men, guns, you name it, you could get it from the Kim company."

"Do you think the Kim family had anything to do with your mother dying?"

"Yes," I answer immediately. "My father's men stole from Adrian's father. They nearly wiped him clean on one of his ocean ports. Before that, he thought he was untouchable."

I squeeze Ellison's hand at the memory of my mother's pleading. Of her begging them not to harm me.

"And... my mother was retaliation for it. But my father... he didn't have the men to take from Andrew Hart. He loaned them, and he paid his debt for the Kim family's generosity with blood. He traded Andrew's assets to clear whatever he owed the Kim's. And when Andrew Hart found out... my mother ended up dead, and the Kim's were wiped out by a mysterious gas leak... all in one night. And the men that were left over from the Kim's... they all scattered, and some are still involved, both with my father, and Andrew Hart."

"Jesus Christ," Ellison mutters under his breath.

"If we can get in on this auction, and actually get something, we may find out more than we want," I whisper. "Every family will want to get their hand on it. To see who was in the Kim's pocket, and who was betraying whose trust."

"It'll be a rich person's bloodbath then."

"Yes," I nod slowly. I turn to face him when he parks the car outside of the new house.

And it stands just like it did before, only now, it somehow looks more beautiful than I remember.

"It would show who is guilty, and who was complicit," I pop the passenger side door open and clamor out, and Ellison is coming around the back of the car to get me before I can even move myself. "Also... yes, we can afford it."

"How?" He balks.

"I've been stealing from our fathers for months now, Ellison," I huff, like it's common sense. "We have like... I don't know, a gazillion dollars?"

"That's so hot of you," Ellison groans, and I laugh, reaching out to push him away with a hand to his chest.

"Shut up," I whisper in exasperation. He reaches out to grab my hand and leads me straight to the door, opening it to usher me inside.

It's just as perfect as I remember it from Angela's tour.

The hardwood floors were a beautiful, distressed oak that paired perfectly with the white and gold marble countertops.

"I love the floors," I find myself saying out loud, and Ellison hums behind me.

"Gives it a nice, warm feel to it," he agrees. "We'll probably need to have this fireplace cleaned out," he crouches next to it and twists to look at the interior. "It's in good shape still."

"Do you like it?" I ask, watching him wipe his hands on his jeans.

"The fireplace? I like how big—"

"Not the fireplace," I laugh under my breath. "Our house."

Ellison stops mid-stride to look at me.

And he does look at me.

Not just looking, but assessing. He looks me over from head to toe before he settles back on my face, and he licks his lips just enough to distract me.

"I like it a lot," he says simply, and then he slowly closes the distance between us, meeting me in the kitchen. "I like seeing you in it."

"What would you change about it?" I wonder, glancing around him to look over the open floor plan. "If you had to change anything."

"If I had to change anything..." Ellison murmurs almost to himself. "Hmm." I turn back to him to see if he's cataloging the entire room like I am, but instead, his gaze isn't on the cabinets or the floor or the countertop that I'm leaning on.

His eyes are fixed on me.

Ellison takes a few steps forward until he's caging me against the kitchen island, and God, he smells so good it's almost dizzying.

He places his hands on the marble countertops on both sides of me and leans his weight against me.

I have to tip my head back so I can meet his eyes, and when I do, he leans forward enough that his lips just barely brush mine, and I suck in a ragged breath, knowing I don't stand a chance.

"Needs to be christened," he murmurs against my lips, his breath warm, voice low and enticing, as if he needs to somehow convince me.

As if he doesn't know my temperature has already ticked up a thousand degrees.

"Is that so?" I manage to weakly whisper.

"Mhm," he brushes his lips against mine again in a teasing little caress. "Gotta properly dedicate the space, right? Declare it as ours."

"And how do we do that?" I whisper, and my pulse that was already fluttering under my skin skyrockets when he rolls his head to the side to look at me.

I hate when he does that.

I hate that he does it often.

I hate that it always turns me on.

The kiss he places on my lips is almost tender, something more of a sigh than meant to drag me into surrender.

It's sweet enough that my knees feel a little bit wobbly.

Enough that my hands move on their own accord, slipping up the solid muscle under his t-shirt before I settle it over his chest.

And then he pushes forward a little bit, like a gradual means to devour me.

His lips part, inviting and hypnotizing. My tongue meets his, and his hands leave the counter to move up to my face, his palms cradling my jaw, thumbs stroking over my cheekbones in a way that feels far too intimate.

And I lose myself in it. In the soft, wet sound it makes. In the scratch of his stubble against my skin. In the way his body towers over mine, all hard edges meeting my softer curves. My fingers dig into his shirt, and he breaks the kiss.

Only to trail his lips along my jaw, down the column of my throat.

"This kitchen," he murmurs against my skin, his voice husky and distracting. "This is where I'm going to make you coffee every morning. Watch you try to cook." A nip to my earlobe makes me gasp and close my eyes. "And I'm going to bend you over this very island and taste you for dessert."

The image, spoken in that rough tone of his, sends a downright disgusting amount of want through me, and my head falls back to give him more access.

"Ellison," I whisper, sounding a little choked up.

"My thoughts all day," he continues, his mouth working its way back to mine "Getting the keys. Signing the papers. Listening to you talk. All I could think about was getting you alone in our empty house. Having you in every room." His next kiss turns hungrier, more urgent. His tongue slips into my mouth and mine moves to meet it, thrilled by his words and the realty that we are here truly alone.

My hips start to move on their own accord, but his do too, a slow seeking grind through the layers of our clothes. The rough denim of his jeans against the softer cotton pants I'm wearing is frustratingly sweet. I can feel how hard he is, pressing against my belly, and I rock against him, wanting more and more.

A low groan bleeds from his mouth, and in one smooth, effortless motion, his hands slide from my face down to my waist, and then under my thighs. He lifts me up, setting me down on the cool countertop with not one ounce of shame. The surface is shockingly cold compared to the heat building between my legs.

He steps between my knees, pushing them wider, his hands sliding up my outer thighs before they dip into my waistband and drag my pants down in one slow glide.

The second he looks down, his eyes darken to that dark stormy gray that I adore, drinking in the sight of me perched on the marble, his hands on my hips, open just for him.

"My beautiful wife." The words are thick with want. "In our new kitchen."

His hands slide up, bringing my thin shirt with it, and he pulls it over my head like he's practiced it every day just for this occasion.

He curses when he uncovers my breasts, snapping my bra loose with quick hands.

He leans in, but not to take a nipple in his mouth like I'm expecting him to. Instead, he places a single, soft kiss over my heart, and then another an inch lower. And then more, tracing a path of fire over my skin. He takes his time, his lips gliding slowly, tongue flicking out to taste the salt on my skin. And when he finally takes a tight nipple between his lips, the suction is gentle, slow and so good. My toes curl against his legs and I know he feels me tensing up.

My hands slip into his hair, my fingers tangling in the dark, silken strands. I hold him closer to me, a soft, desperate sound escaping my throat. He switches his attention to my other breast, giving it the same unhurried devotion. His teeth graze against my skin, a hint of sharpness that makes my entire body jolt, and my hips roll forward, seeking friction against his jeans.

He straightens up at my insistence, his own breathing uneven just like mine. His hands go to the hem of his t-shirt and he pulls it over his head in one swift motion and drops it on the floor. Seeing him shirtless, chest broad, muscles taut with his desire just for me, steals the air from my lungs.

He's perfect.

And he belongs to me.

My hands go to the button of his jeans, and he moves to help me. The snap of it coming undone is loud in the quiet room. The rasp of his zipper coming down sounded like heaven.

He pushes his jeans and boxer-briefs down just enough, freeing his cock until it stands thick and flushed against his stomach, clear moisture already glistening at the tip.

Just for me.

I reach for him and he catches my wrist, bringing my hand to his lips instead. He kisses my palm, eyes holding mine, and guides my hand back to my own body. "Not yet, baby," he rasps.

He steps closer again, the heat of him drowning me. His hands slide up my inner thighs, pushing my knees wider apart. His gaze is almost worse than his touch, roaming over the most intimate parts of me. The vulnerability is almost too much, but the trust that comes with it is a headier drug than any touch could be.

"Perfect," he breathes out, and he leans in, but not to kiss me on the lips.

No, he wants to torture me.

He crouches down, lowering his head between my thighs. His breath washes over me first, hot and damp, and then the first touch of his tongue, a flat, slow stroke from top to bottom.

And I cry out, my back arching off the countertop. My hands reach for purchase on the smooth surface, and he doesn't help me any. He laps at me with a single-minded goal in mind: to unravel me completely.

His tongue traces over ever fold, delving inside of me, circling the aching, swollen bud of my clit with maddening skill. The sounds coming out of my mouth are obscene, wet and hungry, and echoing in our empty kitchen.

I don't have it in me to be polite about it.

"Ellison... oh, God, right there... please." The words come out in fragments and gasps, torn from my lips, and all I can do is move my hips, rocking against his mouth, wanting more.

He holds me steady, hands firm on my thighs, allowing me to move but controlling the angle, the depth, the frustration.

And perhaps I never had an issue with control after all, because I'm willing to let him control every aspect of me if this is the pleasure that I get.

My legs start to tremble, and a high, thin whine escapes my throat, and only then does he pull away from me, lips and chin glistening. Now his eyes are beyond dark, gorgeous, and I could drown in them.

"Not yet, baby," he rasps just like before, voice rough with a command. "I want you to come on my cock. I want to feel you around me when you do it."

Before I can protest, before the ache of denial could even form, his hands are on my hips again.

He tugs me forward, to the very edge of the island. He positions himself, the broad head of his cock nudging through my thighs, not entering yet, but telling me he will.

"Look at me," he snaps in that same low tone, and I force my eyes up.

My vision is blurry with how bad I need him to hurry this up, but nothing in his gaze tells me he'll keep it from me.

Instead, he leans forward and places one lingering kiss on my lips.

And then he pushes forward.

The stretch, the slow, burning fullness he gives me is everything. A choked sob breaks from my lips as he bottoms out, our bodies stuck together at every point.

Home.

That's what this really is.

Not this house or these new walls and counters.

Just him.

That's home.

He holds me there, buried to the hilt, letting me feel every inch. And his hands come to my face, his thumbs wiping away the tears that had escaped before I could control them.

"My Sage," he whispers, and I can't breathe. "Always."

And then he begins to move.

This isn't like the frantic, driving pace from the last time we had sex.

This is different.

A slow, deep, needing rhythm that makes me dig my feels into the firm muscles of his legs to try to pull him closer.

His eyes never leave mine. They hold me hostage, a stormy, possessive anchor, a command for me to surrender to being taken like this.

"That's it," he murmurs softly, encouraging. "Look at me, baby. Feel just me. Every part of you belongs to me in this house."

I can only nods, a shaky, breathless motion. Words are beyond me.

All I can do is feel it.

The thick stretch of him, each measured thrust, the way my body clenches around him, trying to keep him inside. And a warm, heavy feeling starts building in my stomach.

He leans forward, bracing his hands on the counter, caging me in.

His mouth finds mine again, and this kiss is different, too. Softer. But no less intense. A deep, soul-sharing one. I can taste myself on his lips, and that makes even more heat spread through my veins.

He breaks the kiss only to trail along my jaw and down my throat.

"You feel so good, Sage," he breathes against my skin. "Taking me so deep." His hips snap forward with a bit more force on the next thrust, drawing a sharp, surprised gasp from my lungs.

The change in angle makes me tense up, brushing a spot inside that makes my eyes roll back. My fingernails scrape across his back, searching for something to hold me steady.

"There?" He asks, voice dark with knowing.

"Y—yes... oh, God, yes..."

"Not God, baby. Just me," he chuckles against my throat. "Tell me."

"Ellison, I—please, right there, don't stop—" I choke out.

He adjusts his stance slightly, widening his own legs, and the next thrust is targeted.

And the next.

And the next.

The pleasure is no longer a slow-build, but something pulling me under. My cries start losing control, breaking into sharp, pleading sounds.

"I know, baby. I know." Ellison's own control starts fraying, breaths ragged against my neck, and his arms, corded and tense where he held himself with restraint, start to tremble. "Fuck... squeezing me so tight."

He loses his slow pace, and the need takes over for both of us. My head tips back, my long black hair fanning out against the white cold stone.

The world narrows to the sensation of him filling me, over and over, hitting just perfectly, and it's enough to shatter me.

"I—fuck, I love you," I gasp, the words choking out of me. Not a sweet whisper, but a raw, overwhelmed confession forced out by the sheer magnitude of what he makes me feel.

He stills for a fraction of a second, still buried deep, eyes blazing and dark. A look of pure, barely controlled possession.

"Say it again."

And the dam breaks.

The words pour out of me, mingled with sobs and gasps, each now louder with each relentless thrust.

"I love you... I love you, oh, God, I love you, Ellison, I—"

Ellison's fingers dip between us and brush over my clit, and I clench around him in a series of hard, rapid, uncontrollable pulses, sending shockwaves over my body that leave my limbs numb and my mind incredibly blank.

And through the haze of my own climax, I feel his. His own control shattering completely. His hips slamming into me one final, devastating time, and holding there, shuddering as I feel the sudden rush of his release deep inside of me.

It's quiet for a moment as we collapse together, tangled and sweaty, with most of his weight still against me, his forehead dropped to my shoulder, trembling.

My arms, weak and boneless, come up to wrap around him, holding him to me as we struggle to catch our breath.

And finally, the world seems to seep back in.

He doesn't move away, but instead, with a tenderness that makes me want to cry, presses a soft kiss to the hollow of my throat, before he slowly, carefully pulls out of me.

He makes a soothing sound, his hands coming up to my hip as the warmth trickles down my inner thighs.

He looks down at me, his stormy eyes soft now, sated and almost frightening with the conviction there.

"My love," he whispers with a hoarse voice. "My heart."

I reach up and trace the line of his jaw with my fingertips, the hair damp at his temple. And my eyes well with tears again, but this time, from emotion.

"I'm sorry," I whisper. He shakes his head against me as he brings me in for a hug. "I think I—" I swallow and nearly choke on it. "I think I really love you," I admit.

"I know," Ellison whispers against me. "And you are everything to me, Sage." He pulls back to wipe my tears with his thumbs and leans down to kiss me, long and unhurried. "You are all that I want in this life, and I love you."

He holds me until I lose track of time, until he finally pulls away to help me sit up, my legs wobbling a little as he helps me hop off of the counter.

"Our brand new house is empty," he sighs as he reaches for his discarded t-shirt so he can wet it under the faucet. With a gentle touch, he cleans between my legs before he tosses the shirt back on the floor.

"There," he looks down at the mess on the counter, dripping onto the floor, and a pleased smile touches his lips. "Properly christened."

"Shut up," I whisper, because I feel too weak to laugh at his clear satisfaction.

"Yes, Ma'am."

Chapter 13

Sage

Dallas is waiting in the kitchen when we get back.

Of course he is.

He's leaning against the counter like he's been waiting for ages, arms crossed, expression flat, like the concept of patience personally offends him.

Anderson was outside the front doorway, silent as always, gaze sweeping the house in intervals like he never truly rests.

It almost makes me feel bad again over yelling at him the other day.

Ellison's hand is still warm against mine when we step inside, and I can feel the way his body shifts, already bracing for business so we can figure out what to do next.

"You better not have fucked up the Escalade," Dallas grumbles, glaring at both of us. "You look like you fucked up the Escalade," he points out, and Ellison shoots him a downright devious grin.

"It just needs a light detail—" he starts, and Dallas' face falls comedically.

"You didn't," he pleads helplessly, reaching up to rub his face with his hands. "Come on. We just got it back from the—"

"Of course, we didn't, Dallas," I let out an exasperated breath. "Your precious Escalade is just as you left it. Clean and tidy."

"Right," Ellison leans against the countertop. "No come on any of the—"

"Ellison!" I gasp, reaching up to smack my hands over his mouth. "No!"

He wrangles out of my grasp like it's the easiest thing in the world. "Fine," he pants against my fighting hands. "Ruin all my fun."

"Can we just talk about the—"

"Right," Dallas says immediately, and I have to force myself to ignore the blush on his cheeks. "We need to talk. Your text didn't make much sense."

"Yeah, I figured," Ellison exhales through his nose. "Sage can explain it better than me."

I slip my shoes off and hop up into one of the chairs at the island.

"Angela sent us the paperwork," I point out, and he reaches for my phone to slide it over to me. Then he just stands beside me, close enough to brush against my arm each time, but it's not subtle enough to seem like he is trying to see the email, too.

Dallas' eyes flick between us, and then he nods. "Well, let's see it."

I open the email and the screen glares up at me like a bad omen.

"So, it's obviously an auction for the Kim properties, but we have no idea which property, or what might be in any of them. We have no idea what's included, whether it's assets or anything."

"Angela said that the properties would be auctioned as-is, and the email says that the only thing that has been altered in them is they had the biohazard shit cleaned up," Ellison chimes in.

"So obviously, there could be a ridiculous amount of information in the main house," I add, and Dallas places his hands on the counter and thinks for a moment before he shakes his head.

"No," he disagrees. "The Kim's weren't stupid enough to stash all of their intel in the main house."

"Well, hold on," Ellison huffs. "How did they even get these properties back from the police? I mean, there were mass casualties there, so who exactly got it back, and who is auctioning it?"

"You're thinking too much," Dallas shakes his head again. "The people we're dealing with don't care about rules or the law. The law is in their pocket. Hell, even we have two of them on our payroll. I wouldn't be surprised if it's the government themselves putting the auction on."

"So, what? We need to try to buy one of the properties and just hope we get some information from it?" Ellison asks, and Dallas reaches for my phone.

And then he snorts.

"No weapons," he mutters. "That's real convenient."

Ellison's jaw tightens and he nods his head. "Yeah, I said the same thing."

"One bodyguard allowed," Dallas continues. "That would be me," he looks to both of us. "Any objections?"

Neither of us object, so he scrolls his finger up the screen again. "As expected. Arrival time is staggered. Back entrance only. So we'd have a ten minute window so no one sees you come or go."

He looks up and slides his gaze over to Ellison. "You realize that's not hospitality, right?"

"Containment," Ellison says, and Dallas instantly agrees.

"Yes. Good," he says it like he's talking to a child that's finally learning. "It's anonymous, but nothing is truly anonymous. There will probably be scouts everywhere, which means weapons will be hot, so we can't afford to fuck this up. There will probably be people here that are hoping for a fuck up. So we need to go, do what we need to, and leave at our allotted time."

"Yeah," Ellison shrugs in agreement, so Dallas continues reading, voice dry as paper.

"Wire transfers only. No cash. No checks. Immediate verification and agreement." His gaze finally snaps to me. "We ready to move money that fast?"

"Yes," I don't hesitate to answer. "We can move it from our offshore accounts. Buy our way in with Daddy dearest's money."

Dallas seems to like that answer so he keeps scrolling. "Private room bidding. Each property has a ten-minute bid window. No interaction between buyers. No mingling. Each bidder must stay in their assigned rooms."

"So it's a rich person's bloodbath," Ellison sighs. "Just quieter. No one gets dirty in public. All the blood pours from their pockets."

Ellison's hand comes to the back of my neck, thumb pressing gently like he can feel my pulse climbing, and Dallas glances at me.

"This isn't a charity auction, Sage," he says, a little softer. "This is an autopsy. Everyone there is gonna be picking through bones for leverage."

"I know," I whisper.

He nods once, and then returns to the email.

"If there's no agreement after ten minutes, the property goes to a final bid," Dallas reads. "Thirty seconds on last call. Highest bidder takes it."

"So we won't know who won until the thirty seconds is up? We'll just have to hope we bid higher than the other guy?"

"That's when people panic," Dallas corrects. "Panic makes people throw money around. We'll have to bid high."

"And you're sure they won't see Ellison there?" I ask.

Dallas shakes his head. "Not the buyers. But bodyguards will be in the hall for the majority of the bid."

"So they'll know you were there?" I swallow, and Dallas nods.

"And they know you're usually with me. But it's men only," my voice trembles. "So they'll assume you're there with Ellison. And they'll... they'll tell their bosses anyway."

"Yes, but likely not until we're leaving," Dallas answers.

"But will he be safe?" I ask, and the question lands on the counter like a hand grenade.

I look between the both of them, and my gaze settles on Ellison.

"You'll be safe even if they know you're there?" I repeat, and he tilts his head, thinning his lips a little.

"There's no guarantee in a situation like this, but Sage, I can take out a hundred men like this before—"

"No," I spit the word out.

Ellison's shoulders tense up as he looks at me, his fingers rubbing circles into my nape. I know he isn't scared of it. I know Dallas isn't either. They've probably faced men a thousand times more violent.

But I know how unpredictable these people are. They think they're untouchable because they have power.

But we have power too.

"I have to go," Ellison's voice is soft next to my ear.

"No," I refuse, more intensely this time. "No. These people are fucking cowards and you have no idea who will be nearby just waiting—"

"Do you want me to go to the auction or not, Sage?" Ellison halts my words right in their tracks. "Do you? Because I can't get you the answers you want if you don't let me do it, baby." His words hold an edge of frustration in them, and it's the first time he's ever spoken to me like that.

"You have to let me start making moves at some point, baby. And I know this is a shitty way to get my foot in the door, but we *need* our foot in the door. You have to let me prove myself."

"I know," I tilt my head back to look up at him, and he doesn't look like he's worried.

"We'll get what we can, and I'll get you some answers. Okay?" He softly offers, and I nod at him. "And I know you haven't seen it, Sage, but I can hold my own, weapons or no weapons allowed. Alright? No need to worry," he softens his voice again, and it's slow to calm me down, but it does. It does calm me down.

"Okay," I whisper.

"Okay?" He asks and I lean into his palm when he reaches up to hold my face.

"Yeah, okay," I agree finally.

Dallas' gaze softens only slightly. "We'll get in and get what we can, and we'll come straight back here. Once we get back on the main road, I'll have our guys meet us to escort us back just in case we run into any company."

"Okay," I murmur, taking a deep breath. "Anderson stays here with me?" I ask, and Dallas levels his gaze for a moment.

"Is that what you want?"

"Well, someone has to stay here," I point out.

"Yes, but do you feel safe with him after the other day?"

"I'm not a child, Dallas." He meets my eyes, and I don't like the look he gives me. "What if I go with Anderson and we stay nearby in case something goes wrong?"

"You're not going," Ellison says immediately. And it's the first time he's outright told me no.

It stings a little bit.

I turn to him and he doesn't let me say a word.

"No," he repeats, somehow even more firm. "Not this time."

The anger begins to rise and I try to keep it down.

I need to keep it down.

He kept it down when it was me that told him no.

His hand tightens around my neck, not to force my hand, but to hold me steady, and he doesn't so much as flinch when I force myself to swallow my anger down.

"This is worse than doing some shady steals and money grabs," he tells me softly. "There's no weapons here, which means the reward is worth a risk. And men like this are willing to take risks when they're desperate. It'll be a viper's pit. And you're not going in the pit, Sage."

"Are you telling me no?" I ask, willing my voice not to shake.

"I'm telling you no," he answers immediately.

And it feels like the temperature drops in the kitchen.

Dallas doesn't move, and neither do I.

Neither does Ellison.

He holds my eyes, and he stands right there, and he repeats it.

"I'm telling you no."

I open my mouth.

And then I close it again.

Because as angry as I am hearing the word no, I understand what this is.

A line being drawn carefully.

The only compromise he's willing to make.

I'm the one who got him into this mess, and I knew I wouldn't be able to go. Angela said it herself. Men only. There's no room for me there, and men like these... they prey on the lesser.

As much as I hate to admit it, that would be me at this current time.

I see Dallas lean back slowly from the corner of my eye, and still, Ellison doesn't look away from me.

"Alright," I say finally, low, like saying it any louder will hurt me.

Ellison's hand slips from my nape to brush my cheek. "Alright?" He asks, and I nod just once.

"Alright," I agree.

"Fine," Dallas finally speaks up. "I go with him. Anderson stays with you. Everyone stays in communication. The guys will intercept us on the main road and escort us here."

Ellison nods once, and then he glances at his watch.

And Dallas glares like it's the most annoying thing he's ever seen.

"What?" He says sharply. "You got somewhere better to be?"

"Yup," Ellison pops the P sound to make Dallas more agitated. His expression goes flat and his lips twitch like he wants to tell him off.

"Well?"

"Yeah, you fucking prick," he mutters. "I need to cook so I can feed my wife."

I bite my lip so hard it nearly hurts.

And Dallas' eyes flick to me.

He sees it. The tiniest curve of amusement I can't hide fast enough.

His eyes roll so dramatically it should be illegal. "Disgusting," he shudders.

"Get out, then," Ellison doesn't miss a beat. So Dallas pushes off the counter.

"Fine. I'll leave since you clearly don't want to share."

"Yeah," Ellison gestures toward the door. "Get the fuck out. I'm not sharing shit."

Dallas' shoulders shake like he's holding back a laugh as he heads for the door.

And when Ellison reaches out to slam it closed, he opens his mouth again. "And good luck in your Escalade. I'm not telling how Sage and I defiled it this time."

He slams the door just as we both hear a long string of expletives from Dallas.

But Ellison beams at me with all teeth as he turns around and leans against the door.

"Clean up first?" He suggests, and I reach for his hand when he steps forward. "I would've done this when we got home but Dallas acts like an orphan," he spits out. "Doesn't he have a house of his own?"

A laugh slips out of me and he squeezes my fingers as he leads me upstairs. "I... actually don't know," I chuckle. "I think he sleeps in the Escalade because he's literally always here."

"Well, he needs to be here less, then," Ellison petulantly quips.

I probably shouldn't be used to it by now, but Ellison steps behind me into the shower, and his hands reach for me immediately, like closeness is something he requires just as much as I do. It should feel suffocating, but somehow only makes me calmer.

His hands are gentle as he works shampoo through my hair, unhurried and thorough, fingers massaging everywhere.

It's probably mundane to most, but to me, it's something intimate. Something I'm hesitant to share but still do. I tilt my head back as he lathers the shampoo. Letting him take care of me.

I suppose that's become a habit... him taking care of me.

It makes no sense.

And it makes too much sense.

Because each time I let him, it's only because he's the first to do it.

It's quiet for a long time, just the sound of the water between us, until finally, a question slips out of me. One I've been wanting to ask.

"Why do you always wash my hair?"

His hands slow for a second, almost imperceptibly, but it's there. Like he hears the real question underneath it. And then he moves his fingers through my hair again. "Because I like it," he says simply.

"My hair," I ask, "or washing it?"

"Both," he answers back without hesitation, and I glance over my shoulder in confusion.

"Why though?"

"Because I can tell you like it," he murmurs, his lips forming into a smile that I've learned is only reserved for me. "And it makes me feel good to do something for you."

I don't think I've ever heard a man say those words before. Not towards someone they claim to be the object of their affections. "That's... strange," I offer back. And he actually laughs, quiet and surprised at my choice of words, a sound that feels startlingly normal.

"Why would that be strange?" He softly asks.

I hesitate to answer this time. Not because I don't have an answer, but because no one usually cares.

The world that I live in was not built for the opinions of a woman.

My mother taught me that.

The words come out slowly.

"My father never... cared for my mother like this," I carefully explain. His hands still again, and then start back somehow gentler than before.

"Our house was always tense," I whisper. "Quiet. Like everyone was waiting for it to collapse. And my mother..." I trail off, saddened by my tainted memories of her. "I think she only stayed because I was there, and my father never would have let her take me," I shake my head, and his expression shifts into something unreadable as he moves to turn me so he can rinse my hair better.

"My house wasn't like that." The sadness in his voice catches me off guard, and then the thought comes sharp and sudden.

"So, you do have family?" I ask, and a long breath leaves him. I almost regret that I said anything, but he gives me a dull, flat smile.

"No, baby," he says.

My heart drops and he reaches up to rinse my hair before speaking again.

"My father died when I was a teenager," he murmurs. "Cancer."

I turn fully to face him, needing to see his face as he bares himself to me, and he reaches up to brush his thumb over my cheek, like it soothes him.

His eyes are steady on me, despite such a heavy topic. I wonder how he manages to keep it all in when I can barely stand to speak of my mother without feeling like falling apart.

Maybe he feels the same way.

He's just better at hiding.

"He was military," he continues. "So I thought... I'll just follow in his footsteps. Do something that makes sense."

"And your mother?" My question is quieter now.

"Car wreck," his jaw tightens. "When I was seventeen," he explains quietly.

My heart feels like it's physically aching in my chest. I just stand there staring at him while the water runs down my skin like it'll wash the hurt out of his words.

"I enlisted early," his lips thin out, like that fact is frustrating. "Went to bootcamp right before my eighteenth birthday."

"Do you like it?" I ask, staring up at him expectantly.

But this question he seems to think about for a long time.

I let him drag me from the shower while he does.

"I'm good at it," he says simply, stopping to run a towel over my hair so it'll slow the dripping.

"Which parts?"

His mouth twitches faintly with amusement, eyes lightening just a little.

"All of it."

All of it. Such a simple sentence. But the reality of it isn't lost on me.

The honesty is brutal.

The military. The life. The violence. The soldier underneath all of these lies that we're webbing.

It just makes my throat tighten.

"That must be scary," I respond quietly. "Not knowing what will happen or where you're going or if you'll—" I swallow around the fear of it. "Or if you'll come home at the end of the day."

"I suppose it is sometimes," he shrugs.

"Were you scared? When you got injured?" My voice cracks faintly at the thought.

His eyes tighten a little. "Yes," he answers honestly. "But I didn't have any time to be. I had someone else's life in my hands. There's no time to be scared. Only time to move."

That's the reality of it.

The cold truth of it.

I step forward without thinking, my hands wrapping around him until I can hold him against me despite him being much bigger.

And he exhales like something inside of him loosens a little. His arms come up to hold me tight, and my cheek presses to his chest.

"I'm glad you made it home," I murmur against his skin.

His hold tightens on me, hand brushing over my spine as he takes a deep breath.

"Yeah, so am I," he breathes out.

After the shower, the bathroom feels far too cold without the hot water.

I towel off slowly, fingers brushing through damp hair, before I'm reaching for the blow dryer.

"I'll start dinner," Ellison's voice comes from the bedroom, and I call back a quick okay as the dryer clicks on.

He disappears, and yet only minutes pass before he's returning.

Socks are thrusted into my waiting hands, offered with ridiculous seriousness, and I force myself not to smile at him.

"Go cook," I mumble, and his lips twitch into a satisfied smirk.

"If you don't let me take care of my wife," he says, fussy as hell, "I'm going to lose my mind."

A helpless laugh escapes me.

And my palm presses against his chest, shoving him lightly back toward the hallway.

"Go," I twirl my fingers.

"You're being cruel, baby," he points at me, and I turn away from his pouting.

He huffs dramatically and finally leaves, muttering about me being ungrateful, but I know he doesn't mean it.

Dinner passes by like it always seems to do, quiet with conversation sprinkled in here and there.

But later, when we finally crawl into bed for the night, the thoughts creep back in.

I think both of us are a little wary knowing the auction will be here just days from now.

There's nothing we can do to prepare for it.

Nothing we can do to ensure Ellison's safety.

Nothing to distract me from that fact.

Except maybe one thing.

Ellison held me from behind like he always does, his body solid warmth against my back, his arm heavy and comforting around my waist.

But my mind won't settle. It races with the thoughts of what-if, each potential outcome more terrifying than the last.

And I don't want him to go.

I don't want to let him out of my sight.

I just want him here. To feel him. His presence. The fact that he's alive and breathing. That he's here with me, safe.

I shift slowly, turning within his arms, the silk from my nightgown getting caught up a little bit.

But it doesn't matter.

Because he's already there looking at me.

And even though the room is dark, I can see the smooth planes of his face, the dark fan of his eyelashes against his cheeks.

My fingers drift upward to trace the line of his jaw, and he closes his eyes like he loves it, a small, almost absent sigh escaping him.

I lean in, and my lips find his in the dark.

And when he kisses me back, it's a slow, melting kiss. Something craving.

My hand slides up to cup his cheek, my thumbs stroking the high arch of his cheekbone. And his arms tighten around me, pulling me closer until our bodies are flush.

The kiss deepens more than I expect it to. Our lips part, and the warm, tentative touch of his tongue against mine is nothing short of blissful.

He must feel every silent fear, every ounce of my dislike for him going, every worry, because he takes it all.

His hands come up, his fingers threading into my long hair, cradling the back of my head as he takes the kiss even sweeter.

He shifts, rolling onto his back, bringing me with him, guiding me to straddle his hips.

And he pushes my nightgown up, the silk pooling around my thighs as I settle over him.

Through the thin layer of silk and his cotton sleep pants, I can already feel the hard, thick length of him firm and ready for me, and my heart rate accelerates.

He reaches down, his hand gathering in the fabric of my nightgown, pushing it up slowly until it's settled against my waist and hips.

The cool air meets the bare skin of my thighs, and the damp cotton of my panties. His hands smooth over my skin, palms warm and broad as they knead the flesh of my outer thighs, thumbs stroking inward in a teasing motion.

"There," he whispers, eyes wide open now, capturing the little light from the windows, reflecting back in a soft, gray gleam. "Better."

I nod my head, unable to speak. My hands move to brace on his shoulders, and my lips find his again.

This time, the kiss is less tentative, more seeking, more wanting. As our tongues tangle, I begin to move. A slow, rocking grind of my hips against the hard cock under his sleeping pants. The friction is delicious, a sweet, blinding pressure through the fabric.

His hands slide from my thighs to my ass, his fingers digging into the soft curves, helping to guide my rhythm. "Just like that, love," he encourages me, voice thick against my lips. "Use me."

The permission, the praise, sends a fresh wave of heat through me.

I rock my hips harder, my movements gaining a little more intent. My panties grow more damp, breaths coming in short, sharp gasps against his mouth.

And he breaks my kiss, only for his head to fall back against the pillow.

He closes his eyes, brows slightly furrowing in concentration. "God, Sage."

His words only make my desire to please him worse.

I sit up slightly, changing the angle, grinding my hips in a slow circle, and the feeling makes my vision blur. My hands tighten on his shoulders, and his name comes out as a gasp. "Ellison."

"I'm right here, baby," he slides his hands up my sides, through the silk bunched at my waist, back to rest on my hips again, like he's not sure where he wants to touch. "Look at you. My beautiful wife. Riding my lap."

"I—inside... need you inside." The words stutter out of me, and he's moving without me having to say another word. He barely jostles me as he works to push his pants down enough for me to see what I really want.

He pushes my panties to the side, and we both reach down below me to position him right at my entrance, and my head drops back as his cock slides into me, slow and measured, each inch making me feel even more full until I'm back fully seated in his lap, shuddering with how good it feels.

"Yeah, fuck, that's perfect," Ellison's voice is strained, his jaw clenched, like he's so close to unraveling, too.

His hands move back to my waist, and he lifts me just slightly. My hips find that same desperate rhythm before, only now, I'm so full I can barely breathe, and my thighs begin to burn with the effort of how deep I want to take him.

A soft, frustrated sound leaves me, and his hands try to lift me more, to take over the rhythm, to thrust up into me.

"No," I rasp, the word firmer than I intend it to be. I reach for his hands and lace our fingers together, pushing them down so I can brace myself against his chest. "I want to—I want to do it."

"I can help, baby. Hm? Let me help."

"I don't—don't care," I lean down, my lips brushing his. "I want to make you come. Let me do it."

A low, ragged moan tears from his throat, and it makes me clench around him. His grip on me tightens. "Sage, baby, you always make me come," he lets out a desperate laugh. "Always. Just the fucking sight of you riding me like this is enough to do it."

My rhythm falters slightly with his words, but I keep going. I focus on the feel of him, so hard and eager to fill me. On the love I can see in his eyes, watching me, adoring me.

On the possessive way that he grips my waist.

His head falls back again, and his eyes roll back with it. "Do you have any idea what you do to me?" He whispers, voice strained, and I rock down, grinding hard, eliciting a sharp hiss from him.

"Tell me," I whisper back.

His eyes snap up to meet mine, dark and full of fire. "You unravel me, baby." He swallows, hips giving an involuntary upward jerk. "Do you want to feel it? When I come for you?"

The question, so dirty, sends a shockwave through my system, and my breath catches at the thought. My hips stutter, and he laughs under his breath.

"Do you want to be full of my come, Sage? Is that it? Want to be full, even with all of these damn clothes on?"

The image, the filthy, wonderful promise in his words, is what does it.

The slow-building pleasure I was feeling shudders, and I clench around him, a ragged cry pouring from my throat.

My head drops forward, resting against his shoulder, and he groans against my hair. His hands release my nightgown and grab my hips, holding me down against him as he thrusts inside of me, hips seeking the deepest possible contact.

"Fuck, Sage," his voice breaks, sounding choked up. And he holds me there, shuddering as the wet warmth of his come flooded into me, dripping against my sensitive skin.

The world dissolves into panting breaths, and the heavy, sated press of him against me.

I collapse fully onto him, my body boneless, and his arms come up to hold me so tightly that I can barely breathe.

And I never want him to let go.

Long minutes pass, and I count his heartbeat against my cheek, feeling it thrum underneath my fingertips.

His hand comes up, fingers stroking through my tangled hair, and I barely hear his voice.

"You wreck me, Sage," his voice is soft, lips moving against my forehead. "Don't you know I'd do whatever it took to come home to you?"

I can't form a coherent answer.

A deep, soul wrenching exhaustion was pulling at me, the frantic energy of worry finally spent. My limbs feel like they're made of sand, and my eyelids feel too heavy.

I feel him shift slightly beneath me, and I make a soft sound of protest, clinging tighter.

"Shh," he soothes. "I'm not going anywhere. Just sleep, baby."

His voice is the last thing I hear, the solid, steady beat of his heart under my ear dragging me under.

I drift off, wrapped in his arms, still straddling him, with him still buried inside of me.

Safe and sound.

Chapter 14

Ellison

D allas doesn't talk much on the drive there.

Actually, he doesn't really talk much at all.

And I'm not a man of many words either, but this is just fucking sad.

"So, like, are you thinking we'll have any issues tonight?"

He cuts his eyes over to me and purses his lips.

"Let's hope not," he quips, and then falls back into that same silence.

And then he lets out a long, exasperated sigh. "For my sake, I hope not. Sage will flay me alive if you come back with so much as a single scratch."

Ah, the sweet heat of affection. It rushes through me.

Right along with that smug, self-approving satisfaction that settles on my face.

"Wipe that shit-eating grin off your face," Dallas scrunches up his face and shudders in disgust.

"So you think she really likes me?" I beam at him, my smile getting even bigger somehow.

"You see that thing you're doing?" Dallas arches a brow, frustration bleeding into his features. "Where you look fucking stupid and act like we're friends? Stop doing that."

I chuckle at his attempt to shut me up.

It won't do shit.

"We *are* friends, Dallas. You're literally within spitting distance of me for like fourteen hours a day," I point out, and his lips continue to turn downward in a grimace.

"That's only because I'm employed by you. I don't like you; I tolerate you. There's a substantial difference."

"Actualllllllly," I snap my fingers, and he glances at me from the corner of his eye before he looks back toward the road. "You're employed by my lovely wife. Which means you only hang out with me for fun."

"For *fun?*" Dallas deadpans. "There is nothing fun about this, and we are not *hanging out.* We're literally on a mission."

"Oh, so now we're doing missions together?" I dreamily ask, and he shudders again like I'm traumatizing him with every single word.

"You can fuck all the way off."

He scoffs at my pleased laughter, so I decide to give him a break.

"Anyway," I lean back in my seat, watching the city pass by in bright flashes of light occasionally beaming through the window.

I can't help but pity the people playing in the park downtown with their children, going on with their lives since they aren't built around the same violence as ours, like they aren't all just walking around on top of rot and money and blood.

I pity them because they have no idea the greed that runs their city.

And I envy them.

How peaceful it must be to exist not knowing the rivers of evil drowning out the community.

"D'you think Sage was alright when we left?" I ask, and he cuts his eyes over to me again for a second, like he's sizing me up.

"Sage can handle herself."

"I know she can," I agree. "But I also know she doesn't like being by herself not knowing what's going on."

"She knows what's going on," Dallas counters, and I almost roll my eyes.

"Yes, but she isn't here to *see* it," I point out. "She doesn't like the *waiting to find out what happened* part."

"Yeah, well, she doesn't belong around the type of people that attend these kinds of things," Dallas grunts. "Sage doesn't need to be anywhere near these people. They're poison."

The words agitate me a little.

They're right. I mean, I know that.

But sometimes I wonder how this guy means the words he says.

I don't think he likes Sage. Not romantically at least.

But it makes a guy wonder.

"You, uh," I turn my head to glare out of the window, because I know he's about to look at me again. "You really care about her."

"She's my client," Dallas immediately remarks.

"Yeah, but I mean, you're around her all the time. Her life is often in your hands whether she realizes it or not."

"Like I said," Dallas murmurs under his breath. "She's my client."

"So you wouldn't care if somebody killed her?" I throw back, and he hits the brakes a little too hard at the approaching red light. My seatbelt jerks against my chest and I make an embarrassing sound at the sudden pressure.

Dallas turns his head fully to face me, and his expression... isn't one that seems pleased.

"Nobody is going to kill her," he bristles.

"Because you like her enough you'd never let that happen?" I challenge.

"I've been working for this family since birth," Dallas spits the words at me, and the thought settles uneasily in my chest.

What the hell does he mean since birth?

"I've never had a client die on my watch. Including the ones that I wish someone would take a shot at."

"And Sage? Where does she stand on your list?"

"Sage isn't some scumbag fuck-face wannabe gangster," Dallas fumes. "She's not on the same list as those people."

Someone blares their horn behind us and Dallas glances at the rearview mirror before he starts moving again.

"So she's on a super special list?" I prompt him again and I see a muscle jump in his jaw. "Just admit you like her. It's fine if you like her. I mean, she's mine, so don't forget that. I'd *hate* to have to bury you out in some desert because you put your hands where they don't belong, but I mean, it's Sage, so it's alright to look a little-"

"Sage is like my little fucking sister, Ellison," he exclaims in disgust, slamming one hand down on the steering wheel.

"There," I clap, and he looks at me in alarm like I've grown a second head. "You could have just said that to start with."

"Oh my God," Dallas groans. "You are so much more annoying than her first husband."

"But I'm the only one that counts, bud," I click my tongue and roll my shoulders to get the tension out. "You think we'll be able to get a little handsy tonight? I haven't had a good brawl in a couple of months and I'm starting to feel a little fatigued, honestly."

"Do you have ADHD or some shit?"

"Hell, they don't test us for that shit anymore," I sigh.

"Okay, well let's do a test now. Let's see how long you can shut the fuck up for," Dallas exclaims.

I fight my smile as I look out the window.

We drive for nearly twenty more minutes, getting further and further away from the city until we start veering off onto some county roads.

And that's when Dallas finally speaks again.

"You're probably thinking about going for the main property," he points out, and I tilt my head slightly.

"Everyone will," he adds, and there's something almost disdainful in it. "That's where the idiots will throw their money. The Kim family's big house is going to be the trophy. The headline. Everyone thinks that's where the secrets will be."

"So we won't do that," I murmur, and he shakes his head.

"No," he agrees. "We need to go for the third property, most likely. The Kims weren't stupid. They didn't survive that long by keeping the good shit in the first place people would look."

Strategic.

Or paranoid.

The same thing, really, when you live long enough in this world.

The warehouse we arrive at doesn't look like anything special.

Maybe that's the point.

There's no signs. No name. No address. No indication of what's inside of it.

The back entrance is already waiting for us when we arrive, a woman in black stepping forward with a smile that doesn't reach her eyes.

"Mr. Hart," she extends a hand, and I take it. "Thank you for arriving promptly."

"Thank you for the welcome," I tilt my head down in greeting.

The timed arrival is staggered just like Angela said, so no one sees anyone else come in, and no one can pretend this is social.

There's already a line of parked luxury vehicles lining the lot, no doubt all bulletproof and fancy.

Dallas' shoulders are stiff beside me as we're guided down a corridor that smells like fresh concrete. I can't help but think this place will be torn down again once this auction is complete.

They pat us down before they let us into the auction room, even though they had metal detectors at the entrance.

The private room is too clean and sterile.

A massive monitor is mounted on the wall, a console for bidding, a small table with iced wines that neither Dallas or I will be touching.

Dallas takes a seat in the corner, like a fixture that belongs in the shadows.

I really want to point out that he looks like Batman, but I keep my mouth shut. There might not be weapons right now, but I don't think he's above shooting me when we get back to the car.

It only takes a few more minutes before the auction is officially starting, and it begins without ceremony.

The same directions we received on the email are announced, and then properties flash across the screen with sterile descriptions that make my stomach twist.

The biohazards are cleared, but the crime scenes are still intact.

Just cold-blooded evidence on the screen.

The language of professionalism wrapped around something rotten enough to make your teeth ache.

Dallas slips into the hallway within the first few minutes, the door barely clicking shut behind him, and the silence afterwards feels thick.

When he comes back, his expression is colder than before.

"Ledgers are here," he murmurs.

"Sage's father?"

"Yeah."

"And so are the Harts."

Of course.

"Did you see Andrew?" I ask.

"No," Dallas leans closer, voice dripping with amusement. "His main bodyguard is here."

The one who has stood at his shoulder for twenty years like a leashed dog, so Sage says.

"And he didn't look too pleased to see me."

I can picture it clearly in my head.

The stare-off in the hallway, the calculation behind their eyes, the fury that Andrew didn't know his own son was here to bid against him.

He probably thought we wouldn't even know about this auction. Let alone be able to get in the front door.

Dallas slips out again, because he can't help himself, because I can tell he likes the satisfaction, too.

When he returns, he looks more than pleased. "Yeah, they're pissed."

"Good," I simply answer. "Maybe they'll be too mad to hit their little buzzer."

The properties keep rolling, ten minutes passing by excruciatingly slow for each one. And then Dallas straightens.

His entire posture changes, and I reach over to slam my hand on the bidding button.

"Yeah, this is the one," he leans over my shoulder, bracing himself on the back of my chair. "Let's hope this goes in our favor."

The amount on the screen climbs fast, and my pulse ticks upwards with it.

But I keep bidding.

One million.

One point two.

One point five.

Someone else stays with me, matching, pushing, testing to see if I'll fold first, like an animal pacing on the other side of the wall.

I slam my palm down on the button again.

Two million.

The room feels like it freezes and the timer bleeds down without the amount budging.

Nine.

Eight.

Seven.

"Did we fucking do it?" Dallas clamps his hand down on my shoulder a few times in excitement, and I almost smack him.

He thinks we won't be friends and he's full of shit.

The opposing bidder has stopped.

This can't be normal.

This isn't how these men operate.

Three.

Two.

One.

The confirmation flashes across the screen.

Sold.

For a moment, it feels unreal.

"Shit."

"Yeah," Dallas breathes out. "Shit."

"Did we just buy a dead man's family secrets with Andrew Hart's stolen money?"

"Yeah," Dallas swallows. "Yeah, we did."

The attendant appears almost immediately, polite as a banker.

We transfer the money and get the verification back instantly.

A suitcase is placed on the table, heavy in a way that makes my skin prickle.

She tells me the inside contains all of my purchase paperwork, the property details, and a bracelet with a single key attached that feels a little like a noose.

"Would you like to continue bidding, Mr. Hart?"

I look at Dallas once, and he gives the smallest shake of his head.

"No," I tell her firmly. "Pull the car around."

"Yes, Mr. Hart," she bows her head at me, and it feels awfully unsettling.

The hallway is cleared.

Dallas escorts me out like I'm someone important, like I'm not just a soldier wearing another man's power.

And the drive starts calm.

Too calm.

We don't talk this time.

Not one fucking word.

Because we both know something isn't right.

"Car trailing us," his voice is sharp.

I glance in the mirror and see the glint.

The headlights that are off.

The car keeping distance.

"Shit," I turn back to look at him. "Should we kill them?" I ask, and Dallas' mouth drops open.

"What? Are you crazy?" He balks at me. "We can't kill people like the ones that were at the auction. It would start a goddamn war."

"Well," I mutter, shaking my hands out. The itch to get my hands dirty is steadily rising. "Fuck."

"We'll lose them in town," Dallas' jaw clenches.

"You sure?"

"Yes," Dallas snaps.

He turns.

And then he turns again.

And then again.

The car follows.

And then a shot cracks the world open.

There's a ping on the metal and the Escalade shudders.

I duck down instinctively, heart pounding in my ears.

"Motherfucker," Dallas yells.

My hand flies to the glovebox and I pull my pistol free.

I look at Dallas and he looks at me.

"Can we fucking kill them now? Or are you going to let them kill us first?"

Dallas' expression twists with sudden anger.

"Yeah," he snaps. "Fuck it. They shot my Escalade," he hisses. "Now they've pissed me off."

Another shot rings off.

"I just bought this fucking car," he viciously adds.

"Either they're a piss poor shot or these are meant to be a warning," I point out when another shot beams off the rear glass.

The city comes into view fast, and Dallas takes a lot of turns that don't make any sense to me.

But then I see we're heading downtown, turns chosen for absence, for no cameras, for no witnesses.

A rundown stretch of abandoned buildings.

Dallas slams into an old carwash and whips around to the rear.

The brakes screech, and just like we expect, the other car follows.

"Idiots," I chuckle, and Dallas nods his head, glaring at the approaching car.

Dallas moves first, sliding along the wall with a lethal patience.

But I move faster, jagged and hungry, because the moment the car rounds the corner, I fire at the windshield just to make the driver flinch.

That's a *real* warning shot.

And then I shoot both front tires out.

The rubber explodes, and the car veers hard, slamming into the concrete wall with a grinding shriek.

Dallas rips the door open, gun to the driver's face, and drags him out like he's taking out the garbage.

He forces him down onto his knees, and when the man looks up, I laugh.

I laugh, disbelieving and almost delighted.

Because there's no fucking way.

Andrew Hart's bodyguard. Twenty plus years of loyal rot.

His face twists with hatred.

"You're a fucking dead man," he spits.

I throw my head back like this is the best joke I've heard all week.

"No way you're this fucking stupid."

His eyes flash with anger and he moves to lunge at me.

Dallas digs his gun into the man's temple and he settles, vibrating like a rabid dog ready to foam at the mouth.

"You have no idea what your Daddy is going to do to you for this."

I crouch in front of him, smiling wide, and I know I look crazy.

I know I don't look anything like Andrew Hart's whining child in this moment, because this man actually looks scared of me.

"Dead men don't talk, do they, Dallas?"

Dallas' voice is dry. "Nope," he pops, dramatic as hell.

And I point at my mouth, mocking. "Do my lips look like they're moving?"

Dallas tilts his head and smirks at me. "Mmmm. Sure do."

I click my tongue and lean a little closer.

"Well," I murmur. "Guess I'm not dead then."

And then I slam the butt of my gun into his face.

Bone crunches, and it sounds like a sweet symphony to me.

His body drops sideways, unconscious on the filthy concrete.

My breathing is a little heavy, and so is Dallas'.

I stand up, and he uses his shoe to push the man over onto his back.

"We leaving him here?" Dallas asks, and I chuckle under my breath.

"Oh, no. The hardest part of the night is yet to come."

"What?" Dallas scoffs. "What could possibly be harder than the shit we've been doing tonight?"

I beam at him, that same shit-eating grin that I know will piss him off.

"We gotta ask my smoking hot wife for permission to utilize the basement," I smile, all teeth and excitement, and Dallas only groans.

"I need a fucking pay raise."

"Well, that's too damn bad bud, 'cause we've spent a lotta money tonight, and I'm not planning on spending anymore."

"Shut up," Dallas mocks my satisfied smile. "Just get his feet so we can drag him to the car."

"Yeah, yeah," I tuck my pistol into my waistband and reach for the man's scuffed up shoes.

He weighs a lot more than he looks like he does, and it's a little bit of a hassle, but we get him in there.

Dallas and I sweep his vehicle quickly, and when we finally step back, Dallas pulls out a lighter and rips off his suit jacket.

He starts the Hart SUV, and then he rolls the window down.

"This is for fucking up my Escalade," Dallas grinds the words out between his teeth.

And then he lights his jacket on fire and throws it into the open window.

"Dramatic," I fold my arms and start walking backwards towards our car.

"You haven't seen dramatic," Dallas deadpans as he rips his driver's door open.

I get in after him and look toward the backseat to make sure our new friend is still knocked out.

"Just wait until Sage finds out you got shot at," Dallas petulantly grumbles.

I try to push that thought out because I'm honestly not sure what to expect when we walk through the door.

"Fuck, she's going to be so mad," Dallas groans, banging his head lightly on his headrest.

"I'll kiss her extra tonight," I suggest. "Maybe that'll help."

"Nobody wants to kiss your ugly mug," Dallas scoffs.

"Don't be jealous, Dallas. It's not a good look for you."

The tires squeal when he floors it out of the empty parking lot.

And the flames only rise in the rearview mirror.

Chapter 15

Ellison

D allas pulls into the driveway like he owns the fucking place.

I just know his tires leave rubber burn on the concrete, and that'll piss Sage off.

But I get distracted when our friend in the back slings across the seat and rolls slap into the window.

"Oops," Dallas smiles like he's pleased, and now I think I understand him a little better.

Dallas is the type of guy that likes to get even. And he thrives on pettiness while he does it.

I can get behind that.

The headlights sweep across the front windows, across the lawn, across Anderson's silhouette at the door, and for half a second, I get this weird, hollow feeling in my chest.

He should be inside where he can have eyes on Sage at all times.

But knowing my girl, she probably got pissed and sent him outside so she could stress out in peace.

I roll my neck and Dallas throws the SUV into park. He doesn't say a word as the car's engine ticks and cools. He just watches in the rearview mirror, checking the end of the driveway.

"We expecting company?"

I barely get the question out when I see the headlights.

There's a second vehicle pulling up behind us, angled like it's ready to leave in a hurry if need be. The doors pop open, and three guys that I've seen before hop out.

I don't know them. But I know they work for Sage.

Dallas gives me a short look, seeming a little surprised. "They actually followed the directions in my text. A miracle."

I don't bother with niceties when we get out, and neither do they. They don't look like the type anyway.

The first guy that strolls up looks me over quickly, then at the Escalade, and then the back window. "Looks like you guys had company," he points out, and I hear Dallas grumble something that sounds suspiciously like 'no shit.'

"Trevor," he nods his head at me, and then he points at the other two. "Peter and Sam."

"Ellison," I reach out and shake his hand quickly before turning on my heel.

"He pissed about his Escalade?" He asks me, and we both watch Dallas crouch down to smooth his fingers over the rear hatch.

"Yeah."

"I'm starting to think he's having an intimate affair with this car," Trevor murmurs as he brushes past me.

I don't laugh, but something close to it presses behind my lips anyway. We've got bigger things to worry about right now.

Peter and Sam both look like the guys I'm used to seeing. Both standing like they're part of the concrete, faces blank, eyes alert, hands loose at their sides like they're trying not to look armed.

It doesn't work.

These guys are military through and through.

"Alright listen," Dallas gestures for them all to huddle up. "We have a guy in the car that... quite literally could start a war," he breathes out.

"Aw shit," Peter's face finally cracks, and I tilt my head at him. Just a second ago he was trying to look all stonewalled, and now he's scrunching his face up like this is a tragedy. "I didn't bring my big guns."

"Your big guns aren't needed right now, Peter," Dallas quips back in exasperation. "Because no one knows that we have him, alright?"

"Sure thing, boss," Peter crosses his arms and closes his eyes.

"Listen," Dallas snaps his fingers repeatedly. "Sage is in that house, and we have to go in that house, which means we have to face Sage who is not yet aware that we have said man locked up in our car. So here's the plan," he gestures to me.

"What?" I deadpan, taking a hesitant step back.

"What do you mean, 'what?' You fucking idiot," Dallas whisper-yells. "She's your wife, so what's your plan?"

"Aw, shit, we ain't even got a plan?" Peter brings his hands up to his hair and tightens his fists into the strands.

"Listen," I hiss, waving my hands back and forth in a no gesture. "My plan is to go in there and calmly tell her what the hell happened and then beg for forgiveness if she doesn't like it."

"That's your master plan?" Dallas snaps, his face incredulous, eyes wide with frustration.

"Do you have a better one? It's the only one that's worked for me so far!" I throw back, and the other guys all turn back to Dallas.

And he takes a very long, very annoyed breath, eyebrows knitting together. He purses his lips for a moment, and then he slowly smooths them back out into a thin line.

"Actually, no. Okay, here's what we will do. Ellison and I will go in and talk to Sage. You three guard that asshole, and if you see me open the door and give a thumbs up, then you drag his ass in the house."

"Okay, fine," I turn and start walking toward the house.

My heart starts fluttering away the closer I get.

The house lights are on.

All of them.

Every window.

Sage's version of a flare shot straight into the sky.

Anderson shoots me a look when I reach the door, and just before I open it, he mutters a quick, "good luck."

And it hits me as soon as I step inside.

Sage is already there.

Pacing a hole in the floor.

Barefoot with her hair in a messy ponytail, arms wrapped around herself like it'll make any of this move faster.

Her eyes snap to mine and the relief in them is so apparent that it makes my insides burn.

Because I can tell she means it.

"Oh, thank God," she breathes out, her posture deflating violently as she starts making her way to me.

Her hands bury in the back of my shirt, her face pressed against my neck as she clings to me.

Her lips brush my throat before she lets out a relieved breath. I wrap my arms around her and pull her in closer, extinguishing the little space between us.

I don't care if anybody else can see it. Not the guys outside or Dallas standing awkwardly a few feet away. Not Anderson just outside the door.

I don't care who sees it.

Because Sage is relieved that I made it home to her.

And that's all that matters.

"I'm fine," I murmur into her hair, lips brushing her temple. "We're fine."

Her hands move frantically, brushing over my shoulders and down my arms as she steps back a little, like she's cataloging me for injuries that aren't there.

"Did you—" her voice cracks, and she swallows hard. "Did you get anything? Were there any problems? Is everything okay?"

"Everything is just fine, baby," I take her hands and pull her back a little closer to me. She tips her head back to meet my eyes, and I reach up to brush her cheek with my fingers. "We're good."

She's so worried it's almost insulting.

I love it.

Dallas clears his throat behind us, and Sage steps back again, just enough to look past my shoulder at him.

"What?" She demands, the relief evaporating a little bit. Her hands shake as the worry starts seeping back in. "What happened? What did you find? Did you get it?"

"We got the property," I cut in, trying to lessen her spiral and all of her shaking and tension and fear. "We got the one we wanted."

Her eyes widen, and for a second, she looks almost stunned.

"You... you won it? Really?" She whispers.

"Yeah," I say, squeezing her hands. "We did."

Her lips part like she's about to ask more questions, like what the place looked like, who was there, what they said.

But she pauses, her lips closing again as she looks at me and then back at Dallas for a second.

Then she settles her gaze just on me.

I let out a long breath and glance down the hall towards the stairs and then back to her.

"What happened?" She whispers up at me.

"Sage," I say it softly so it doesn't frighten her more, but she stiffens like she can already hear something bad in my voice. "Dallas and I were wanting to utilize the basement... if that's alright with you?"

Her expression changes so fast it's almost alarming.

Almost.

Her brows knit together, and her lips tighten for a moment. Her eyes move past me again, through the doorway, to the guys outside, to both vehicles, to the darkness.

"What did you do?" She whispers, and the words aren't an accusation. They're dread.

Dallas steps forward, hands raised like he's walking up on a wild animal.

"Now, wait a minute. We didn't do anything more than necessary. It's not what it sounds—"

"It's exactly what it sounds like," I interrupt him, because there's no point in pretending. Sage wants to know, so she'll know. "We were... tailed on the way home. And we intercepted the person."

Sage's throat bobs and she looks to Dallas who remains silent this time.

"Ellison," she says my name like it tastes bitter. "What the hell does *that* mean?" She stresses with her hands.

I glance at Dallas and he looks at me like he wants to strangle me, but I don't care. Sage deserves the truth.

"We got followed from the auction," I say quietly. "After we left the warehouse, a car started following us with its lights out."

Sage's eyes widen.

Her hands fly up to my face, forcing my head to tilt, scanning me like she's looking for injuries again.

"Did they do something? Did you catch them? What happened?"

"It's alright, baby," I soothe, moving to stop her hands. I lightly tug them from my body and hold them, squeezing a few times to show her things are fine. "Look at me," I ask, and she does. Her eyes are wide and anxious.

"I'll explain. Just stay calm, alright? I'm not injured, and Dallas isn't injured. None of the people who matter are injured. We're all safe, and all home. So there's nothing to panic over, okay?"

"Okay," Sage whispers, so I squeeze her hands again.

"We went downtown to try to lose them, but they followed us. They fired a few shots off at the car and—"

"He shot at you?" Sage's voice rises so much even the guys outside go silent, their quiet chatter filtering to nothing. "He tried to *shoot* you?"

"Yeah," I answer, and I hate how small it sounds compared to what it was. Compared to how fast my world narrowed into instinct and the pistol in my hand. "A few times."

Her face goes pale, and her breath stops.

She looks like she's about to slap me. Or cry. Or both.

"Ellison—"

"I'm fine, baby," I repeat, gentler this time, because I can see the panic on her face. "Dallas is fine. We're home. The only injury we have is to Dallas' insult, because they fucked up his Escalade."

Dallas snorts behind me, but Sage doesn't look like she likes the joke.

Sage's hands reach up to my cheeks again, turning my head slightly back and forth even though she's shaking.

"How did you catch them? And what are you planning to do? Whose man is it? My father's? Or Andrew's?" She looks back and forth between Dallas and me.

Dallas opens his mouth, probably to soften the blow, probably to say something diplomatic and acceptable so Sage is less likely to combust.

I don't let him.

"Get him," I say, and Dallas tries to subtly shake his head. "Get him," I repeat, and we have a silent stare off for a minute before he finally moves like he's on autopilot towards the door.

It only takes a minute, but Anderson steps aside, and suddenly the hallway fills with Peter and Sam dragging something heavy through the threshold.

A body.

Limp and unconscious.

A man in a suit that's too expensive for the way he's being hauled across the marble floor.

They drop him like a bag of trash, and the sound is sickening.

A dull thud that reverberates through the room.

Peter leans down and grips the man's hair, and hauls his head back so Sage can see the man's face.

She makes a sound I've never heard from her before. A half gasp, half choked swear, like her brain can't decide whether to scream or shut down entirely.

"Oh my God," she whispers. "No. No, no no."

Her hands fly to her mouth, and she stumbles backward one step, only for me to follow and grab her wrists to keep her from running.

"This—" she looks at the man again in disbelief, like he's a bomb sitting on our floor. "Ellison, this can't be here! He can't be here!"

Her eyes dart back to me, wild.

"This is Andrew's—" she swallows so hard it looks painful. "This man is practically a Hart, Ellison! What did you do?"

My hands reach for her hips, and I squeeze once before I look her right in the eyes.

"He shot at us. Remember?" I ask, and Sage's eyes tighten just a little, her eyes frantically moving between us.

"Andrew will kill us," she whispers, her voice thin. "He will kill all of us, Ellison. He will burn this house down with us inside of it. He—"

"We didn't seek him out, baby. He followed us. He chased us down, and he pulled a gun, and he shot at us. He shot at me. Multiple times, Sage. It wasn't warning shots. He was shooting at me with intention of me not coming home."

Sage jerks away like the words sting to hear.

Like they slapped her across the face.

I slide my hands up and hold her face in my palms, forcing her to look at me.

Forcing her to see that I'm standing right here.

Alive and breathing.

Unhurt.

"You think I'd let anybody kill you, baby?" I ask softly, and her lips tremble.

My thumbs brush the wetness gathering at her lash line.

"No," I shake my head, taking a deep breath. "It's nothing, baby," I softly tell her. "He's nothing. Nobody knows we have him. And nobody will. He's officially missing. Andrew knows he went after us, and he'll know he's missing. But he won't find him. Do you understand? He won't ever find him."

The words land heavy between us.

Her breath shakes out of her, and she reaches up to clutch my wrists like she's holding on for dear life.

She stares at me, like I'm the lifeline.

The fear doesn't vanish. I can still see it.

But something shifts underneath it.

Under the trembling hands and the moisture in her eyes.

The worry.

Something colder slips in.

Something meaner.

Her gaze slips toward the bodyguard again, and the panic starts to harden into something sharp.

Something delicious to see.

"He..." she whispers. "He *shot* at you."

"Yeah," I say again, and her eyes move back to me.

She holds my gaze for a moment, and I see it. God, do I see it.

The thirst for violence.

It mirrors mine.

Only it looks so much sweeter in her eyes.

"Kill him."

The words are clean.

So simple.

Absolute.

The foyer goes so silent it feels like the entire house holds its breath.

Everyone freezes.

And everyone looks like they're recalculating everything they knew about Sage and how dirty she was willing to get. How low.

Dallas steps forward, closer to us, like he's a little anxious. His expression is almost unreadable.

"...What?" He asks.

He doesn't need the clarification. He heard her.

They all did.

Sage doesn't cower from it.

"I said kill him," she repeats, and there's something in her tone that makes pride bleed into my veins. "He shot at you," she turns her gaze back on me. "He shot at you. He tried to kill you. He tried to follow you home."

She looks back at the man, his nose smeared with blood and head lulling.

"Kill him."

Dallas' eyes slide to me, and for a moment we just look at each other, communicating in the way only we can, silent, fast, and full of implications.

I didn't expect this either.

Not from my sweet Sage.

The irony spreads through me so fast I almost laugh.

Sage is the one supposed to be human.

Sage is the one who's supposed to keep her hands clean.

And yet her pretty fingers are dripping bloody orders as she points them at Andrew's right hand man.

My mouth curves into a smile, slow and dangerous, smug, because something in me likes it.

The violence.

Dallas looks like he might try to soften her, but I don't let him.

"Are those your orders?" I ask, and Sage's shoulders drop a fraction, like she didn't realize she was holding her breath until I agreed.

"Those are my orders," her voice trembles a little, but she doesn't falter.

She's too strong to falter.

"Okay, baby," I brush my finger across her cheek again. "Would you like to join us in the basement?"

Sage makes a face at that.

"No," she says immediately. "No. I don't want to see it. Just—I don't want to see it. Do what you think is best."

"Are you sure?" I ask one more time.

"It's gross down there," Sage shivers at the thought, and then she glances around the room.

Like she's looking for an out.

"I'm just—I'll just order food," she announces, her voice a little high. "For everyone. It's late and I didn't eat because I was waiting for you to come home and now I—" she pauses, her hand briefly pressing to her stomach, and then dropping. "I'll just order food. You guys do... whatever it is you're planning to do with that man."

Sage steps forward and grabs my face with both hands, and she kisses me.

Hard, and with a little too much force, and then she hugs me tight.

She looks like she's about to whisper something sweet to me.

Something about how she loves me and she's happy I'm home and not injured and is so happy to see me.

But instead, she holds my face and looks me dead in my eyes. "And someone better clean his blood off of fucking marble flooring."

The smile that slips onto my face is nothing short of that shit-eating grin that Dallas can't stand.

"Yes, Ma'am," I tell her.

Nobody breathes as she walks around all of us and heads to the kitchen.

Like she didn't just order this man's execution in the foyer.

Like she just didn't change the temperature of the entire house.

Dallas watches her go, and when she's finally out of earshot, he exhales through his nose.

"Did she just give us permission to kill him?" He asks, and I stare after her for a moment longer than everyone else.

"Yeah," I let out my own long exhale. "God," I whisper. "She's so fucking hot. I think I'm a little hard."

"You're a fucking freak," Dallas shoves past me. "Shut the fuck up," he mutters, and then he points to Peter and Sam. "Basement," he cocks his head toward the hallway.

They lift the man off of the ground, careful not to rub him any further into Sage's floors. And Trevor follows behind, pulling gloves on like he's ready to get messy.

Anderson is slow to make his way over to me.

"She's been stress-eating," he murmurs, and I glance towards the kitchen.

"Just let her," I tell him, nodding. "Make sure she actually eats though. Not that grazing stuff she tries to do."

"Copy," he nods and bounds off toward the kitchen.

And then I turn toward the basement.

The air down here is damp and cold, smelling awfully metallic like blood.

There's a single overhead bulb that flickers dramatically, and I almost laugh at that, too, because it seems nervous.

Andrew's lackey hits the chair with a dull thud, and Dallas grabs a bucket.

The others step back, and Dallas looks at me.

"Think it'll do?" He asks and crouches to fill the bucket with the faucet on the edge of the room.

"Only one way to find out."

All we hear is running water.

And then cold water slams into the bodyguard's face.

The man jerks away like he's been electrocuted, sputtering and choking, eyes wild, trying to orient himself to what the hell is going on, and what fresh circle of hell he's landed in.

And then his eyes land on me.

"You—" he spits, water and blood mixing on his lips. "You're a dead man. Just like that fucking whore of yours!"

I tilt my head, crouching just enough to meet his eyes.

"What did you say?" I ask, and my voice sounds eerily murderous even to my own ears.

"Andrew will—"

"Andrew will what?" I cut in, my voice soft enough to make him cower a little. "Kill me? You keep saying that but you're the one tied up, and where is Andrew? Does anybody see him?"

I look around like I'm searching, and then I turn back to the man.

"It's just us here," I warn him. "Just us."

"He'll kill you, and he'll kill that fucking—"

"That fucking what?" I press, leaning closer. "Say it."

His eyes flash with fear.

Because he's fucked up.

And he knows it.

He's a man about to choose his last words.

And he better choose them carefully.

"He'll kill... that fucking bitch," he sneers. "That Ledger whore. Poisoning you, turning you into this! He'll kill her! And he'll kill you along with her! Bury you in the same shallow fucking grave along with her dead mother!"

I don't let him say another syllable.

The gunshot is loud in the basement, a flat crack that eats the air and leaves it echoing.

His head snaps back.

His body goes slack.

And the world narrows into something bitter.

Dallas stares at the man for a long moment, and then he kicks off the wall.

"What the hell," he mutters.

My chest rises and falls, heavy.

My jaw aches from clenching it.

And Dallas turns toward me, eyes wide with irritation.

"You couldn't let me get a hit in, at least?" He snaps, voice laced with frustration. "For the damage to the Escalade?"

"He called my wife a whore," I cut in, my voice so calm it surprises even me. "He doesn't get to breathe."

Dallas drags a hand down his face, furious, but understanding.

"Jesus Christ," he mutters. "I can't argue with that."

I stare at the bodyguard's empty eyes.

At the pool of blood spreading on the concrete.

At the mess that can't be cleaned up with soap.

"Should we clean up before or after we eat?" I ask, and Peter laughs. "I'm a little hungry."

"I had a big dinner," Peter pushes between me and Dallas, making room for himself. "Excuse me, boys, but I've got a date with this here piece of shit."

Dallas exhales hard and steps back, shaking his head.

The thought hits me so sharply it almost makes me dizzy.

Andrew wants to kill Sage.

He wants to kill my wife.

The one person that I love that is still living.

And whatever lies within the Kim property... he wants it.

"Let's go," Dallas tells me, and his hand lands hard on my shoulder, easing me forward a little. "And put that away."

The gun is warm in my hand, like it's made itself a home there.

Bloody and ready to do my bidding.

I tuck it into my waistband and move towards the stairs. Dallas' hand stays planted on my shoulder until we reach the top.

Andrew Hart has made himself my problem.

But for now, I'll go to Sage.

Because she's waiting for me.

And I won't make her wait.

I slide my palm around her hip when I reach the kitchen, finding her stabbing some helpless honey sesame chicken straight from the takeout container.

She leans back against my chest, and I lean forward, hovering over her protectively, even though the immediate threat is still bleeding out downstairs.

"Did you take care of it?" She tips her head back to look at me, and I could drown in her eyes, so trusting and sweet.

"Yeah, baby," I murmur.

I place my hands on the counter on each side of her hips and watch as she devours an entire takeout box worth of chicken.

Dallas' eyes meet mine over the kitchen counter and he holds my gaze until Sage starts asking about the damage to the Escalade.

I don't move from her side all night.

Even long after the guys leave and she burrows into my chest where she's most safe.

Even then, I stay awake long after her breathing has evened out.

Thinking.

Because this is just the beginning.

And tomorrow will likely be harder.

But Sage will stay safe.

And Sage will stay untouched.

Even if I have to kill every man in the country to be sure of it.

Chapter 16

Ellison

D allas sleeps like the dead.

Not the peaceful dead. That borderline concerning kind where a man's brain shuts off because if it doesn't, it's going to start eating itself from the inside out.

I don't know if he's doing it on purpose or if his brain just does it to survive, but I've been staring at him for nearly twenty minutes while I've been sipping my morning coffee and he hasn't budged. When the sun starts bleeding through the blinds and beaming him straight in the face, he's still out cold on the couch.

I can't sleep like that.

Well, I don't sleep much at all.

Not unless I'm wrapped up snug and tight in Sage's arms.

But that wasn't even enough for last night.

I stayed awake long after Sage drifted off, long after her breathing evened out and the tension in her shoulders loosened as she melted into me and the mattress.

Because I couldn't stop replaying the night in my head. And I keep hearing the crack of that gunshot in the basement, and the way I felt like my heart imploded when he said her name like it was something he could spit on.

The way my finger didn't hesitate because the world can keep its morality and its civility and its ethics and all of its neat little rules, but Sage is mine, and I'm not interested in negotiating her safety with people who don't deserve oxygen.

It's a little frightening, in all honesty.

I've killed plenty of men before.

And I'll kill plenty more.

But this one... it's sticking to me like a poison dart.

Not the killing itself. Not even the words that came out of his mouth.

It's the implication that I keep running back.

Now the thought has settled deep under my skin and I can't shake it.

The real question is how far is Andrew Hart willing to go before he tries to eliminate Sage? And how far has he already gone?

Has he planned it? Has money exchanged hands? Is the target already planted on her back, dead center on the tattoo I like to trace?

The endless questions plagued me all night long.

So by morning, my body felt heavy in a bone-deep way, tense like my body has been stuck all night and forgot how to let it go.

Sage was still curled up next to me when I finally pulled myself out of bed.

I had stared at her for a minute too long, noticing the softness in her face that never shows up during the day. Something unguarded and honest, like she's finally not holding the world together with her bare hands.

Even now, drinking my coffee and staring at Dallas' stupid face, I think about her.

My chest aches like something stupid because my wife ordered a man's death in our foyer last night. The same woman who also tugs the blanket tight around the both of us, like I might get cold even though her body temperature is making me sweat.

I love her.

And I want to keep loving her.

So I might have to kill Andrew Hart soon.

We'll have to talk about that.

I polish off the rest of my coffee and head back upstairs.

My fingers slide through the ends of Sage's messy hair, slowly, because I don't want to wake her.

But she wakes anyway, like she always does, refusing to fully rest if I'm awake. Her lashes flutter open, and the moment she finds me staring, something shifts in her expression.

The relief from last night is still there, faint under the surface.

"Good morning," she whispers up at me, and I card my fingers through her hair again.

"Good morning, baby."

Sage closes her eyes and lets me brush over her hair, so trusting and relaxed even though she knows today won't be easy.

"Are we going to the Kim property today?" Her voice is still rough from sleep, so I only hum in confirmation. "We got the third property, right?"

"Yeah, baby," I confirm softly. "We got the paperwork and a key, but we didn't get much further than that because of our little scuffle."

"Dallas," she murmurs, "is he awake?"

"He's dead on the couch," I tell her. "Maybe quite literally. I can't really tell." The tiniest hint of humor twitches at her mouth before it disappears again.

"Anderson?"

"Outside," I answer, and she looks towards the window like she might be able to see him there.

Sage's hands slide down her stomach absentmindedly as she sits up, not quite rubbing, not quite holding. Just pressing like she wants some kind of reassurance.

"You want me to make you some coffee?"

"Mmm, maybe later," she shakes her head.

"Really?" I huff a little surprised laugh. "But you always want coffee."

"Maybe we can get some on the way to the Kim's?" She suggests.

"Okay, baby. You wanna get ready now?"

I leave her for a while so she can shower, and I lug myself downstairs so I can kick Dallas with my foot, shaking him awake finally.

I sip on another coffee while Dallas has his first, and when Sage comes out to declare she's ready to go, I shake my head.

"Eat first," I tell her, because I'm not letting her walk into this shitty day without at least that.

"I don't want—"

"Sage," I cut in gently, and she pauses, her eyes lifting to mine. "You didn't eat all day yesterday until we got back. I know you're under a lot of stress, but eat something please?" She narrows her eyes at me, offended on principle because that's just who she is. But I lean in and place a kiss on her forehead and then reach for her hand to pull her towards the kitchen.

She follows me, even if she glares daggers at the back of my head.

"Fine," she mumbles under her breath.

It's ridiculous how much that one word satisfies me.

She eats the strawberries and bananas that I cut for her, and I stand behind her, close enough that my chest brushes her back when she moves, because I can't help it. After last night, having any space between us feels catastrophic.

Anderson is waiting with the keys at the edge of the room, quiet as a mouse like always, watching us.

I glance over at Dallas and grimace.

Dallas is still sprawled on the couch in the living room, one arm thrown over his face, looking like he fought a war with the blankets and lost. Anderson meets my eyes and gives the smallest shrug, like yes, he's alive, yes, he's breathing, no, he's not ready to be a person yet, so I'm driving.

"Can we stop by Starbucks on the way?" Sage tilts her head back to look at me. And God, she's the most endearing creature I've ever seen with her mouth full of fruit.

"We can stop wherever you'd like," I lean down, my mouth near her ear. "We can also leave Dallas here so we won't have to hear him be insufferable—"

"Shut up," she makes a sound that's halfway between a huff and a reluctant laugh, and then she turns her head back to her empty plate. "Happy?" She glares at me again, but I know she doesn't mean it.

"Ecstatic," I beam at her, and I see her fight the smile that threatens to meet mine.

Dallas only stirs when the front door opens and closes again, and he sits up slowly like his spine is made of rusted metal, hair a mess, face creased with sleep and irritation.

He looks around the room real fast, and then he starts patting himself down, likely in search of his keys.

"We aren't taking your bullet hole filled Escalade, dude," I deadpan, scandalized that he'd even think of it. "Anderson's driving."

"My car," Dallas rasps, and I roll my eyes.

He drags himself up and then turns around, nearly running into Sage who's pulling her jacket on.

"What?" She says sharply, and Dallas flinches a little.

"What? I didn't say anything," he throws back.

Sage simply stares at him until he drags a hand down his face. "Why is everybody so pissy today?"

"I'm always pissy," Sage crosses her arms. "I just don't like people."

"Yeah, and he's always horny," he gestures to me. "And I'm always overworked and underpaid, and Anderson's always like a silent ai robot regurgitating information. Perfect, and here we all are, living in hell together, one big happy family!" He chipperly barks.

Sage makes a face like she wants to throw something at him, and Dallas ignores her in favor of fishing out his cellphone.

He stalks out the front door as he makes a few calls, and shortly after, Trevor is showing up, along with Peter and Sam, the whole crew moving slowly in the early morning light.

Nobody mentions last night.

Nobody also mentions when we run through the drive-thru at Starbucks either.

Though Dallas also seems surprised when Sage orders this large ass strawberry drink instead of a coffee.

At least I'm not the only one that thinks it's odd.

But I file it away to bring it up later, wondering if she'll end up wanting one later in the day.

The rest of the drive out to the Kim property is quiet. Sage leans on my shoulder for most of it, drifting in and out of sleep until we turn off of the main highway down a long, winding drive surrounded by trees.

It's not the main house. Not the trophy place people would brag about, but still looks expensive in that empty, dead way that all rich people's houses do.

The gate is locked when we arrive, but thankfully my new handy dandy briefcase has a code for that. It's the first thing that makes the hairs on the back of my neck rise.

It feels all too welcoming.

Trevor radios our car, saying nothing odd is showing up on his scans.

I really need to ask what exactly he does here, because I have no fucking clue what all of his little gadgets do. I just saw him loading them up in the car before we left.

When we finally park the car, Sage gets out and stands there for a second, staring up at the big house like it's studying her.

Her arms fold over her chest and I step up behind her, my hand sliding over the small of her back. I feel her exhale, long and strained.

"I don't like it," she murmurs, and yeah, I get it.

"I don't either. Fucking creepy," I whisper back, and she gives me a relieved smile. At least my humor is doing something for her.

"Here," I hold my hand out, and Sage takes it. Her lips press together, but she walks alongside me anyway until we reach the top step.

It unlocks with my new fancy keys, and I push the door open and take a step back.

Inside, the air is stale.

You can tell it hasn't been occupied for a long while, but still, it's all cleaned up despite the fine layers of dust.

The rooms are all too neat.

The furniture is minimal, expensive, and catered for appearance rather than comfort. It makes my skin crawl because there's no softness here, no warmth, no proof that anyone ever lived here in the first place.

"Does it not look like a staged house?" Sage whispers, and everyone instantly agrees.

She moves slowly, eyes tracking everything, her gaze catching on tiny details that I catalog right after her.

There are papers stacked in every drawer, ledger-looking things, numbers and codes, financial trails that make my head hurt just looking at them. And when she flips through them, I watch her face shift, the tension deepening between her brows as names repeat and patterns emerge, showing connections she didn't want to see.

Dallas whistles under his breath. "Jesus."

Peter steps in closer behind him and peers over his shoulder, careful not to touch anything with bare hands. "This is... a lot," he murmurs, and for a man like him to sound unsettled, it means it's worse than it looks.

Sage doesn't answer.

She moves room to room, hallway to hallway, each step a little too loud for this empty house, amplifying us like it's listening, like it knows what we're doing here.

At one point, she pauses in the middle of the room, the light from the windows cutting across her face, and she turns her head slightly like she hears something.

"What is it?" I murmur, and her eyes flick up to mine.

"I think... that I'm going to find things I don't want to here."

"Nothing here can hurt you, baby," I tell her, the words coming out before I can stop them. "Whatever has happened has already happened."

"That's right," Sage whispers softly, her hand reaching up slightly to brush down the back of my shirt. "The hurt happened years ago." Her voice is so flat that it scares me more than when she cries. "When they took my mother."

My throat tightens.

There's no good answer to that.

No comfort that can undo what's already long been done.

I let my hand slide into hers instead, fingers threading together, and she holds tightly to me.

And then, like she can't stand the added pressure, she pulls her hand away and keeps walking.

It doesn't take long.

We find the safe in what looks like a back office, tucked behind a false panel like it was never meant to ever be found.

It's massive and industrial-grade.

And I don't think we'll be able to get to whatever is inside.

The metal feels cold enough to bite when I brush my fingers over the keypad.

"That's not a house safe," Dallas murmurs, leaning in to look at it. "That's a fucking vault."

Trevor crouches beside it, studying its hinges and seams, the way it's set into the wall like it's part of the structure.

He shrugs out of his backpack and unzips it, pulling a UV light from the bottom, and he moves all along the edges and keypads before he lets out a long hum.

Sage stares at it like it's the doorway to hell.

Her voice is tightly controlled when she speaks. "Can you open it?"

Dallas tries the handle like he's testing a door, and his gaze slides over to her. "Maybe."

"Oh, I can open it," Trevor drops his light back into his backpack and quickly zips it up.

All eyes turn to him.

"How?" She asks, and he seems confident as he tugs his backpack back on with a pep in his step.

"Because I'm me," he smiles at her with all teeth, a little too deadly proud. If I wasn't looking at him, I'd think blood were dripping from his canines with how sure he is in his abilities.

Sage's eyes move toward the rest of the room, toward the papers scattered on the desk, like whoever was flipping through them left in a rush.

I watch the decision form behind her eyes.

"Haul it," she murmurs.

"Yeah?" Dallas steps forward, his brows lifted in surprise.

"Yeah," she repeats a little steadier. My chest tightens with pride. "Call a truck in. Get it out of here. Bring it to the warehouse. Call Ramos and Kline," Sage orders.

"Who are Ramos and Kline?" I interject, and she looks at me for a moment before she looks back at Dallas.

"I want them to escort you all the way to the warehouse. All clear intersections. I don't want anyone wanting to know what's in there."

Dallas nods once like he respects the decision, and then he steps away, already pulling out his phone. "I'll make the call and get a truck in as soon as possible."

He leaves the room, boots echoing down the hall, and the second he's gone, the house feels even more quiet, like it noticed one less heartbeat in the room.

Sage and I stand alone with the safe, and she looks at it like she can feel the truth inside trying to claw its way out.

"Ramos and Kline are on our payroll," Sage finally answers me, still looking at the safe. "They work for the police department task force. We pay a lot of money for them to pull strings and make sure nobody asks any questions."

I stand behind her, not touching at first, letting her have her space, but my hand eventually lands on her hip anyway, unavoidable when I ache to soothe her.

Her voice comes out soft, almost embarrassed. "It's unsettling," she admits, honest as ever.

"I know," I murmur back.

Her head tilts back just enough that she can lean against my shoulder, and she closes her eyes when I step closer to wrap my arms around her.

"Ellison," she murmurs, and I gently rock her back and forth a little, bracing myself for whatever she's about to hurt me with. "I think my father had my mother killed."

I don't say anything at first.

I don't want to agree, because if I do, she might lose it a little.

But I know she needs me to say something.

"If he did, then we'll do whatever you want us to do to make it right," my lips brush her hair when I speak, a little too intimate for a conversation like this, but she leans further into me, like she wants me closer.

"What if I want you to kill him?" Sage whispers.

It lands like a match struck in the dark.

Like a light to a truth that can't be undone.

I feel like a moth being led to a funeral pyre as I chase after it.

Because I know that I will do it.

"Then I kill him."

The words come out so softly, quiet, like they're the absolute truth.

And they are.

I've always been the matchbook, waiting patiently for Sage to set me alight.

Her head rolls on my shoulder, and her eyes meet mine.

The intensity there could drown me, and I'd let it.

She looks like she believes me. And she should.

"There is not a thing that you could ask of me that I would not see to the end for you," I whisper to her, and I know she believes it.

I know she does.

Sage closes her eyes when I lean down to place a featherlight kiss to her lips.

And when we part, she turns her head back forward and looks at the safe again.

Sage is the most dangerous person I have ever met, precisely because she knows when to turn her humanity on and off.

And I am the means to an end because when it comes to her, I have no humanity to give.

I will do what she needs me to do, and I will do it with pride.

"Whatever is in that safe is going to change everything," Sage whispers.

My hands tighten around her, and she breathes out like it pains her to admit that.

"We'll do what we have to do," I promise.

Down the hallway, Dallas' footsteps return again, and he doesn't even blink when he sees me holding Sage.

"Alright," he announces as he steps back into the room and looks at the safe. "I've got a crew on the way. We're pulling it out and hauling it back to the warehouse. Ramos and Kline will meet us when we leave out. We'll have clearance and I'll have Samuel trade off their cash. Cameras will all be down so we can get it moved. Trevor said it'll probably take all night to get it open. Can I have the night off? There's this woman at the bar who I've been dying to—"

Sage's stare turns icy.

"Kidding," Dallas lifts his hands quickly, surrendering to the fact she might murder him. "Mostly."

I watch Sage's mouth twitch, just barely, like the amusement fought its way through the dread for half a second.

"You can have all day tomorrow off," she finally answers.

I follow after her when she starts walking toward the doorway.

"What?" Dallas scoffs when Sage trails right past him and starts walking back to the front of the house. "I don't need the entire day. Two hours will do."

"Two hours?" Sage slows her stride just to look at him. "That's it?" She clicks her tongue. "Poor girl."

A laugh chokes itself out of me.

Sarcastic, brutal Sage is somehow still an angel to me.

"Sage!" Dallas' voice is positively scandalized.

"Touch break, bud," I clap my hand over his shoulder as I pass in front of him.

Following after Sage, leaving behind the house of secrets.

Chapter 17

Sage

T he park smells like freshly cut grass.

It's nearing winter, but that doesn't dampen the spirit of the kettle corn covered children.

I'm not sure where I expected Ellison to take me. To the house maybe, given everything that's happened in the past twenty-four hours.

But somehow, we ended up at a park.

It feels almost embarrassing.

Ellison walks beside me a bit awkwardly, even though he clings to my hand still. His shoulders are a little tight, gaze sweeping every which way like he's expecting a hit to go down in broad daylight with dozens of kids running around every which way. Maybe he thinks the chaos will make them bold.

There's kids shrieking and tumbling all over each other, parents chasing after them and hoping they won't bust their heads open on the slide over on the playground side.

And for a moment, I almost hate them for it.

Because they don't know.

They don't know what kind of city they're playing in.

They don't know what kind of blood runs under the sidewalks and gives life to all of the pretty flowers that will be dead come next month.

Ellison's hand squeezes mine, fingers tight like he's pulling me back from the depths of my racing mind.

He said we were coming here for fresh air.

Like it'll fix something.

Like it can un-kill my mother.

Like it can un-write my father's name on the papers from the Kim home.

We walk in silence for a while around the track, the sound of laughter and passing cars and a woman calling after her dog and... I find myself staring.

At a man pushing his toddler in the swing.

At a woman leaning her head on her husband's shoulder like they have no worries.

At two teenagers throwing a football with a younger boy who keeps dropping it over and over again.

And yet they keep throwing it to him, even though they know he won't catch it.

It's all so simple.

It's all so unbearably simple.

"Would you be like this?" The words slip out of me before I can stop them. "To be like these people?"

Ellison's leisurely pace slows to a stop as he glances around at all of these people.

"To be normal?" He asks, and I huff out something that almost resembles a laugh, except it doesn't feel like humor.

"What do you think it would be like?" I ask, and his lips twitch with amusement.

"I think it would be incredibly boring," he deadpans, and I glance up at him, offended on principle, and he catches it immediately.

"And incredibly enriching," he softens his voice, tracking the families again.

The words feel a little heavier than I'd like them to.

"To live like that," he continues, tugging at my hand to pull me along the concrete track. "With the people that you love. Your family and friends. Without all of the shit we deal with."

I swallow around the lump that settles in my throat.

"If you could," I ask quietly, "would you want your life to be like that?"

Ellison's steps slow again, just slightly.

And then he turns to me fully, like he's forgetting the chaos around us just so he can look at me.

"If I were with you," he says in a way that makes my chest ache, "yes."

I blink fast, rapid as a butterfly's wings.

And yet the tears come anyway.

It's humiliating, honestly, the way it floods me.

Ellison stops completely.

His hands rise without any hesitation, cupping my face in his palms like he can't stand to see me cracking under the pressure.

"Hey," he murmurs, thumbs brushing under my eyes. "No, let's not do that."

My breath stutters, cold in the open air, in the middle of the park filled with people moving with nothing but happiness, having no idea my world is collapsing in slow motion.

I try to swallow it down.

I try to push it back where it belongs.

But Ellison's hands don't let me.

His palms are warm against my cheeks, making all of these feelings a million times worse, because it does nothing but make me think of why I'm so devastated.

How badly I want to pretend we can be normal.

"I'm sorry," I whisper miserably, voice breaking. "I don't know why I'm so—"

"Don't," he cuts me off softly. His eyes stay on mine, storm-grey and holding all of me together. The noise seems to all blur away, turning distant, and his hands tighten just slightly like he refuses to let me fade out with it.

"Things are difficult right now," he says, and his voice is quieter than before, rough like he's choosing each word carefully even though they're heavy. "And scary. And a lot."

I let out a breath that trembles.

"I know," I manage. "I just... everyone else—"

His jaw tightens instantly, like the concept of anyone else irritates him, and he rapidly shakes his head.

"Everyone else doesn't fucking matter, Sage."

The words don't come out cruel, but I go still at how firm they are, stunned silent, still sniffling in a way that is quite frankly pathetic.

His hands stay on my face, eyes searching mine to see if it's sinking in. If I'm grasping what he's saying.

His thumbs keep brushing away the tears as if he can erase them with sheer will.

His voice breaks when he speaks again.

"Baby, everyone else doesn't matter. We are all used to the smoke and the fire and the life on the line, but you just lit the match for the first time."

My throat tightens so hard that it burns.

The reality settles harshly. And yet his gaze doesn't waver.

"This is the first time you're really playing in the fire," he murmurs. "And the smoke is gonna choke you up a little, but we're gonna breathe through it, and do what needs to be done."

I stare up at him like he's the only thing holding me upright.

Because he is.

The park keeps moving around us.

The children all keep laughing.

The dogs keep barking.

Life keeps being simple for everyone else.

But my lungs feel so terribly full.

"Okay," I whisper, barely audible.

Ellison's brows lift slightly. "Okay?" He asks.

"Okay," I repeat, leaning into his palms like they're the only safe place I can be.

His fingers brush the lingering wetness away one last time before his hands slide down, slow and steady.

He takes my hand again, threading our fingers back together.

He starts to tug me gently back toward the car.

And my feet stop moving.

His body stills immediately, and he turns back, his attention snapping to me like a tether pulled tight.

And the words come out before I can reconsider them.

I've said them before.

But that was during sex.

And this is different.

This is more than different and I need him to know.

"I love you."

Ellison looks at me like I pushed his world onto its side.

Like something inside of him melts so fast it floods him with affection.

His lips part, and his eyes soften so much I nearly start crying again.

"I love you too, Sage."

But that isn't enough.

He isn't understanding and I need him to understand me right now.

"No," the word slips out, trembling.

"What?" His brows knit together, the confusion apparent.

And I just shake my head, my breath catching in my throat.

"No," I repeat a little firmer. "You don't understand."

"Sage," he murmurs in a careful tone. "What are you talking about, baby?"

The crying creeps back in like it never left.

Like it's been waiting this entire time.

"I—Ellison, I really love you," I rasp. "I really do. I—I feel like I can't breathe because my lungs are full of it, and it's overflowing, and I need you."

Ellison's face breaks open completely.

His hands rise immediately to cup my cheeks again, like he can't help himself.

Like he needs to hold us both together.

"Sage," his voice is wrecked when he says my name. "I know, baby, and I need you, too."

But I'm shaking my head again, desperate.

"No, I—I really don't think I can do this without you," I whisper.

His thumbs brush harder now, wiping at tears that keep pouring.

His voice lowers, firm with a promise that I know he means. "I'm right here," he tells me. "I'm right here, and I'm not going anywhere."

My chest hurts.

I know he means it.

I know he does.

And his voice breaks as he continues.

"You aren't doing this without me, Sage." His voice cracks like it hurts him to even imagine it. He swallows thickly as he looks me right in the eyes.

"Every part of me is tailored for you," he whispers. "To care for you. To love you."

I squeeze my eyes shut and his hands don't move.

"I'm in this life for you," he says, voice even more raw somehow. I never would have chosen any of this. I'd still be out there, in the desert, waiting for the wrong bullet to catch me..."

A sob catches sharp in my throat.

"... if it wasn't for you."

He leans forward and kisses me on the lips, soft and trembling, a little wet from my tears.

"From the second I saw you," he breathes out in a rush, "from the second I heard your voice on Adrian's screen, I was done."

My heart feels like it kickstarts into overdrive.

"I was in it for you, Sage," he whispers. "I didn't even get a choice."

I make a broken sound, and his mouth finds mine again, sweet and insistent, like nothing else matters.

When he pulls back, his eyes are shining.

"I know you love me," he murmurs fiercely, like he needs me to understand it, too. "I know you do. I can feel it in every touch, in every word, in every look you give me."

I can't bring myself to say anything to that.

I can't.

"You never have to doubt that I know," he says, voice shaking. "Because I feel it. It mirrors everything that I feel for you."

My breath trembles out of me.

And the truth that I've been choking on finally slips free.

"I'm scared."

The words hurt him instantly.

I see it in his eyes. They make him ache just like they make me ache.

His eyes water too, like my fear is right there in his heart too.

"I know, baby," he whispers. "I know you are."

His fingers slide into my hair.

And his thumbs brush over my cheeks again.

"But you are not alone," he promises me. "Not for one second. I'll hold you together whenever you need it. I swear I will. And I know you'll do the same for me when I need it."

My eyes burn with the sincerity in it.

I want him to tell it to me all the time. Not to worry.

To trust in the time that we have together, where we can hold each other through it, and that I won't wake up on my own because he will be there when I open and close my eyes.

But I don't ask him to do that.

I don't ask him.

Even though I know I will one day.

So instead I ask him the only thing I can right now.

"I need you to keep loving me," I whisper. "I need you to. Okay?"

"You don't need to worry a day in your life that I'd stop, Sage."

"You—" I take a deep breath. "Do you promise me?"

Ellison's lips are soft on mine again.

And when he pulls away, he doesn't have to promise me.

I can see it in his eyes.

"I promise you," he says it anyway.

"I promise you that I will always love you. And there won't ever come a day where I will stop."

I believe it.

Chapter 18

Sage

"Come on," Ellison murmurs quietly. His thumb brushes the underside of my jaw, lingering like he's memorizing the hurt on my face so he never has to see it again.

I let him lead me back to the car, where reality sinks back in the second his hand touches the passenger side door to open it for me again.

The drive to the warehouse is suffocatingly quiet. The music is playing low on the radio, but I don't hear a word of it.

I hold Ellison's right hand between both mine, brushing my fingers over the pulse point of his wrist, letting the steady thud of it keep me sane and silent.

He glances at me every few minutes like he's checking that I'm not drifting too far into my head, and sometimes I meet his eyes, offering him a tired smile that I know doesn't quite meet my eyes. Sometimes I just stare at our conjoined hands.

Sometimes I just stare out of the window at the passing neighborhoods that have so much life in them.

At the little houses with porch swings.

At the Christmas lights going up far too early.

At people raking up the falling leaves with their children playing in the yard.

I watch them and feel something hollow in my chest. I watch them and think of how unfair it is that the world keeps being simple for them while I have to fight the decisions of men made years ago.

"Are you okay?" Ellison asks eventually, his voice low and soothing.

I want to say yes.

I don't want to be a liar on top of everything else, too.

"I just want to get this all over with."

"Me too, baby," he murmurs back.

He tightens his hand once around mine, and I squeeze it back.

Dallas' voice slices straight through all of my practiced calm the second we walk through the doors.

"Finally."

Ellison pauses with his hand still on the door. Dallas is leaning against the wall like he's been standing there for an hour, sunglasses on despite the fact he's inside.

I can tell immediately that something is wrong.

Because Dallas never paces, and he starts pacing the second we step out of the elevator.

"I thought we were going to have to burn our entire warehouse to the ground," he huffs out a sound of frustration.

"Did you get it open?"

"They've been working on it for hours. Trevor's losing his goddamn mind. There's torches involved. And Peter's been trying to sweet talk it like he's in a whorehouse."

Ellison's tense expression doesn't change.

His hand finds the back of my neck anyway, holding me steady.

"Did you get it open or not, Dallas?"

Dallas hesitates to turn back to me, just barely.

And the hesitation is enough to make my throat feel like it's closing up again.

"Not yet," he admits. "But it's really fucking close."

Close.

The truth is close, stuck behind the other side of burning steel.

Ellison's fingers press gently against my nape.

"You wanna go now?" He asks, and my lungs feel full again.

Not of love this time.

But of the smoke.

The fire.

The match I lit and can't put back out.

And I nod.

Because I'm not a child anymore.

Because my mother is still dead.

Because my father's name was all over those papers.

Because I have to know.

"Yeah," I whisper. "Let's go."

He moves to meet my gaze head on and his thumb brushes my cheek just once, and he nods at me.

"Sage," Dallas' voice is quieter when he speaks again. And when I look at him, his expression is strange.

Not his usual irritation or his sharp tongued sarcasm.

Something a little careful.

"We might find... things in that safe that you don't want to see. It might upset you."

I already know.

I already knew the second we went into the Kim house.

"I want you to be prepared just in case we find anything... particularly damning about your past."

"Alright, Dallas," I whisper, and he nods once, tight and non-committal before he shrugs the words off and puts his usual mask of indifference back on.

It doesn't take long.

By the time we get to the lower levels, it feels like walking right into a lion's den.

It's louder than usual, and the second we step inside, everything feels wrong.

Trevor is crouched beside the safe, sleeves rolled up, face smeared with sweat and something that looks like grease, looking far too pleased with himself.

Dallas moves to stand behind him, arms crossed and focused on whatever dread is about to be revealed.

Ellison's hand grips mine tightly.

And then Trevor looks up at me with bright eyes, voiced edged with excitement. "Oh, good. You're here."

My pulse skyrockets and Ellison's hand tightens.

"Are you in?" I ask, and my voice is shaking a little.

"Just... one... ah," the steel makes a high-pitched whine before it cracks, the sound catastrophic. And Trevor falls back to land on his rear end. "There we are."

Dallas' gaze meets mine.

And there's something in it I don't like.

Something like pity.

"Open it," I whisper.

Trevor's tools scream against the metal as he pries it back.

The sound is unbearable, making my teeth feel like they're prickling, like the safe itself is fighting back. Like whatever is inside was buried for a reason and the universe doesn't particularly enjoy the idea of it being unearthed.

Ellison doesn't move from my side.

His hand stays at my back, firm and grounding, so close I can feel the heat of him through my clothes. Close enough that I can cling to the fact that I'm not doing this alone.

Trevor leans in again, muttering to himself, the concentration of a man who knows what he's doing.

Dallas exhales and it sounds like disgust.

The seam gives with an abrupt metallic groan, a deep reluctant sound, and then Trevor steps back, wiping his hands down his pants as if he's just finished changing a tire instead of excavating a grave.

"There," he says simply.

The door swings open.

And for a second... for the briefest, most stupid second, it's cash.

Stacks and stacks of cash, wrapped in tight bands, packed so neatly it's almost unreal, like a movie prop.

Hundreds of thousands of dollars.

My breath catches because of the sick absurdity of it.

Because this is what they worship.

Greedy paper bills.

The ability to buy suffering with the same ease that normal people buy gas.

Dallas lets out a low whistle.

Peter shifts closer, eyes narrowing as he reaches for a stack of it and thumbs over the edges. He shoots me a surprised look and taps it on the back of his hand. "Real," he beams at me.

Ellison doesn't look at the money.

Not once.

Because he's looking past it.

And Trevor reaches in, tugging something loose from behind the stacks, the sound of paper sliding against the smooth metal sounds louder than anything I've ever heard.

It's a folder.

And then another.

Then several, packed behind the cash like it was meant to disguise them, like someone thought the money would soften the blow behind it.

My hands go cold when Trevor flips one open without thinking, the careless confidence of a man who doesn't yet understand that the truth of my entire life is in these folders.

He peers down at it, and then he freezes.

The warehouse seems to freeze with him.

His excitement disappears.

And Dallas pushes forward to snatch the folder from Trevor's hands.

Whatever he reads first drains the color from his face.

My heart begins to pound.

"Give me that," I whisper, stalking forward, dragging Ellison with me.

Dallas hesitates to hand it over, but then the folder is in my hands.

The top is nothing but numbers.

Money transfers and accounts.

Dates and wire confirmations.

A trail so clean and deliberate it makes me want to vomit.

And then my eyes catch the name.

IAN LEDGER.

It's written right there.

My father. Stamped and typed and undeniable.

My breath stops.

I stare at it, blinking like my vision is lying to me, like maybe I'm too tired and too haunted, like I'm misreading something that cannot possibly be real.

But it is.

It is real.

The next page is a text-message printout.

A phone number I could recite in my sleep.

A number that has called me my entire life.

A number that has told me goodnight and good morning.

A number that has threatened me and wished me declarations of love.

A number I used to call when I needed help.

[Payment Confirmed.

Authorization for wife received.

Child is not to be terminated.]

My fingers go numb.

The warehouse tilts.

The air leaves my lungs in a thin, broken exhale.

Ellison's voice comes low beside me. "Sage, baby, take a deep breath."

I don't.

I can't.

Because the words are still there.

Authorization for wife received.

Child is not to be terminated.

My mother.

Me.

My life memories, my trauma, my terror and fear, carved into terms as a business agreement.

Dallas mutters something vicious under his breath. "Fucking pieces of—"

I don't hear him as I read the next page.

Because there it is.

The second wife.

Another name.

ANDREW HART.

My stomach is dangerously close to letting go of its contents.

The Kim family didn't just take one payment.

They took two.

They double dipped in blood.

[Payment Confirmed.

Authorization for child received.

Injury only]

My throat constricts, and Ellison's hand is no longer simply at my back.

It's bracing me now. Holding me. Because my knees feel distant.

Because my worst fears are finally valid.

I flip again, frantic now, desperate, as if turning faster will change what I'm seeing.

But it only gets worse.

Invoices.

More dates.

Security schedules.

Photos.

A grainy still of a little girl being dragged down a long hallway, her face blurred, and blood staining her clothes.

Me.

[Payment Confirmed.

Authorization for injury confirmed.

Termination preferred.]

The scar on my stomach burns like it's fresh.

Like the blade is still there.

I can suddenly feel it again. Phantom sharp. The memory I have spent years locking down behind my skull.

The blood.

The way everything went white.

The way someone stopped it before it finished.

It wasn't mercy. Or kindness. Or care.

It was just changed orders.

Collateral kept alive for later.

My hands shake with the knowledge, and I drop the pages onto the concrete like they've burned me.

I stare at them on the floor.

I stare at my father's name.

At Andrew Hart's name.

At the Kim family's change of heart.

They didn't just kill my mother. My father purchased her death. He paid for it. And Andrew Hart paid for mine.

And the Kim family orchestrated everything. Baiting one empire against another.

Lighting the match and stepping back to watch two bloodlines burn each other down before they could ever threaten the Kim throne.

My chest rises in shallow, broken breaths, and stillness settles over me, eerie and total.

It's not shock.

Not denial.

Something colder settles in.

Anger, so deep it feels ancient.

And it's not just mine.

Dallas stares at the documents like it's his name written in blood instead of mine.

"Jesus Christ," he murmurs finally, voice rough with emotion. "They've been playing around like they're God."

It wasn't Dallas' anger I was worried about either.

Ellison's head turns slowly, and his expression is blank.

And when his voice comes, it's quiet. Low.

"No," he murmurs.

His hand slides from my back to my shoulder, steadying me as if he knows my soul is trying to leave my body.

Along with all of my humanity that I've tried to cling to.

"They have not seen God yet."

My eyes lift to his, and in them, there's no soldier there.

No assassin.

No borrowed Hart heir.

Only something vast and violent and holy.

Something that won't stop.

Because my life was made collateral.

And my mother was currency.

And the men who arranged it are still alive and breathing, trying to collect a debt.

I look at my husband and my hands shake.

Because I know that the debt will be paid in more bloodshed.

And it won't be mine when it's all said and done.

Chapter 19

Sage

The warehouse doesn't feel real after the truth is uncovered.
Nothing does.

The air is still the same air. The fluorescent lights overhead are still the same. Trevor is still incredibly awkward. Peter is trying to make himself scarce because he talks too much when he's anxious. Sam and Anderson left the room the second Dallas started snatching papers.

But I'm not in it anymore.

I'm somewhere else.

Somewhere quiet and hollow.

Because my mother is dead in ink.

And my father's name is on the receipt.

Because Andrew Hart's money sits right there beside it, paid neatly into the same pit, because the Kim family didn't care whose blood they bought as long as it spilled.

And because I'm still standing here, alive and breathing, married to a man who will kill all of these people, moving through the aftermath and unsure what to do next.

I don't remember telling them to pack the documents up.

I don't remember my hands moving.

Or my voice.

I only remember the weight of Ellison beside me, the way he never once lets space open between us, like if he does I might evaporate into the concrete.

Dallas keeps talking, and I hear him distantly, like his voice is wading through water.

"Lock this shit down."

"Move it."

"—want this safe disintegrated."

"—can't know we have this. Do you understand?"

Trevor nods rapidly, swallowing any argument he might have to Dallas' commands.

Peter starts running around looking for something to put the cash in.

And I... I just stand there.

Still and quiet.

Listening to the sound of my own blood in my ears.

Ellison's hands are the only thing reminding me that I'm still here, that I'm upright and breathing.

My mouth opens and words come out.

But they don't feel like mine.

"Put the cash into payroll," I hear myself say, and Dallas turns his head sharply like he didn't expect any orders. "Give—" I swallow around the lump in my throat. "Take a stack for each of you, and then—then give bonuses out on the upcoming payroll." It's blood money, filthy, but it needs to be turned into something else. "Put it on the payroll as a holiday bonus. At least two—" my words trail off and I feel Ellison's fingers flex against my spine. "—two thousand per person at least."

Dallas studies me for a long moment, something proud, and almost tender underneath all of his anger. "Yeah," he says quietly. "Done."

I tear my eyes away from him, feeling sick to my stomach.

Because if I look at any one of them for too long, I might crumble in front of all of them, and they're trying very hard not to show me any pity.

So instead, I force my feet to move.

Deceptively composed.

The way I was raised to be.

The way my mother had to be.

The way my father demanded I be.

We leave the warehouse with the crew cataloging and getting rid of all of the evidence, sealed up like we can put the truth back in the dark.

The night outside is colder than it should be.

Ellison helps me into the car like I'm made of glass, and Dallas drives.

No one talks.

The city passes by in smeared lights, streetlights flashing across the window like blinking eyes, like the world is trying to shut it out while something catastrophic sits in my chest.

Somewhere downtown, people are eating dinner.

Somewhere, someone is laughing.

Somewhere, someone is kissing their wife goodnight.

And I sit in the backseat, hands folded in my lap, staring as it all passes me by, like if I look out of the window, I might see my mother's ghost reflected back at me.

Ellison's hand wraps around mine.

He doesn't let go once.

Not at the stoplights.

Not when Dallas turns onto the long road back toward home.

Not when the gates open.

Not when the house appears, warm-lit and deceptive.

Anderson is waiting at the door again, and he dips his head when we pass by.

Inside, everything looks the same.

The marble floors.

The lamps.

The air conditioner kicking on and off.

It all seems so normal that it almost makes me sick.

Dallas approaches cautiously, like he doesn't know what to say. And he takes one last look at me before he clenches his jaw. "I'm going to make some calls. Make sure Ramos and Kline got their money."

I nod.

Ellison doesn't nod.

Ellison doesn't even look at Dallas.

He looks at me.

And Dallas hesitates just a fraction. "Are you good?"

The question is ridiculous.

I give him a bland look anyway.

"I'm fine."

Dallas' jaw tightens like he wants to argue.

But he doesn't.

Not yet.

So he just exhales and turns away, footsteps heavy as he disappears back down the staircase.

And then it's only me and Ellison.

His hands slide to my waist, and he pulls me in to lead me into our bedroom, shutting the door softly behind us.

He stares at me for a minute, and then he takes a deep breath.

"Baby," he murmurs.

And the word cracks something.

My throat tightens instantly, like barbed wire is constricting my airways.

I don't answer.

His palms slide over my sides again and he gives a small squeeze around my hips.

"Sage," he says again, softer now.

And I don't know what it is.

Maybe it's because the door is shut and we don't have any witnesses.

Maybe it's because the way he always says my name undoes me.

Maybe it's because I love him and only feel safe when it's just him and I and four enclosed walls.

But my face scrunches.

My breath catches in my throat.

And the sound that comes out of me is ugly.

It isn't graceful.

It isn't contained.

It's a sob that tears from somewhere locked down, something wounded and devastated, something I've been holding back since I was a child.

Ellison's arms come around me immediately, firm and unyielding.

And I break down.

I break so completely that my knees nearly give, my hands clutching at his shirt like I'm dissolving into nothing.

"Oh my God," I choke out, barely able to breathe. "Oh my God, Ellison—"

He holds me tighter.

"I know," he murmurs, voice low and wrecked just like mine. "I know, baby. I know."

"He—" I can't even say it.

My mother's death and my father's orders.

The casual cruelty of it.

I shake my head violently, sobs pouring out in waves.

"He—he had her killed," I rasp. "He ordered like she was—like she was in the way. She was—she was nothing to him."

Ellison's hand slides up the back of my head, cradling me.

His mouth brushes against my hair as I shake.

"I know."

"I was there," I cry. "I was there, Ellison. I was there and he—he still—"

He holds me tighter and the air in the room feels too thin. "Baby," he whispers. He pulls back and cradles my face. "Look at me."

I can't.

I can't do it.

I can't bear whatever pity I might see.

But Ellison tilts me anyway, gentle but relentless, until my wet lashes lift and meet his eyes.

And they're furious.

And soft.

And devastated.

All at once.

"You are here," he firmly tells me. "You are alive and safe, and with me. And he will never get access to hurt you again. Do you understand me?"

My breath shudders and I shake in his hold, melting under the weight of it all.

My chest aches fiercely.

"I don't know what to do," I whisper, and his thumbs wipe my tears just like they always do.

"We do what we always do, baby," he murmurs. "We keep moving forward."

"But what do we—what do we do, Ellison? He killed my mother," I rasp, reaching up to hold his wrists.

"Listen to me," he tightens his hold just a little, and I brace for whatever words he's about to say.

"I'm going to kill your fucking father."

Those aren't the words I'm expecting.

They aren't the words I'm expecting at all.

But they're from Ellison, so I have no doubt that he means them.

Because he's here.

Holding me.

Loving me.

Promising that the world hasn't won yet.

"I'm going to kill your father, Sage. I promise you," he repeats more firmly, shaking me a little as he says it, like it'll shake the words into me enough to make me understand it.

And eventually my sobs start to slow.

Not because the hurt is gone.

But because I trust him.

Because he rocks me gently like he can teach me how to breathe again.

"And before I do that," he murmurs, and he leans in and kisses me firmly on the lips before pulling back again to look me in the eyes. "I'm going to bury Andrew Hart somewhere that he won't be found."

"I want him dead," I whisper, the words still full of my tears. "I want—God, Ellison, I want them both dead. What does that make me?"

"It doesn't matter, baby," Ellison whispers back. "None of it matters. None of it. Look at me," he commands, and my eyes snap back up to meet his.

"No one is gonna take anything else from you. And no one is gonna take you from me," he whispers. "Do you understand? I promise you, Sage."

No one.

No one is going to take from me. And no one is going to take me.

No one.

"Do you understand?" Ellison asks again, and my eyes fill with tears again as I nod my head.

"I love you," the words tremble out of me.

"I know, baby," Ellison's voice breaks. "I know you do."

He takes a deep breath and pulls me into his chest to hold me.

"And I love you."

Chapter 20

Sage

I don't sleep.

Not the way people in that park sleep, tucked into safe lives with clean consciences, rolling over in warm sheets while their biggest worry is whether their kid will catch a cold from being out too long.

I lie in a bed that feels too big and too quiet, and somehow still not quiet enough, because the truth keeps echoing in my skull like a gunshot ricocheting off the wall.

When morning comes, it doesn't feel like morning.

It feels like the night just stretched thinner.

A new shade of exhaustion painted over the same uncovered horror.

Ellison is up before I am, or maybe he never went to sleep either, because the second I open my eyes, he's already there, propped up slightly beside me, watching me like he's been guarding the line between my nightmares and waking life, his hand resting on my hip, like the only thing he can do right now is keep me tethered to him.

His gaze drags slowly over my face, reading the damage.

"Good morning," he murmurs, voice quiet and rough.

My throat hurts, the kind of ache you get after crying too hard, after swallowing too much down.

I don't know what to say.

I don't know how to say good morning after everything we discovered last night.

But Ellison doesn't demand any words from me.

He just shifts closer and presses his lips to my forehead, a soft kiss that lingers like he's trying to replace whatever bad memory is currently there with another one.

"Let's eat breakfast," he says after a moment, and I know it isn't a suggestion.

I'm too tired to fight him on it.

I almost argue on instinct, because I always do, even when the orders are built on love. but I feel too heavy for the fight, too hollow to even try.

So I let him pull me out of bed.

He keeps a hand on me the entire time, guiding me down the stairs, watching me take each little step.

Dallas is gone by the time we reach the kitchen, the house quiet except for the distant hum of the air conditioner.

There's already food waiting, and I know it has to be Dallas' doing, because Ellison never once left my side this morning.

It's nothing but toast and fruit, but it nearly makes me cry.

Ellison sits next to me, his knee touching mine, gaze never leaving my hands as if he's waiting for them to start shaking again.

I pick at the food while he watches.

He doesn't nag me. Not yet. But I can feel him deciding how much pressure to apply.

"Eat," he finally murmurs, and his voice is still gentle, but there's an order tucked underneath it.

So I force a bite down even though it tastes like nothing.

And Ellison's mouth tightens when he sees it.

When he uses his own fork to feed me, I let him.

And the only things that seem to have any taste are the strawberries.

He gives me every single one from off of his plate.

It settles something in my stomach, so I finish them all despite the nausea and the discomfort.

The rest of the day moves wrong.

I stay in the living room so no one will worry, and I watch countless movies, even though I don't pay attention to a single one.

Ellison takes calls in the study that I barely register, his voice calm and clipped, his tone turning into that cold, controlled thing that he's learned to turn on and off.

Anderson brings me some water every so often.

He doesn't say much, but he only usually sticks around when he wants to, and he's hovering in the doorway like he's waiting for me to freak out.

At some point, Ellison crouches in front of me and lifts my face up with his hands, forcing my eyes to his.

"You want to talk?" He asks softly, and I stare at him for a moment too long.

The words pile up behind my eyes, and there are so many things I could say. So many. And I know he'd listen to every single one, but all that comes out is... "I don't know."

Ellison's gaze softens, a flicker of pain slicing through it like he hates it, too.

"That's okay, baby."

My eyes burn again, but I don't let the tears fall.

Not when Ellison is already making plans with the kind of calm that scares me.

I just let him do it.

A few days pass like that.

Heavy and wrong.

And Ellison does everything.

He handles the warehouse.

He handles Dallas.

He handles me.

He keeps things running like nothing has changed, even though everything has changed, even though I'm walking around feeling like my bones are fractured.

He brings me food and he keeps me hydrated.

He pulls me into his lap sometimes to rub my back.

And I let him.

Because it's easier than admitting how much I need him right now, because needing him so badly feels like another weakness stacked on top of all the others.

On the fourth day, when the quiet starts to finally feel like it's too much, when my own mind starts feeling like a room with no windows, I find him in the study while he's on the phone.

He turns to me immediately. Always immediately.

Like he's been waiting for me to say something. Anything.

"Can we go to the new house?" I say, and my voice comes out steadier than I feel. "I want to... work on it."

Ellison's eyes search mine, and he doesn't ask me why. He knows I just need something to do.

He doesn't tell me I should rest.

"Okay," he says. "We can go right now."

He drives me by himself, somehow convincing Dallas that we don't need a bodyguard with everything going on around us.

The new house is still just as beautiful as it was before.

It should feel exciting, a fresh start, a new chapter, a clean space.

But right now it just feels empty like me.

I roll paint onto the walls all afternoon, concentrating on covering every little edge and line, because that's something small and controllable I can do.

Ellison moves around me quietly.

He reaches all of the spots that I can't before I even need to ask.

He doesn't hover or treat me like I'm fragile.

He just exists near me, a steady presence, sometimes painting, sometimes just standing behind me with his hand on my waist to keep me from tipping off of my stepstool.

At some point, I end up in what will be our bedroom.

The room is empty still except for the drop cloths and paint trays and the smell of fresh primer.

But I can already picture it, can already imagine waking up here, can already see the version of myself that will love the paint and the furniture and the silly little decorations.

Ellison comes up behind me and wraps his arms around my waist, pulling me back into his chest.

He rocks me gently.

Back and forth.

Over and over.

And something in my body finally loosens, just a fraction, like my nervous system is recognizing safety.

I lean into him without thinking.

I tip my head back against his shoulder.

The silence isn't empty.

It's full of things we aren't saying.

Full of the life that keeps trying to exist around my fears and anger.

Finally, my voice comes out quiet.

"Okay," I whisper.

Ellison's lips brush my temple. "Okay?" He murmurs, the echo of the question he asked me in the park, as if he's checking whether it's real.

My throat tightens, but I force the words out.

"Okay," I repeat, and I turn around in his arms to face him. "What do we do now?"

"We just keep moving forward, baby," he murmurs.

"Okay."

"Sound like a plan?" Ellison asks softly, and I'm slow to nod my head.

"It's a plan."

Chapter 21

Sage

Angela's email shows up so late in the afternoon that it feels like it lands on the tail end of my nerves, sliding into my inbox like a harmless little thing.

I'm standing in the kitchen when it comes through, phone in hand and a glass of water in the other, staring at the subject line with an awful sense of detachment.

Community Outreach Opportunity – Children's Event Tomorrow!

I almost delete it.

Almost.

But then I remember we are supposed to be laying low, pretending that we're living normal lives and haven't gotten in too deep over our heads.

That's the only reason I open her email.

Angela's email is cheery and professional, the way she always is, especially when dealing with people like us.

It's just an orphanage.

Just a carnival and some fall games and the need for extra hands because turnout is expected to be high.

She conveniently tacks on a piece about the media being there to take pictures and videos for the local news stations.

And then there's that little line near the bottom that makes me take a deep breath.

"It would mean a lot to the kids, and it would mean a lot to the community!"

I stare at it for a while, unsure why it bothers me so much.

It's this same community that turns a blind eye to men like my father and Andrew Hart.

The same community that accepts payment to brush evidence under the rug.

The same community that cleans the roadways with blood.

Why would I give them anything?

Behind me, I hear the slightest movement approaching and I know it's Ellison.

By now, I've learned even the way his footfalls sound on the marble floors, like he's part of the house.

His hand settles on my shoulder, warm like always, and he leans over the back of my chair, lips brushing my cheek as he leans in to kiss me there.

"What's that face for?"

"You don't like my face?" I ask, and he turns my barstool to make sure I see the offense in his expression.

"Quite the contrary. I love your face," he leans in and kisses me quickly on the lips. And then again. And again. Until I start to smile despite my best efforts not to. "But why are you looking like your phone personally offended you?"

I swallow and reach for my phone again, handing it right over.

"Angela emailed me," I sigh, and he browses over the email while I stare at him.

His hair is a little windswept, falling in his eyes in a way that almost seems intentional.

I reach up to brush it back with my fingers and he glances up at me over the phone for a moment. He switches his hold so he can place his other hand onto my thigh, leaning a little closer so I don't have to reach up so much to brush his hair.

It does nothing but remind me how considerate he is toward me.

Even though this world can be awful and kindness is forgotten, he keeps reminding me, even in the confines of our home, that it exists between us.

That kindness exists between us.

"There's a children's event tomorrow," I tell him as I run my fingers through my hair. By now, he must have gathered that through the email, but he still hums. "Angela said the turnout is supposed to be bigger than they expected, so they need volunteers to help with setting up."

"You want to go?" He asks, rubbing circles into my thigh.

"We probably should," I murmur.

The thought of staying in this house, running circles in my head, replaying the memories of my childhood to try to see if there were signs of my father's deception... I can't keep doing that.

"I don't know," I admit, and the honesty burns my throat a little. "Do you think we should?"

Ellison leans in and places a small kiss on the lips and I sigh into it.

"I think we should go," he answers, and he sets my phone back on the countertop to pull me in for a hug. "Get some more fresh air. Have a little fun. Be *deceptively* normal," he suggests in a conspiratorial tone.

"Deceptively normal?" I tease back, though I can't quite bring the same enthusiasm that he had. "I think everyone knows nothing about you is normal."

"Oh," he playfully scoffs. "Oh, I see how it is."

"You know it's true," I murmur, and he stares at me for a moment with the sweet, playful look in his eyes before he holds his hands up in mock surrender.

"Alright, alright," he laughs quietly. "You know best."

"Good thing you know that," I quip and he yanks his hand back like I've burnt him.

"God," he chuckles. "Sassy this afternoon."

"You like it," I murmur, and he nods his head eagerly.

"Yes, I do," he beams at me, and then he softens his hands when he brings them back to my waist. "Alright, we'll go and do our socializing." He plucks the phone back from the counter and shoots a response back.

And Angela's reply comes back within minutes, enthusiastic and grateful, and suddenly we're committed to something normal for a change.

Something that will actually benefit the community.

The children.

I think back to the selfish question I asked myself just minutes ago.

Why would I give them anything?

And I think... why wouldn't I?

Why wouldn't I give to someone that needs it?

I never would have second guessed it before.

Why would I now? Just because my heart is hurt?

That isn't me.

I can't let that be me.

While Ellison cooks dinner, I try to do more than pick at it.

Even when Dallas comes in to go over tomorrow's plans with us both, I try to finish my plate, and I ignore Dallas' insistent stares as he glances at me when I take a sip of water after every single bite, like I'm trying to keep it down.

Even though halfway through my plate, something sharp twists in my stomach, and I pause with my fork halfway to my mouth.

Thankfully it happens when Ellison is running upstairs to my office to look for some paperwork he was emailed.

Dallas looks at me immediately in alarm. "What's wrong?"

I shake my head and try to swallow it down so he doesn't blow it out of proportion.

"Nothing," I lie.

"Liar," he glares at me, and I give him a pleading look.

I don't know how to explain that my body has been going a little haywire, acting like it's not sure what it wants, that my appetite has become unpredictable from all the stress.

The thought of the strawberry drink from a few days ago flashes through my mind, sweet and cold and delicious, and my mouth waters pathetically.

Dallas watches me for another moment like he doesn't believe me, and we both snap our heads to the side when we hear a door shut upstairs, meaning Ellison is coming back.

"If you're sick then you better fucking tell me," Dallas warns, and he whirls around to reach for the coffee pot right as Ellison bounds down the stairs.

My throat tightens up with the fear that he'll say something else, but he keeps his mouth shut.

Once Dallas finally leaves, I barely sleep.

And when I do, I dream of a hallway I haven't been in for years, dream of my own blood on someone else's ears, dream of my mother's voice screaming my name from behind a door that won't open no matter how hard I pull on it.

By the time morning arrives, my body feels wrung out, hollowed and refilled with newfound nerves.

Ellison dresses in black like always, looks like himself like always, and I just put on a sweater and jeans, something warm just in case we're stuck outside all day.

When we leave the house, Anderson's already outside, keys in hand and looking bored as usual, and Dallas is Dallas.

Except now he's looking at me a little too intensely, leaning against the hood of his car like he's been there for an hour, sunglasses on again despite the fact the sun is barely awake.

"About time," he mutters at Ellison and I, and Ellison rolls his eyes and pats him on the shoulder.

"Don't act like you have anything better to do."

"Did you both eat breakfast?" He asks, and I avert my eyes the second he glances at me.

"No," Ellison shakes his head and opens my car door. "You wanna stop and grab something?"

"Was gonna grab a coffee at Starbucks if we aren't strapped for time."

He says it almost like he's testing me, and I can feel him staring at me for a long minute before the pressure eases a little.

We decide to go inside we get there, and Ellison rattles off his order at the register, only stopping to glance at me.

"You want your ice coffee?"

"Can I get the—" I turn my head to see Dallas staring pointedly at me, and I quickly look back at the menu like I can't decide. "Um... the strawberry lemonade refresher?"

"What's with you and your strawberries lately?" Ellison laughs under his breath, leaning into me so he can dig his wallet out of his pocket.

"I like them," I murmur, and I wander off to look out of the window.

And I feel it.

When Dallas steps up beside me and stares out the same windowpane.

At first, he doesn't say anything, but my hands are already shaking when he turns his head toward me.

"We need to talk immediately," he says quietly so no one else can overhear it.

"No, we don't," I whisper in irritation.

"Sage, yes the fuck we do," Dallas snaps under his breath.

"I can't do this right now, Dallas," I breathe out in a rush, snapping my head up to look at him. "I just need to make it through the day, so can we please not fucking do this?"

"I'll lay off for right now," he lowers his voice even further. "But only because you and I aren't alone right now." He turns away and faces the people waiting in line, looking over Ellison and Anderson talking back and forth.

"But we will be talking. And you will tell me the fucking truth, Sage."

"I'm your boss, Dallas," I whisper as I turn around too. The venom isn't lost in my voice. "Or did you forget that?"

It's a low blow, especially for me.

"You're my boss, yeah," Dallas whispers back. "Which means your safety and health are my priority. Or did you forget that?" He throws my own words back in my face.

"I'm fine," I lie again, and he shoots daggers at me.

"You're good at a lot of things, Sage, but you're a shit liar."

"I'm not lying, Dallas, I—"

"Haven't had coffee in nearly two weeks now, nor any alcohol. You've been nauseous every day, barely eating, and have an insistent craving for fruit all of a sudden."

"Dallas, I can't do this with you right now," I whisper, and the fear is ever present in my voice.

I know he hears it.

I know he does.

I'm ten seconds away from exploding into tears and I need him to fucking hear me.

"Please just let it go."

I walk away before he can say anything else.

Chapter 22

Sage

By the time we make it downtown, the street is already busy. People are moving in clumps with drinks and sticky-fingered children.

The orphanage is decorated like a fall fair, paper leaves taped to windows, banners strung across the entrance, balloons all over the place.

The outside is overwhelmingly cluttered too.

There's various bouncy castles being set up, and booths all over with hand-made crafts being sold.

It's cute, all things considered. Cozy, fitting for the fall weather.

The moment we step inside to look for Angela, the noise increases tenfold.

There's children everywhere, adults ushering them all over the place, music a little too loud.

It's overwhelming in a way I wasn't prepared for, like my nervous system is getting slammed by the joy in the air and doesn't know what to do since it isn't terror.

Ellison's hand stays on me.

Angela spots us nearly immediately and her face lights up, a bright smile that I know isn't anything short of genuine.

She is one of the only genuine people we have met in this town.

"Sage!" She gushes, rushing over to greet us both. She hugs me quickly, even though we don't really... do that unprompted. For a second, I stiffen out of reflex, but then I force myself to soften because I know she means well.

"Thank you so much for coming," she says softly, and then her eyes sweep over Ellison. "Oh, and you brought your husband," she points out, and Ellison reaches over to shake her hand, giving a friendly smile.

"Yes, the one and only," he beams at her, all of his perfectly sharp teeth on display.

I laugh before I can stop myself.

His response to her is a little unhinged, but it makes me truly laugh for the first time in days.

Because why the hell would he say that.

"Yes," Angela awkwardly looks between us. I reach up to cover my mouth with my hand and Angela just points around the room. "The... one and only," she trails off. "Anyway, the kids are so excited! We do this event every year, and it's a favorite of theirs."

We follow her from section to section as she points out all of the events inside, then heads outside to show us the reading corner, the painting tables, and all of the games.

She put genuine effort into this event.

Anyone can see that.

This is something that she cares deeply about.

"It's lovely Angela, really," I murmur.

"Oh, thank you, Sage! You're so sweet!" She claps in excitement. "All of the proceeds from the admission fees and the booth sales go to the orphanage to help keep in running."

A few of the kids run all around and in between us as we follow Angela, some a little shy and some a little too curious.

A little girl with pigtails runs slap into Ellison's leg, nearly falling down with the force of it.

And when she gets her balance back, she stares up at him like she's trying to decide if he's scary or not.

Then she sticks her tongue out at him and runs away.

Dallas makes a strangled sound like he's trying very hard not to laugh, and Ellison's lips twitch, almost imperceptible, but I see it.

It makes something in me loosen just a little.

This isn't a chessboard.

This is a charity event.

Nothing is dangerous here.

Angela guides me toward the reading corner outside before she ushers Ellison off to go play with the kids out in the fenced in yard.

He gives me a quick kiss before he goes, and he brushes his palm over my hair.

Within minutes, I'm sitting on a bright rug with a book in my hand while some younger kids settle around me like they do this every single day.

They lean into each other all too comfortable and trusting.

So I wait until they're calm before I start my reading.

For a few minutes, it feels like I can breathe a little.

This is calm.

This is normal.

This is something kind that I can do.

"Excuse me," a little hand tugs at my jacket when I reach for a second book, fingers far too covered in something colorful that I fear knowing the name of.

"Yes?"

"Is that boy your boyfriend?" He points his sticky fingers towards where Ellison is throwing a football with some of the older children.

"Why would you ask that?" An exasperated laugh falls from my lips.

"We saw you kissing," the boy scrunches his face, and I laugh again. "So that means he's your boyfriend."

"Yes," I chuckle at him. "It does."

"Well, that's gross," he shudders like the act of kissing is truly a crime, and then he's running off to fight the older boys for the ball that Ellison is throwing.

Angela picks that convenient time to pop back up beside me, and I flinch at her sudden appearance.

"Don't mind that one; he's our resident troublemaker," she smiles at me.

"He's just curious," I laugh under my breath. "It's okay."

"You're very good with them," she says softly. "The kids."

I swallow because I'm not sure how to respond.

"Have you thought about them? Having your own?"

"I—" I start, and then I stop because I'm not sure what I want to say.

I've never planned for children.

I've never even let myself picture it because my life has always been too unstable, too dangerous, too full of men making decisions that could ruin everything.

Angela watches me for a moment, and then she flicks her eyes to Ellison, running around with a bunch of kids chasing after him, laughing like it's the most carefree thing he's ever done.

And I wonder if it is.

He had a childhood with parents. At least for a while.

He grew up in the south where being outside is normal.

He knows how to do it.

The sight hits me a little hard, a strange ache settling in my chest at the thought of it.

Angela follows my gaze and her smile turns a little more understanding.

"Have you talked about it?"

Ellison looks up suddenly, like he can feel my eyes on him even from a distance, and even though he's running around and it's chilly and he's out of breath, he smiles big at me like he's thinking the same thing I am.

What it would be like.

To be this normal.

"We haven't," I murmur under my breath. "Maybe we'll discuss it at some point."

"That would be lovely, Sage," Angela softly rubs my arm.

But then a woman walks up and starts talking to her, and Angela follows after her as I watch Ellison.

And a warm ripple of nausea rises again, a little abruptly, and my hands tighten around nothing as I try to force it away.

For a second, I can still convince myself that it's still just stress.

For a second, I can still convince myself that it's simply my body reacting to the last forty-eight hours the way any normal human body would.

But then the nausea creeps higher, sour and insistent, and the world tilts just slightly off balance, and I abruptly sit down.

Dallas is beside me instantly.

Of course he is.

He's probably been watching this entire time, waiting for something to go wrong.

His hand finds the small of my back as he tries to calm me down, and it's so different than the Dallas I usually deal with. The one who would rather die than be physically affectionate with anyone else.

"Sage, do you need to go to the restroom?" He asks, voice low but threaded with something worried underneath it.

I force my expression into something neutral, because the next thing I know, Ellison is crouching in front of me.

"Hey, baby. Everything okay?" His hands reach up to hold my face, and I pray to God that my expression is neutral.

"Yeah, everything's fine," I lie automatically, because the last thing I need is Ellison's attention sharpening into violence in the middle of a charity event with dozens of children running around.

His hand presses into my forehead to check my temperature, and then he looks over my face like he's looking for damage.

"I'm fine, I promise."

"Adrian!" Angela suddenly calls out as if summoned by the Devil herself. "Do you mind helping us with some tables? And the bounce house will need to be taken down soon. We want to usher the kids back inside since it's getting colder."

"Yes, of course, Angela," he smiles back at her, but then he turns his attention back to me.

"Sage," he murmurs, and I manage to smile at him.

"Nothing is wrong. I was just aggravated," I lie again, and I can tell he doesn't believe me.

"Why would you be aggravated, baby?"

"The warehouse," Dallas interrupts like it's obvious. Even he sounds irritated. "Trevor texted me and said something was wrong with the security installs. All of the passwords are in Sage's office and the door is locked."

Ellison stiffens at Dallas' words, and he looks at me again.

But Dallas keeps going, relentless now, covering for me like his life depends on it.

"Why don't you help out with Angela real fast? Anderson can drive you home," he says in a measured voice, pointing to where some other staff are already moving chairs. "I'll just run Sage by the warehouse and meet you back at the house."

Ellison's eyes narrow, his suspicion flickering, but he looks down at me for a long minute.

"I'm fine, Ellison," I whisper. "I promise. I'm just tired and this shit is irritating enough. I thought we'd have one normal day. But this can't wait."

"You're sure you're okay?" Ellison asks again, eyes roaming over me again. He leans forward to feel my head again, and then he lets out a controlled breath.

"I'm okay. I promise," I murmur, and I lean into his palm when he places it against my cheek. "I'll call you as soon as we're done at the warehouse."

That seems to settle him a little.

"Okay, baby," he murmurs as he stands back up. "Just call me and let me know what's going on."

"I will."

Angela's voice rings out again, and Ellison gives me a quick kiss before he's bounding off to help her.

Dallas steers me away immediately.

And the nausea follows.

He rips the passenger door open with a rough yank as soon as we reach the car. "Get in."

I do, but my hands shake as I pull the seatbelt across myself.

Dallas slides into the driver's seat, shutting the door with too much force, and for a moment the car goes strangely quiet.

He starts the car, but he doesn't start driving yet.

He just turns his head slowly toward me.

And his expression is different now.

There's no sarcasm. No sharp-tongued bravado.

No frustration.

Just a man seeing the cliff edge and wondering if I'm about to throw myself off of it.

"Okay," he says finally. "What do you want to do?"

My throat closes and my stomach rolls again, panic blooming hot and poisonous.

"I don't know," I whisper, and my voice cracks like I'm a child again, like I'm back in the hallway and freaking out and screaming for help. "I don't know, Dallas. I don't know."

His jaw clenches as he looks at me.

And then he reaches for the gear shift.

"Alright, shit," he says under his breath. "We're going to the doctor. And then we can figure it out after that."

"Okay," I whisper.

The fear settles right back in alongside the nausea.

And I'm not so sure that it's the only thing that's settled in.

Chapter 23

Sage

The doctor's office is entirely too bright.

The kind that doesn't feel clean, but sterile.

The lights feel like they're trying to expose everything whether you want them to or not, like you can't hide yourself for even a second.

Dallas sits in the corner with his arms crossed.

He looks like he belongs anywhere but here. Not in a place with pamphlets about prenatal vitamins and cartoon storks and zoo animals painted onto the walls.

I don't really remember coming in, and Dallas ended up taking the clipboard to fill the rest of my paperwork out.

I don't really remember being led back into a private room.

All I remember is the nausea that keeps creeping up like a tide.

The thin sweat coating the back of my neck.

The way my fingers keep drifting down to my stomach, pressing absently like I'll be able to feel if the answer is yes or no.

The doctor asks me a lot of questions, and for a good while, I just watch her mouth move in disbelief.

Because the words slide past my ears like I'm underwater.

And the only one that actually sticks is, "Congratulations."

Congratulations.

Congratulations.

"What the fuck," I whisper in shock, and she looks at me in alarm.

"Oh, is that—is it not—oh," she stutters through her surprise, suddenly realizing her news might not be good news to me.

"I'm—I'm pregnant?" I rasp, looking between her and Dallas with wide, fearful eyes. "Are you sure? You're really sure?"

"I—Yes, Mrs. Hart," she slowly tells me. "You are certainly pregnant. I'd say... about nine weeks? Give or take."

"Nine weeks," I whisper, and my eyes fall helplessly to the floor as I stare at the bright colored tile. "Nine weeks."

It doesn't feel real.

It doesn't feel real.

And yet it has to be.

Because when have Ellison and I literally ever used condoms?

Never.

That's the answer.

The answer is never.

I don't even think we own condoms.

Oh God. What do I do?

"You're sure?" I whisper again, eyes pleading for... I don't know what.

"Yes, Mrs. Hart. I'm sure. Would you like to discuss your opt—"

"Thank you," I cut her off in a stunned whisper. I don't mean it to sound harsh, but it does.

Because no. No, I do not want to discuss any options. There are no options to discuss.

The paperwork they hand me feels like a loaded weapon.

And Dallas keeps his hand over his mouth while they go over all of it with me. Like he too is in shock.

Like he too can't believe it.

His eyes find me and don't move.

The doctor keeps talking, rambling on and on about stress and alcohol avoidance and food choices.

Avoid, avoid, avoid. Don't do this. Don't do that.

But my hands are still shaking.

My hands are still shaking and they feel useless.

So useless that Dallas pays when we leave the clinic.

And when we step back out to the car, my legs feel distant.

Everybody else is still moving through the motions. Walking down the sidewalks sipping coffee and making small talk.

And Dallas is guiding me to the car with a hand at my elbow.

The door shuts, and that's when it hits me.

It's not tears.

Not fully.

Just panic, thick and immediate, rising so fast it makes my vision blur.

My breath comes out too shallow, feeling like I'm being crushed from the inside.

And Dallas doesn't start the car yet.

He just sits there, staring forward, hands resting on the wheel like his brain is trying to piece this shit together.

Then finally, he turns his head.

"Okay," he says carefully.

"What the fuck do I do?"

It feels so similar to the conversation we had before the clinic, only now, the words are small and shaking, humiliating in their helplessness.

"We just gotta—" Dallas swallows and nods his head like he's trying to convince himself. "Let's just breathe through it and—"

"I can't," I cut him off. "Dallas, I can't!"

"You can," he says immediately. "You can. You're doing it right now. Just keep doing it."

My hands clutch tightly to the seatbelt like it'll somehow help me.

"I'm pregnant," I rasp in disbelief. "Oh, God. I'm fucking pregnant."

Saying it out loud makes it worse somehow.

He only nods once, like the truth doesn't scare him the same way it's swallowing me whole.

"Yeah," he murmurs. "You are."

My stomach rolls again, nausea braided with terror because I can't separate them right now.

And Dallas simply starts the car.

"Where are we going?"

"Just... sit there and breathe," Dallas shakes his head.

And I do.

That's all I can do as the city passes by in streaks of light and passing cars.

Until finally we pull into a parking lot, and I nearly smack him upside his big head.

"Dallas!" I practically yell his name, scandalized through my impending tears. "I can't go to a bar, you idiot!"

Dallas glances at me like he pities me, but in a way that doesn't quite feel cruel yet.

"Relax," he hops out of the driver's side door.

"Relax?" My voice somehow rises ever more. "I'm carrying a child and you brought me to a—"

"I own it, Sage," Dallas sighs in frustration.

"What?"

Dallas sighs again like he cannot believe the universe keeps requiring him to explain himself.

"I own this bar, Sage," he repeats. "It's closed and empty. No one's here."

"You... own a bar?" I rasp as I climb out of the car.

"Mind your business, kid."

I follow helplessly inside, and he's right.

It is closed and empty and quiet.

Dallas moves behind the bar and pops open a fancy-looking bottle of liquor.

He pours himself a shot and knocks it back immediately.

Then he pours another, slower this time, and leaves it sitting on the counter, like he isn't sure if he'll need it yet.

Then he opens the fridge, and he pulls a bottle to slide it over to me.

It's a strawberry cream root beer.

My eyes burn so fast it's embarrassing.

Dallas watches my face shift like he regrets being a person at all.

"For the record," he starts in a rough voice, "I don't do this shit with my clients."

"I'm sorry," I whisper miserably. "I know I'm messing everything—"

"No," he laughs once under his breath, awkward at emotions. "Don't apologize. Jesus."

Silence stretches for a second and I use the time to take a few sips of my drink. The strawberry taste is so good that I almost start crying even more.

"Sage, listen."

"What?" I sniffle, and it sounds so pathetic.

Dallas hesitates for a moment, like he isn't sure how to say whatever it is he's thinking.

"I don't do this shit with my clients," he murmurs, looking down at me like he's frustrated. "But you knocked my world off its axis a little."

I look down in shame at his words.

"And you keep doing it, kid."

"I'm sorry," I whisper, and he shakes his head.

"You're a client. Yeah. But you're the first one that I actually... care about," he admits quietly.

My eyes fill with tears and Dallas looks like he wants to hide under the bar top.

"Don't cry."

"That was a horrible thing to say if you didn't want me to cry," I rasp, and he laughs a little helplessly.

"Fair," he admits. And he leans forward slightly to place his hands on the bar. "You're a good person, Sage. No matter how much the world around you tries to change that."

My chest aches at the words and my fingers tighten around my drink.

"You're honest, and you're strong, and you're doing a good fucking job at dealing with all of the shit we've gotten ourselves into. And regardless of what you choose," Dallas gives me a measured look, his lips thinning out a little. And I can see the moisture in his eyes, too.

I lick my lips and try to force myself to keep breathing around the tears clogging up my throat.

"I will protect you," Dallas murmurs. "And I will protect your child."

"How can I raise a child in this world, Dallas?" I whisper.

"You raise it the way you wished you would've been raised," he says simply. "With love and kindness. You keep it away from all the bullshit."

"But what will Ellison say?" I whisper desperately.

Dallas lets out a short laugh. "Sage," he mutters. "When will you learn? Come on, kid, keep up."

"I'm not a kid," I whisper petulantly. "Lean what?"

His eyes meet mine as he tilts his head.

"Ellison loves you," Dallas chuckles. "Like, God, it's borderline concerning how much he loves you."

A sob threatens to come out of me.

"He'd die before he let anything touch you, or your child. And it'd be worse once you tell him."

He pauses to let me process his words, and then he sighs.

"I know you had a shitty family. But I'd like to think you're building a new one."

My tears spill again.

"With people who actually care about you. So it can't be the end of the world, right?"

I wipe my cheeks with trembling fingers. "Right," I whisper.

"I usually am," Dallas reaches out to take his second shot, and then he hisses like it burns his throat.

"Come on," he tosses his shot glass in the sink like he doesn't care if it breaks open. "Let's take you home so you can do the adult stuff."

I close my eyes and breathe through the drive home.

And Dallas lets me sit with it.

He doesn't try to make me talk, and I'm grateful for it.

Because I don't know what I'll say to Ellison.

But I know I have to say something.

He's waiting when I walk through the door.

Not pacing. Not angry. Just there, waiting for me.

Standing in the foyer like he hasn't moved since the moment I left his sight, shoulder a little too tight, jaw set in a way that tells me he's been restraining himself from a thousand different possibilities of where I've been.

His eyes drag over me like he's searching for bruises that aren't there, for blood he can't see, for cracks that might have opened when he wasn't looking.

Ellison's voice comes out low and careful but stressed.

"Baby."

The word alone makes my throat tighten again. Because this time it isn't tender for tenderness' sake.

It's him reaching for a lifeline.

"I trust you," he says, and his brow furrows like it hurts to keep from touching me. "I do. I know you wouldn't lie to me unless it was something important. Unless you thought you had no choice but to carry something by yourself."

I blink away the tears rapidly building on my lash line.

My hands feel useless by my sides again.

Ellison takes a few slow steps forward, like he doesn't want to startle whatever fragile thing is happening inside me.

"But I went to the warehouse," he continues, voice tightening just slightly. "And they told me nothing was wrong. No security systems down. No emergency. No calls made. Nothing."

His gaze holds mine, steady and pleading underneath all the calm.

"So if something is wrong..." his throat bobs. "If something happened, Sage, I need you to tell me."

My lungs feel too full again.

He shakes his head once, frustrated in a quiet way.

"I can't help you if you don't tell me, baby."

The words land like hands on my shoulders.

I try to breathe. I try to open my mouth.

But suddenly, sitting down feels like the only way to keep myself from falling apart completely.

So I do.

I sink to the edge of the couch and Ellison follows immediately.

He crouches in front of me without hesitation, like he belongs there, like his place is always going to be at my feet if it means keeping me upright.

His hands hover for a second, uncertain, before the settle gently on my knees.

His voice drops softer.

Almost desperate.

"Just tell me what's wrong," he pleads. "Tell me what you need and I'll do it."

My eyes burn as the tears slip out.

"I can't—" I whisper, trying to swallow my fear.

"Yes, you can," his voice breaks slightly. "You can. I'm right here. Let's do it together." His hands tighten, not hurting, but desperate. "I can't help you if you don't tell me, Sage. Just tell me."

The air leaves my lungs in a trembling exhale.

My mouth opens.

And the truth comes out before I can talk myself out of it.

"I'm pregnant, Ellison."

Silence.

A real one.

Like the universe paused to hear me.

Ellison goes completely still as he stares at me for a full minute.

And then his brows knit, confusion flickering so fast it's almost childlike. "What?" He whispers.

The tears keep falling. "I'm..." I swallow. "I'm pregnant, Ellison."

His face doesn't change all at once.

It seems to fracture.

First into shock.

Then into disbelief.

Then something so devastatingly confused that it makes my chest hurt just to look at it.

"I've been nauseous," I whisper, the words tumbling now. "And I thought it was the stress. I thought it was all of this, everything happening, the safe, and my parents and—" my voice cracks and I choke on a sob. "And my appetite. I thought it was just... I don't know. I thought it was stress."

Ellison doesn't even blink as he stares at me.

He doesn't even look like he's breathing.

"But it isn't," I whisper helplessly. "It was a baby."

My hand presses against my stomach without thinking, like I need to prove it to myself as much as him.

"It's a baby, Ellison."

The words make me feel dizzy.

"I'm pregnant, and we're..." I laugh once, a broken, ragged sound. "We're going to have to figure out what to do because I'm pregnant, and I don't even know where your head is at or—"

"Where my head is at?" Ellison cuts me off so sharply that it startles me.

His voice is wrecked.

Awe-struck.

Like he can't believe I could even ask.

"Baby," his eyes fill with tears instantly, fast and shocking, and I freeze.

Alarm rushes through me.

He's crying.

My hands fly up automatically, cupping his face so I can brush his tears like he's done to me countless times.

"Oh God," I whisper, panicked. "What's wrong?"

He shakes his head, breath trembling, and he moves to take one of my hands from his face.

He kisses my palm and he gives me a tight-lipped, watery smile.

"Where my head is at?" He repeats and it's all choked up, followed by a half laugh, half sob. "What's wrong?" He echoes, disbelieving. His eyes lock onto mine as he looks up at me.

"My wife is pregnant."

My throat tightens.

"My wife is pregnant," he repeats, like he needs to say it out loud for it to be real.

And my fear surges up again so quickly.

"Is it so bad?" I whisper, devastated without even meaning to be.

Ellison's face breaks.

He almost looks offended by the idea.

"Bad?" His voice turns so haunted with tenderness. "Nothing could ever be bad about it. Where's my head at?" He laughs again, full of tears. "My head's in the clouds, baby."

"Ellison," I whisper.

"I'm so happy," he whispers back, breathless, shaking his head as he looks up at me, struggling like it's hard just to hold my eyes.

Like it's hard for me to see him cry... like he's not allowed to break in the same ways that I do.

"I—God, Sage, I can't even breathe. My heart's beating so fast I think it might stop working."

He's slow to rise, but he gets up from the floor so he can take my face into his palms. So he can hold me steady.

"You are such a blessing," he whispers, voice shaking as the tears slowly fall. "Do you understand that? You are such a blessing in my life," he cries.

And he leans down to kiss my forehead.

And my cheeks.

And my mouth.

Everywhere he can kiss me, he kisses me.

"You are such a blessing," he shakes his head, and his lips are trembling like he doesn't know what else he can say to express it. Such a blessing. And I love you, Sage."

His hands slide down slowly, like he's afraid he'll somehow startle it.

He settles them against my stomach, and his fingers spread out, warm and protective, possessive in the gentlest way.

"I really love you," he repeats in a strained whisper.

His voice drops into something unbearably soft.

"And I love our baby, too."

A laugh breaks out of me around my tears.

"You just found out about them," I whisper shakily. "How can you love them already? You couldn't possibly."

Ellison chokes on a laugh, his eyes meeting mine, bright and unwavering and so full of happiness that I can see it.

"You can tell me what to do any other time," he murmurs, reaching up to brush my cheek. "I'd swear by it that you're always right any other time," he shakes his head. "But you're wrong just this once," he smiles even bigger.

"I do love them. I already love them."

His lips find mine again, trembling, and then he leans back so he can look me over again.

"I love them, too," I whisper.

"I know. I know you do," he whispers back.

Chapter 24

Sage

For a long time after I tell him, I sit on the couch like I've been anchored in place.

I expected panic.

I expected silence or yelling or something like dread.

I expected fear and anger and restraint.

But Ellison doesn't give me any of that.

He gives me awe.

He gives me this stunned, trembling kind of joy.

He looks at me like I'm a miracle.

Like I'm the only thing that matters in a world that's been nothing but blood and smoke and counterfeit love.

His hands stay glued to my stomach all night, spread wide, and I can feel his warmth and the faint tremor in his fingers like he's trying so hard to be steady and calm even though the emotion in him is too big to contain, even though his eyes stay wet and he looks like he's fighting not to laugh or sob or both.

"My wife," he whispers when we crawl into bed after the exhaustion creeps in, like he can't let it go. "My wife is pregnant."

I give a shaky laugh as I nod into his chest.

Because he's so happy.

He's so happy, it makes me realize how badly I was bracing for the opposite.

How badly I was prepared for anger.

How badly I was expecting him to react like my father would have.

Like it was a burden.

My eyes burn again as he holds me, and I swallow hard, trying to keep it all contained.

"Ellison," I whisper, and he pulls back only so he can see my face, his attention careful like it always is.

"Yeah, baby?" His voice is soft.

"What if this is..." I start, and my voice catches. "What if this is... dangerous?"

"Dangerous?" He repeats, and there's this quiet, lethal promise underneath the words, like he's already thinking of a list of people he wants dead.

"I mean," I whisper, trying to explain myself, trying to make him understand that I'm not talking about my body, not really. "Everything is dangerous. We're in the middle of a war that I didn't even know I was born into. And we just found out my father is—"

"Baby," Ellison cuts me off softly, and his hands move again, one sliding up to my cheek to brush my skin. "I hear you."

He leans closer, forehead nearly touching mine, voice dropping lower. "I hear you, and we're gonna talk about all of it. Every piece of it. I'm not ignoring it."

My lungs burn as I breathe in.

"But," he continues, and there it is again, that warmth. "This baby is ours. And we're going to protect it. I promise you. I'm going to protect both of you."

I swallow, trying not to cry again, because I swear to God I've done enough crying to fill an ocean in the last week alone, and yet my eyes keep betraying me.

Ellison watches my face shift, and his expression softens even more, like he can somehow be gentler than he already is.

"You were scared to tell me," he murmurs, and it isn't a question.

Shame slides through me fast, hot and humiliating, because yes, I was scared.

"Don't worry," he whispers immediately, like he can see the self-loathing. "I get it. And I know you're probably scared. You don't have to be ashamed for being scared."

His voice drops even lower. "I'm not upset with you. I'm worried that you felt that I'd react badly," he takes a deep breath. "And I hope it isn't because of anything I did or said. But I have a feeling it's because of things you found out this week. And I just—I just want you to know that this baby won't be raised like you were," he whispers. "This baby will be raised loved, and happy, and cherished. With good manners and ass-whoopings if need be."

I laugh despite the heaviness of what he's saying, and I see him light up with a smile, too.

He leans in and kisses my lips, slow and sweet, like he's begging me to feel he means it.

"You don't ever have to fear that I won't accept something you have to tell me. And I promise, the love that I have for you will never be moved by anything else that we have going on. You will always be my first priority."

He tugs me in and my head ends up against his chest.

I can hear how hard his heart is pounding. Fast, frantic, and almost disbelieving.

"Ellison," I murmur into his chest, the words smushed into his clothes. "Your heart's beating like, really fast."

"Yeah," he lets out a breath that's halfway a laugh.

I tilt my head slightly, looking up at him. "You're gonna pass out."

"Probably," he says, dead serious, and then his mouth builds into a smile. "Worth it. My wife's pregnant," he repeats excitedly.

It should sound scary still.

It should.

But hearing him say it makes me feel relief.

"A baby," I whisper again.

"A baby," Ellison echoes, sounding a bit like wonder.

"I don't know anything about babies," I admit quietly, and it feels awful. Because I'm Sage Ledger, and I'm supposed to know everything. I'm supposed to have control over every moving piece.

"We don't have to know everything, baby. We can learn."

We.

The word steadies me.

Because we're in this together. I'm not alone, and we're in this together.

The word steadies me so much that it almost scares me.

Because it makes my brain reach for the edges of a future that I don't know we'll get to see, like I'm allowed to think about tiny socks and middle-of-the-night cries and little hands that will reach for mine without knowing they're covered in blood.

I don't say that out loud, though.

I just nod into his chest, and Ellison kisses the top of my head again and pulls me in closer. "We'll figure it out," he murmurs again. "We'll figure everything out."

I choose to believe it because the words come from his mouth and that's how I know they're the truth.

When sleep finally crawls over me, I take it greedily, clinging to the heaviness of Ellison's body pressed to mine, warm and safe and ever present.

And when I wake in the morning, it's to quiet.

Ellison is propped up on one elbow, hair messy, eyes wide open, gaze already on me.

The second my lashes flutter is the second that his smile starts to build.

"There she is," he whispers, like he's been looking for me.

"Hi," I rasp, still half asleep, slow, and I can't help the way my lips form into a smile too.

"Hi," he whispers back, and then, like he can't help it, his hand slides over my side and settles back where it apparently plans to live from now on.

My stomach.

I stare at him for a second, letting the reality settle again, letting my tired brain catch up to my body, and all I can feel is his happiness seeping into the room.

"You're gonna annoy it," I rasp under my breath, and his laugh shakes my entire body.

"It'll get used to it," he snorts. "Besides, it's like a little animal stuck in a cage right now. It needs some enrichment."

I laugh despite myself, and my entire body shakes again. I reach up to cover my face, and he snorts again.

"Okay, I said enrichment. Not a damn earthquake, baby."

"Stopppp," I can't help but keep laughing, making it even worse. "Stop making me laugh."

"No can do!" He quips back, and then he rolls over and stretches, dramatic and groaning before he's hopping out of bed and leaning down to reach for me. "Come on. Let's get you fed and see what Dallas is doing before he starts whining."

"Be nice to him," I groan as he pulls me upright.

"Never in a million years," Ellison teases.

"He helped me a lot yesterday," I murmur, and Ellison pauses, his face turning serious for a minute.

"I know he did," he softens his voice. "I'm grateful for it, baby."

"You better be," I grumble, smacking him on the chest softly as I walk to the bathroom.

We brush our teeth side by side, stealing glances through the wide mirror in front of us, and it feels so childish considering the things that have happened in the past week.

It feels stupid.

But I fight my smile the entire time because it's nothing but domestic bliss.

It's a moment where I get to feel normal just like those people at the park, and the people at the fall fair.

It's just a glimpse of it, before this small chunk of time, I get to feel it, and it's all mine.

A memory no one can take from me.

A knock comes from our bedroom door right as I reach for it.

And when I pull it open, Dallas' gaze drags over me, sharper than it should be, checking my face, my hands, the look on my face, and I know exactly what he's doing.

He's testing my temperature.

Making sure I'm not falling apart.

Trying to see if I look like I'm hiding a secret still or not.

It's so infuriatingly tender that it makes my eyes burn a little.

And then Ellison exhales through his nose, like he's restraining himself from laughing while he pretends to be furious.

"Dude," he finally mutters, voice low, fake-glaring at Dallas. "I know Sage is like your little sister or whatever, but you could have given me a fucking warning or something."

Dallas tilts his head, unimpressed as he glares back.

"Sage is my priority," he says with a snort, like the statement is so obvious it shouldn't even be spoken. "So fuck off."

Ellison's lips tug into a smile.

"What happened to bros before hoes?"

My hand smacks the back of his head sharply enough to make the sound echo.

And Ellison barks out a laugh, rubbing the back of his head like he's delighted he got hit.

"That's spousal abuse, Sage," Dallas deadpans, and Ellison laughs harder.

"Why am I getting ganged up on first thing in the morning?" I question, the words dripping with sarcasm. "I don't like you two being friends."

I push between the two of them and start making my way downstairs, and I hear both of them speak at the same time.

"Did you hear that, bud? We're friends!" Ellison smirks.

"We are not fucking friends!" Dallas hisses at the same time.

Ellison bounds down the stairs a little too chipper for first thing in the morning, and he reaches for my hand and kisses my knuckles like I didn't smack him a minute ago, like he's proud of it.

And Dallas finally clears his throat, a little too loud.

"So, are we gonna talk?" He asks, which is code for *we're talking about this right now because I'm not waiting.*

"Yeah," Ellison says, voice losing a little of its happiness. He still moves to the fridge to pull out some strawberries and bananas, and

I nod when he looks at me and holds them up. "You want me to make a smoothie or just cut them up?"

"Smoothie, please," I rasp. And I hop off the counter to run back upstairs to the bathroom.

When I come back down, I place a little pill on the countertop and they both look at me in confusion.

"Prenatal," my voice is reserved as I say it, but they both hastily make themselves busy doing other stuff while I take it.

My stomach flips, not with nausea this time, but just nerves.

Dallas looks between us, and meets Ellison's gaze, and Ellison turns away after a second to start cutting up my fruit to put in the blender.

"Relax, Dallas," he finally says, voice reserved like he's trying not to step on a landmine. "I'm not mad. I just—I wish one of you would have warned me or something. I walked into the warehouse yesterday thinking something was wrong with our systems and then walked out of it thinking something was wrong with Sage."

Dallas' eyes cut to me again and he shifts his stance slightly.

"Something was wrong with her," Dallas mutters, and his voice is almost defensive, like he's daring Ellison to argue. "But we got it figured out. I stand by what I said. Sage is my priority."

Ellison's stare goes razor sharp as he looks at Dallas.

"I get it, and that is the way that it should be, but I would appreciate at least hearing that she isn't in immediate danger."

"I wouldn't put her in immediate danger."

"And I wouldn't either. But I need to know that she's fine. If she doesn't want to tell me something, that's fine. But for both of our sakes, I would appreciate you tell me that. I trust you, and I trust you most with Sage, but if my wife goes missing, it might not be good for anyone if I go looking for her. I might start looking and not ask questions until later."

"It's my fault," I murmur finally, my voice small, and Ellison immediately moves to comfort me.

"No, absolutely not," he shakes his head, reaching out to take my hand. "You did nothing wrong, baby, and I'm not mad. I'm not mad at all, and I told you that I understand you were scared and worried and didn't know what to do. I'm not mad at you for it."

"But you are mad? About—about Dallas taking me?"

"No," Ellison shakes his head again, and squeezes my hand again. "That's not it at all, baby. I just—it's okay if you need to do some things on your own, or if you need some time by yourself or—or whatever other reasons you may have. That's fine. But I'd appreciate if the two of you give me a head's up. Just a, *hey, Sage has some things to do, but she's safe, and she's fine*. That's all I'm asking. I won't ask you to tell me anything else about it. I just wanted to know you were safe. That's all I'm saying."

"Okay," I murmur. "We can do that."

"Yeah?" Ellison asks. "You okay with that?"

"Yeah, I'm okay with that."

He reaches up to brush my hair behind my ear and then squeezes my hand one more time before he steps back over to the blender.

"Okay..." Dallas awkwardly grimaces, shifting his stance again before he crosses his arms. "Now that we've settled that. What do you want to do?"

"Why?" I ask quietly. "Did you have an idea? Because I've got no clue," I admit shamefully.

"Actually, yes I do," Dallas surprises both me and Ellison. We both turn to give him our full attention, and Ellison instantly seems to dislike his suggestion.

"I think we should plaster your pregnancy all over the place."

"Absolutely not," Ellison spits the words out between gritted teeth, and Dallas immediately puts his hands up in his defense.

"Now, wait just a minute," he shakes his head. "Hear me out first."

"What could possibly be good about that?"

"Sage is carrying a baby in the middle of a war," Dallas says, and Ellison goes still for a second.

"I don't want to... I don't want to hide my baby, and I don't—I don't want it to be something stuck in the shadows. But it's our baby, Dallas. We can't just put a target on it."

"That's precisely what we need to do, Sage. Think about it," Dallas earnestly stresses with his hands, leaning forward to place them on the counter. He takes a deep breath and then he lifts just one, holding it up to stress each point.

"Public opinion is high on you right now," Dallas says bluntly. "You want it, and you need it. These people need to know you exist as a person and not just a pawn."

My mouth goes dry and Ellison's gaze sharpens again, thoughtful now as he listens.

"Think about it," he says. "Both Ian and Andrew have been operating in the dark. They do everything in the shadows because they think secrecy equals control. They think they can move pawns without anyone seeing the hand that moved them."

Ellison's jaw tightens at the mention of their names.

And Dallas keeps going anyway, because he's fearless when it comes to the same landmines that Ellison tries to soften over.

"They don't know what you found at the Kim property," he continues. "But he knows you got the property. They have no idea what you pulled out of the safe. They don't know who you're allied with right now, because Ellison's been keeping that close, and you've been keeping that close. And that's smart, but it also means they're sitting back waiting to see what the hell you're doing."

I swallow and Dallas' gaze pins me down with something a little reckless.

"So why don't we make moves they can't predict?" He asks. "Why don't we do something that takes the shadows away from them and put the light on you?"

Ellison's voice is low and annoyed, but not entirely against it.

"You want to publicly announce it?"

Dallas gives a one-shoulder shrug before he crosses his arms again. "I want to weaponize it."

My stomach flips again, and I instinctively move to hold my stomach. "Our baby is not a weapon," I whisper, horrified.

Dallas' expression tightens like he regrets his phrasing, like he's trying and failing because he's emotionally inept.

"The baby isn't the weapon," he shakes his head. "The announcement is."

Ellison's hand reaches out to squeeze mine, steadying and unified.

"You've been volunteering. You've been running a legitimate business and Ellison's been getting us more clients. You're turning a profit in a city where men control the chessboard, Sage. People saw the two of you at Angela's ball. They saw your donation and your standoff with Andrew."

Ellison's mouth twitches and I can tell he's putting together what Dallas is saying.

"Right now, to the public, you look like a young couple chipping away and stealing your own pieces on the board, and you're doing it while making it look clean and good and normal, while they've been making moves in the dark like rats," Dallas spits the words out.

"Right now, it looks like you two are separate from your fathers. Everyone is curious about the two of you. You announce you're pregnant, and suddenly you're not just Sage Ledger with all of the rumors. Now you're a wife. A mother-to-be. A person running an empire. A person the community recognizes and roots for. And your husband is a combat veteran, medically discharged after serving his country and saving a life. If anyone tries touching you, there will be public outcry. And you have the perfect person who can paint you in the light."

"Angela," I whisper, the name forming like an answer before I even mean to say it.

"Exactly," Dallas snaps his fingers. "Angela has pull. She has access. She can put something front page without it looking like propaganda. She can make it look like a human story. A community story."

"That's so lame," Ellison mutters automatically, and Dallas shoots him a look.

"So is breathing," he says dryly. "And yet we all insist on doing it."

Ellison stares at him for a second, and then his mouth twitches again, unwillingly amused.

I drag a hand down my face, overwhelmed.

And Ellison's voice softens.

"Baby," he murmurs, leaning against the counter. "I hate to say that Dallas might be right, but..."

"If either Ian or Andrew make a move against you," Dallas cuts in sharply, almost eagerly, "then they make it publicly, against a pregnant woman that the community now supports, and it'll back them into a corner. It forces them to be careful, because now the light is on them, too."

Ellison exhales through his nose, thinking.

"My father and Andrew," I whisper, and the names taste like poison. "They don't like losing control."

Ellison's hand slides to the small of my back, moving in small circles, encouraging.

"And... me having the spotlight on me backs them into a corner, too." I whisper, brows furrowing as I piece things together. "It might drag them into the light with me, and they can't have that. And we..." I swallow, looking up at Ellison. "We also have another weapon."

"What's that?" Dallas asks and Ellison looks at me in confusion before his eyes start to tighten a little bit, lips thinning.

"I don't like that," he murmurs, and I plead at him with my eyes.

"I don't either, but it makes the baby untouchable."

"What exactly are you talking about?" Dallas demands in frustration. I turn to meet his gaze, and I swallow before I open my mouth.

"Andrew is getting older. He was grooming Adrian to eventually take over the Hart family. But he claimed Adrian was weak and couldn't do it. And now... now people think Ellison is different. He's different from the way that Andrew painted Adrian to be."

"What are you saying?"

"I'm saying," my voice trembles. "I'm saying... that Adrian was supposed to take over when Andrew stepped down, and now... now we have a potential heir. We have... we have a potential heir, and Ellison, who is still young and fit, and becoming more favored by the public, too. And Andrew is struggling to keep his control. His son is outwardly turning against him, gaining public opinion. His profit is struggling. His product keeps going missing. His right-hand man is missing because we killed him."

"You..." Dallas starts and then pauses, his eyes wide like his parted lips. "You are... deceptively genius, Sage."

"If we announce the baby publicly," I sit up straighter, my voice trusting what I'm saying now. "And then we announce it in front of the family... we can announce the baby as the next heir, the Hart family future. And the control will flip to our favor."

"Jesus Christ," Dallas whispers under his breath.

"It would help protect me, and it would keep our baby safe. They're the future of the Hart family. Anyone who harms me, including Andrew, will be public enemy number one, but also a traitor to the Hart family."

Dallas watches Ellison for a second, reading him like he always does, and then he slowly starts nodding his head.

"We need to do what we can to make this happen." Ellison nods along, too, like he's trying to keep calm. "All eyes need to be on Sage and I so we can find out who is moving sideways hoping no one will see." His hand presses over my stomach and he takes a deep breath. "Especially now... we need to stay ahead of this."

"So we call Angela," I whisper. "We call her, and see if she'll help us. We'll leak it ourselves." I turn to look up at Ellison. "And you're okay with that?" I ask.

He doesn't hesitate.

"I'm okay with anything that keeps you safe," he murmurs. "Anything that keeps you and our child safe."

They sit still while I make the call to Angela.

And she's absolutely elated that I called her first.

I barely have to explain our plan before she's throwing in suggestions and begging to set up a photo shoot for Ellison and me to be on the front page of the paper.

It's painful to hear how excited she is, gushing about how she just knew the look on my face at the fall fair event wasn't longing but anticipation.

I don't see how Angela was able to see something I wasn't, but when I hang up the phone I sit there for a second in silence, and I hear Ellison's voice, back in its playful tone.

"Dude," he says, voice half annoyed and half grateful. "Next time you find out my wife is pregnant, give me a fucking warning."

"Next time?" Dallas repeats dryly. "Let's survive the first one. Don't get too confident in yourself."

Ellison barks out a laugh, and I can't help it. I laugh too, shaky and nervous.

And Ellison leans down to kiss my forehead.

"Now we wait," he murmurs.

Chapter 25

Sage

The newspaper goes live two weeks later.

It isn't dramatic at first. It isn't a loud commotion. It doesn't get delivered with trumpets and fireworks and cries of joy. Not the way you'd think something like this would.

It shows up quietly through a phone screen.

Through Angela's enthusiastic message with far too many exclamation points.

Through a link I stare at for nearly ten full seconds before I click it, my thumb hovering awkwardly over it.

Ellison is behind me in the kitchen, shirtless, leaning over the counter with his arms braced beside me, watching with that constant, impossible attentiveness, the way does all the time now, like any micro-expression I make might mean something is wrong with the baby or I'm going to throw up all over the counters, which honestly... could happen.

"Is it up?" He asks, a little too excited.

I open it, and yeah, it's up.

And... wow Angela, what the fuck.

I don't think either of us have ever looked so clean and polished.

It's a photo of me, reading to the children, my eyes bright and at ease, with a smaller child's hand gripping my jacket seem like they want to climb into my lap.

And Ellison, standing just to the side, arms crossed, his gaze angled down toward me like I'm the center of the universe.

And I have... no idea how Angela made this photo, because Ellison was never once near me while I was reading to the children, but I can admit... it does look terribly good.

"How do you look this good?" I mutter, almost to myself.

"I know," the smile is evident in Ellison's voice. "You are so beautiful."

"I was talking about you," I roll my eyes, and he beams at me like he knew that already.

The headline is glaringly soft.

Community Leaders Support Children's Outreach Event – The Hart's Attend Fall Charity Fair

Angela's name sits beneath it like a stamp of approval. And I really have to ask her what all it is that she actually does because wow.

The words underneath are warm and carefully chosen, full of community and dedication and generosity, making it difficult to imagine blood on marble floors or money transfers or bribery tucked away in steel vaults.

Ellison's chest brushes my back as he steps closer, his hand sliding around my waist, one palm settling against the faint curve that has started to exist there, barely noticeable unless you know exactly where to touch... and only Ellison has that special privilege.

He reads over my shoulder for a long moment, quiet, and then he exhales.

"It's still lame."

I huff out something that might be a laugh if I had more energy.

"It's kind of sweet," I murmur, and he sighs again.

"Only a little," he agrees. "But make her email us that picture so we can print and hang it up."

"You... do know it's photoshopped, right?" I teasingly ask, and Ellison looks offended.

"Who cares? I look hot and you are God's gift to the Earth, so we should print it."

"Whatever," I roll my eyes again, but I still turn my head away so I can hide my smile.

I look over the article again, and a little trepidation settles in.

Because this is what the world sees.

This is what my father will see.

This is what Andrew Hart will see.

"Do you think they've seen it?" I whisper, and Ellison hums over my shoulder.

"Only time will tell, baby."

Behind the scenes of our announcement, the world doesn't stop.

Dallas and Ellison don't stop.

The shipments keep coming in.

Andrew's empire keeps moving through the city, spreading drugs like a disease, packaged neatly, disguised as business and wealth and something inevitable.

And then one night, three days after our article goes live, Ellison comes home with blood on his knuckles and a satisfied smile.

Dallas strolls in behind him, rolling his shoulders like he just went to the gym for the first time in twenty years.

And I stand in the hallway, one hand hovering over my stomach.

"Is it done?" I whisper, and Ellison reaches out to brush his thumb over my cheek.

"Shit ton of product," Dallas lets out a humorless laugh.

"Millions of dollars worth. One of the biggest he's had moving this year. He must have been desperate to move that many pills at once," Ellison points out.

"And?"

"And it no longer exists."

Ellison's hand slides lower, moving over my stomach in protective circles.

"This one's gonna hurt him."

"I know," I whisper.

And then... nothing.

There's no retaliation.

No screaming.

No threats.

No bodies dropping as a message.

Andrew Hart does what my father does best.

He disappears into the shadows.

And the silence stretches for days until it becomes its own kind of terror.

And by the end of the second week, my body begins to betray me in new ways.

A fullness in my chest that feels unfamiliar.

An exhaustion that settles into my bones.

The faint curve of my stomach is there more often than it's not, and I take to wearing Ellison's t-shirts around the house.

Ellison notices.

He always notices.

He notices the way I pause on the stairs, tired beyond belief.

He notices the way I stand there to hold my stomach, internally begging this baby to chill out for a minute.

He notices the way I wake up at night with shallow breath, staring at nothing and feeling sick.

So he schedules an appointment without asking, telling me in the morning while he fastens his watch.

"We're going to the doctor today," he says, and my lips part on instinct to argue. "No," he cuts me off gently. "No arguments."

His hand slides over my hip.

"It's just a checkup," he murmurs. "Let's just make sure everything is alright."

So we go.

And the clinic is too bright, just like the first time I went.

Ellison holds my hand the entire time, his foot impatiently tapping on the floor.

When the ultrasound wand moves and the screen comes to life, I feel my breath catch so sharply it almost hurts.

There it is.

A heartbeat.

Ellison goes utterly still beside me. His grip tightens until I can feel the tremor in his fingers.

And the technician smiles, speaking gently, pointing out the baby moving around a little bit.

She prints it out for us, and he doesn't say anything, but I can see the sadness in Ellison's eyes when he brushes his fingers over the name on the film.

Baby Hart.

I hate it too. How badly I wish it had no attachment to the Hart name.

How badly I wish it were Gray instead.

The appointment ends with smiles and pamphlets and dates for future visits since the gender still too early to tell.

Ellison doesn't speak much on the drive home, but he takes me to lunch anyway, insisting I eat, his hand never leaving mine under the table, his eyes on me more than anything else.

And that night, he coaxes me into soaking in the bathtub, pressing kisses along my nape as I lean against him.

His hands stay on my hips or my stomach, alternating between the two like removing them will be personally horrifying.

"I can't believe it," he whispers against my throat.

"Well, believe it," I laugh. "Your child is killing my ribs," I groan.

He huffs out the smallest laugh. "I'm trying to believe it. And is he even big enough to be up in your ribs?"

"He?" I echo softly, leaning back so I can tilt my head to meet his gaze.

"Don't you feel bad calling him it?" Ellison whispers, and I laugh again, smiling softly as I think about it.

"He can hear you, but he doesn't know what you're saying," I tease. "And yes, I feel bad that we've been calling him it."

"Then we'll just call it a boy for now," he shrugs and places his hand back over my stomach. "Knowing our luck though, it'll be a girl with an attitude to rival yours," he softens his voice, and it makes my heart warm.

"Let's hope not," I murmur.

I reach up to brush my hand through his damp hair.

"I have a surprise for you tomorrow," I softly tell him.

Ellison tilts his head slightly, curiosity flickering in his eyes. "A surprise?"

I nod and he kisses my throat again.

"I'll gladly take whatever it is you're offering," he chuckles.

That night, I sleep curled up on top of him, a bit dramatic, suffocating him, no doubt, but it's the most comfortable I've been in days, and he lets me do it.

And when morning comes, I nearly strangle Dallas when his agitating voice carries up the hall before he even reaches our door, sharp with frustration.

Ellison sits up instantly beside me, body going alert.

The bedroom door swings open as soon as Ellison reaches for it.

Dallas stands there in sweatpants and a coat thrown over his shoulders haphazardly.

His sunglasses are missing, so it must be bad news.

"We've got a problem," he says flatly, and Ellison gestures for him to spit it out. "Andrew sent an invitation, demanding that you both come to a family event."

The room goes very still, but I sit up slowly, my hand sliding over my stomach.

"We'll deal with it later," I say, and surprisingly my voice doesn't shake.

"Sage—" Ellison turns to look at me.

"I told you I have a surprise for you this morning, and I'm not letting Andrew Hart of all fucking people ruin it, so I said no!" I snap.

They both stare at me like I've lost it.

But I get up and reach for my sweater, pulling it on slowly, forcing the sleep from my bones.

"Baby, let's just—"

I step closer and reach up to grip Ellison's cheeks, and he instantly shuts up to look down at me, stunned.

"No." I repeat, and then I walk around him and into the bathroom.

I shut the door behind me, but I still hear Ellison when he turns to Dallas.

"She's so hot."

"Shut the fuck up," Dallas throws back.

But he doesn't.

Chapter 26

Sage

The car ride is mostly quiet, still too early as far as both of us are concerned.

Dallas stays behind at the house.

That's the first surprise.

He makes up some flimsy excuses before he shoves us towards the door, so Ellison ends up driving.

He keeps one hand on the wheel and the other drifting over to my thigh every few minutes. He follows every little direction I get him, taking each turn slowly and glancing around at all of the street signs like he's trying to figure out exactly where we're going.

The city starts to fall away, thinning out as we start heading more toward the countryside.

I picked this area for this specific reason. There's less traffic, less people to go snooping, and I knew Ellison wouldn't have a clue where the hell we're going.

"You're being weird," Ellison points out when he sees me getting a little antsy the closer we get to the destination.

"I'm not being weird," I argue back, but I laugh anyway, because I know I'm being a little weird.

"You're being suspiciously quiet and moving around too much, which is weird for you."

I huff out a laugh, staring at the passing trees, and let him keep staring at me.

"I'm letting it breathe," I murmur, and he snorts.

"Oh yeah?" He laughs. "Are you planning to murder me or something?"

God.

This is what I wanted.

Him laughing instead of stressing over Andrew Hart and his stupid summons.

He reaches over at the next stop sign, taking my hand so he can lift it to his mouth.

He presses a kiss to my knuckles like it's nothing. Like it doesn't make me dizzy.

"I've been thinking, Sage," he starts, and I laugh again.

"I didn't know you could do that," I joke, and he kisses my hand again.

"Give me a break, baby. I'm doing my best," he chuckles. "But I have been thinking."

"What about?"

"You."

"You're always thinking about me," I point out, and his smile is infectious.

"That's true... but I was thinking... should we go on a small vacation or something?"

"A vacation?" I laugh, leaning back against the headrest so I can look at him.

"Mhm," he hums. "Think about it. The beach. Couple massages. Lots of unhealthy food. Super sexy pregnant wife in a bikini."

"You're ridiculous," I playfully smack him. "You'd have to pick every grain of sand out of all my crevices, because the thought of that right now," I shudder in discomfort.

"Oh, I assure you, baby, I can do that for you," Ellison beams at me.

"Shut up."

"Yes, Ma'am," he smiles even bigger. "Also, is there like a baby class we can take or something? Shouldn't we do that? I don't know shit about babies. That's a little too adult for me."

That startles a laugh out of me.

"You're over thirty years old!"

"I'm grown, Sage, but I'm not that grown. The only shit I know how to do is kill people and file my taxes," he says solemnly. "Babies are completely different."

"I'll see what we can do," I tell him.

"So," he says again, voice warm with amusement. "Are you going to tell me what we're doing?"

"Nope."

"Okay, great. Love that for me."

"Oh, stop!" I yell out suddenly, and Ellison practically slams on the brakes.

"What?" His voice rises, and he reaches over to feel my stomach. "What is it? Are you okay?"

"Yes!" I rapidly nod my head and reach for my seatbelt. "Park the car! We're here."

Ellison looks around, and his eyes narrow.

The cemetery is eerie with the overcast skies.

The gate is old and iron, framed by bare branches and dying leaves since the weather's getting colder.

"Sage," Ellison murmurs as he pulls up by the curb.

I just let him park instead of answering.

He hops out and comes around to my side automatically, opening my door with theatrical courtesy.

"Ma'am," he says again, like he's escorting me into a ball instead of a graveyard.

I roll my eyes, but I thank him anyway.

We walk together, crunching leaves under our shoes, the world feeling a little pale and depressing.

Ellison's hand stays tucked into mine.

"Okay," he says finally. I'm surprised he lasted as long as he did. "You cannot bring me to a cemetery and not explain."

"I'm explaining," I throw back.

"Uh, when?"

"Now?" I laugh, and he looks at me with lifted brows.

And suddenly, I feel nervous.

Which is absurd.

I've survived blood and lies and betrayal.

And yet this feels bigger.

We pass a countless number of headstones. Names and lives all reduced to carved out letters.

And then I lead him toward the back.

Toward the newer graves.

Toward the place I've been planning quiet and carefully, sending Dallas out to make sure it's all perfect, even though he came back a little morbidly traumatized with every update.

Ellison's steps slow as I come to a stop and gesture forward.

He looks at what's in front of us and then over at me again.

The structure is all dark stone and clean lines, still unfinished, but already carved how I want it to be.

Ellison stops completely, and his hand tightens around mine.

"Okay," he drags the word out, and then he looks at it again and back at me.

"Do you like it?" I ask softly, and he just stares at me for a minute.

"... Like it?" He repeats, and now I'm even more nervous.

"Yes," I say far too quickly. "Do you like it?" I insist again, and now my voice cracks a little because he's probably thinking I'm like eight degrees past insane.

Ellison looks at the tomb again, and then back at me.

Then back at the tomb.

"Baby," he starts softly, and then he pauses. And the pause makes my hands shake. "So I know I joked in the car about you murdering me... but is this like... are you about to do it *now?* Is Dallas about to jump out of the woods and stab me? That's kind of a shitty way to go out."

Oh.

Oh God.

He doesn't understand.

He thinks I'm about to murder him in the middle of a graveyard like a lunatic. And oh my God, I even showed him the tomb I'm gonna stuff him in.

He thinks I've lost my mind.

"Wait a minute, baby!" He says urgently, voice both rough and confused. "Can you just explain what I'm looking at?"

"I got it for you," I whisper, and my breath catches when he reaches out to brush his thumbs under my eyes.

"You... got me a tomb?" His brows knit deeper.

I nod, and tears well up in my eyes.

"Are you planning to... put me in it right now?" He asks, and he seems like he's genuinely trying not to insult me by holding in his laugh.

The thought is so ridiculous that I let out a wet chuckle.

"No, stupid!" I lightly smack his forearm. "Did you not read it?"

"Read it?" He murmurs, and then he slowly turns his head back towards the tomb.

"I just wanted to have somewhere," I whisper, my voice breaking. "For us. That wasn't touched by them."

Realization starts to pour into his expression, and he looks like he might cry.

"And I wanted... I want to be with you until we die... whenever that might be. And after... I don't want to be stuck somewhere in some awful graveyard with a bunch of dead people that I don't know. And I just thought... I just thought..." I trail off.

Ellison reaches up again, and his grip tightens gently on my face.

"I know it's morbid, and I swear I'm not about to murder you or whatever. But I just wanted..."

"I love you," he cuts me off softly. "You're right. It's totally morbid, and it's perfect because it's definitely something only you would think of."

"Did you read it?" I rasp, and he turns his head back again to glance at it.

I know he sees it this time.

I know he does.

Because his eyes fill with tears so rapidly that I know they'll spill over.

And they do.

The tears spill over and drip down his shirt, and he doesn't say anything as he pulls me in, wrapping his arms around me to hold me tight.

"I wanted it to be ours," I whisper against his chest, and I feel his breath shuddering as he tries to stop the tears from spilling.

"You put my name on it," Ellison wetly whispers over my shoulder, and his arms tighten around me even more. "You really put my name on it."

"It's your name," I whisper. "It's the only name I call you by, and I know everyone thinks you're Adrian, and I know you hate it. I hate it, too. But whenever our end comes, I don't want to have to fake it. I want you to keep your name."

"You really put my name on it," he rasps, and when he pulls back, his lips are trembling, and his lashes are wet with tears he rapidly tries to wipe away.

"I put *our* name on it."

Ellison turns around to look at it again, and his laugh is watery and full of disbelief, but I can tell he's happy.

Because right there at the top, overlapping the entrance to the tomb is our names.

Ellison and Sage Gray.

Not Adrian.

Not Hart.

Not Ledger.

The real us that we would love to be.

"You put our name on it," he repeats, still choked up. "I love it."

"You do?" I whisper.

"Yeah, I love it," he leans down to kiss me a few times, and my nerves start to dissipate a little bit. "I thought you were going to murder me," he laughs shakily, looking repeatedly between me and the tomb.

"I mean, I've thought about it, but we got past that."

Ellison's laugh is so beautiful that it makes my heart skip in my chest.

It's so carefree and happy that I know I made the right decision by doing this.

"I couldn't change your name on the ultrasound," my voice trembles. "But I wanted to," I tell him. "I would have. If I could have."

"I didn't know you even noticed that," Ellison wipes his face and leans in to kiss me again.

"I notice everything about you, baby," I murmur, and he takes my face in his palms again to kiss me.

It's full of so many things. So many things I know he wishes he could express and can't find the words.

I know because I feel it too.

"I love you, Sage."

I know.

"And I love you, Ellison."

Chapter 27

Sage

A ndrew's party comes too quickly.

   I'd like to say I'm not about to throw up at the very thought of having to see his face... but that would be a lie.

I've been replaying the graveyard in my mind, turning over and over it. I can almost still feel Ellison's tears dampening my sweater when he realized what I'd done, what I'd built for him in secret.

I cling to that memory and to the life we're building.

Because that is the goal.

To live and die alongside my husband. To have a life without Andrew or my father controlling any aspect of it.

To be with Ellison to the very end, no matter how fast that time is approaching.

The thoughts carry with me through breakfast, through the way Ellison keeps smiling at me like he's not the least bit worried.

He's in a better mood than he has any right to be.

He accepts all of my complaints about being tired and him forcing me to eat.

He laughs every time I roll my eyes at him.

And his chipper mood does nothing to ease my fears for this party.

I know he'll protect me.

I know he thinks he will.

I don't doubt him at all.

But I've lived this life.

I've seen this play out.

I've watched the light leave my mother's eyes within her own home, thinking no one would ever harm her because she's the wife of someone important.

And the very man she trusted not to harm her is the one who put her in her grave.

While I trust Ellison... the same men who sought to put a bullet in my head, the same people who killed my mother... those people will be there.

And I would never put my trust in them.

I remind myself of this throughout the afternoon. Through Ellison holding me. And kissing me.

And murmuring sweet nothings to my belly.

And then, as if the universe knows I haven't suffered enough, it sends Dallas to me with that look on his face.

The look that says playtime is over.

The invitation... if we can call it that, sits on the kitchen counter in a threatening manner, staring at me. Andrew Hart's name is printed in elegant script as if we couldn't figure out it came from him without it.

The Hart estate is lit up like a palace.

We arrive early, and already, it's flooded with people here to socialize and tip a Hart opinion in their favor.

It looks like wealth on purpose, like Andrew is trying to remind his own men that he's the one in charge.

The driveway is lined with black cars.

There's security everywhere. And this isn't like the auction.

Weapons are encouraged here, even though they're kept hidden underneath fancy clothing.

The house itself is flowing with music and wine and who knows what kind of monstrosities underneath it all.

It's a party, but it's not a celebration.

It's a courtroom disguised to look inviting.

Ellison adjusts his cufflinks beside me in the car, calm and maddeningly handsome, his suit cut sharp, hair carefully crafted like he's walking into a magazine shoot instead of a potential war zone.

He glances at me and his expression softens immediately.

I'm wearing all black as usual, a dress that fits over my hips and thighs, elegant and simple, the fabric gathering perfectly to highlight my baby bump.

It's no longer hypothetical.

It is real, and visible, and most definitely a statement.

Ellison's hand slides over it one more time, like he's grounding himself in the fact that this is why we're doing this.

"This is insane. Do you want to just go home?" He murmurs, and I laugh despite myself.

"I know," I whisper.

His hand reaches up to brush along my jaw.

"You look..." he exhales, shaking his head like words aren't enough. "Kind of like you're about to ruin a man's entire life."

I lift my brows, trying to fight the smile threatening its way onto my face.

"That is, coincidentally, on the schedule."

His lips twitch too, and he eventually gives it up and smiles at me. "That's my girl."

Dallas snorts from the front seat.

"God help everyone inside."

Ellison leans between the two front seats and bats his eyelashes repeatedly at Dallas, softening his voice.

"My dear, Dallas," he clicks his tongue. "Is that cold-hearted jealousy I'm hearing?"

"My dear, Dallas," Dallas mocks in a higher pitched tone. "Shut the fuck up and get out of the car."

Ellison beams at him with the same stupid expression that pisses Dallas off, and he steps out of the car first, turning back immediately, offering his hand to me with theatrical ease.

"My lady," he murmurs, and I smirk as I take it.

I try to breathe through my nose as we approach the door.

And when it opens... I know that we truly are about to ruin things tonight.

I can feel it in my soul.

And I cling to the memories from the graveyard as we walk in together.

My first thought is that there are too many people.

My second is that I might throw up.

Because everyone in the room immediately starts whispering as they outright gawk at Ellison's hand on my lower back, leading me through the room like he knows exactly what he's doing.

That's her! She actually is pregnant!

Did Andrew invite him here?

Is Andrew stepping down?

The whispers are scandalized.

People look at my stomach with open curiosity.

And they look at Ellison with something like awe.

He isn't the scrawny little alcoholic that Andrew used to beat all over these halls for everyone to see it.

No.

My Ellison is strong. He's solid. Dependable. Confident.

He works around the room with ease, shaking hands with men he's spoken to on the phone.

Showing he's been involved.

This time, the same people who seemed to want me gone now openly speak to me... mostly about my baby. And some about how I must be so proud of my husband.

Yes, I am proud of him.

"And I'm so proud of Sage as well," Ellison gushes over me with affection, brushing his fingers over my stomach. "Poor kid is already kicking away in there."

"A son, then?" One of the men dressed in a suit that looks like it cost more than Dallas' fancy Escalade asks. "Ah, getting started on building your legacy then?"

"Oh, our legacy has long been started," Ellison chuckles back in good nature. "Just because you haven't seen it doesn't mean it isn't there," he winks at the man, and then he steers me away towards the edge of the front stage.

I have no idea how he figured it out, but the room seems to shift.

Like a predator is stepping into the territory.

And Andrew Hart appears at the top of the staircase, one hand on the railing, his suit immaculate, expression carved into something cordial.

The applause is polite and obedient.

But Ellison's hand tightens around my hip.

Andrew's gaze finds us immediately, and his smile sharpens by half a degree.

"There's my son," he says, voice carrying easily through the room. There's mock pride in it, and it grates on my nerves. "And my beautiful daughter-in-law, look at you!"

My stomach twists with the hatred of those words.

Andrew descends the staircase slowly, looking over everyone.

Every step is power, especially when he reaches the bottom and turns, lifting his glass.

He doesn't immediately speak though.

Instead he keeps glancing around the room.

Because he likes the silence and the fact that his presence demands it.

"Thank you all for coming," Andrew begins slowly. "I know rumors travel fast in our world."

There's a hush of laughter, and he smiles as if he's amused.

"I'd love for this to be merely a social call tonight."

The laughter dies.

"There have been... disruptions," his voice sharpens just slightly.

Ellison tilts his head faintly when Andrew's eyes cut toward him.

I'm certain Andrew takes his movement as a challenge.

"Targeted attacks," Andrew continues, teeth grinding beneath his words. "Against our shipments. Against our product. Against our stability."

The air thickens.

"And," he adds, his voice darkening, "my dearest companion and right-hand man is missing."

A ripple of surprise runs through the crowd, and Andrew sweeps his gaze over the room.

"He was loyal to me. Eternally loyal," Andrew's jaw clenches. "So, I pray that if he has met his untimely demise, then he was loyal to the end."

Ellison's lips twitch just slightly, and I can tell he's fighting a smirk.

Yes, Andrew's right-hand man was loyal to the end.

Up until the very second that Ellison put a bullet in his skull.

Andrew lifts his glass higher.

"But," he says, smoothing his face back into one of control, "with the recent reveal of my son and his wife expecting a child..."

His gaze slides deliberately to my stomach, and I place my hand over it as Ellison smiles at those who turn my way.

"It is more important than ever that we remain vigilant."

The room breaks out into whispers again.

Andrew's voice becomes honeyed and poisonous.

"We must keep the Hart family safe." He pauses, and then slowly, he looks directly at Ellison. "As we find the culprit behind these devastating attacks."

Silence follows.

And Andrew and Ellison stare at each other from across the room.

Long enough for others to glance between them, sensing the discomfort and animosity between them.

And then Ellison moves.

He lifts his glass, and the motion is casual, but the room's attention snaps to him immediately, like they can't help it.

Ellison smiles, and this time, it's not warm or friendly.

"Yes," his voice carries, calm and clear. "With our heir finally here..."

Andrew's expression drops.

And Ellison continues, unbothered.

"I will do anything necessary to protect my child."

He pauses and extends his hand toward me.

Mine slips into his palm, and he turns slightly, looking down at me like I'm a jewel in his palm.

"And my beautiful wife, whom I could not accomplish half of the things I set out to do without her by my side."

Then he lifts his glass higher.

"I'd like to thank all of you," Ellison says smoothly. "For coming out to support us during this time."

Andrew's face tightens, turning red as he nearly shakes with anger.

Ellison is stealing it.

All of it.

The room.

The narrative.

The control.

"Please," Ellison adds, voice almost playful now. "Drink. Celebrate the approaching arrival of our child. Enjoy the evening in honor of the Hart family."

He nods once, and he brings his glass to his lips.

Andrew's mouth opens slightly.

He is furious, and he can't even hide it this time.

Not in front of all these eyes.

Ellison takes a solid sip of his wine, and the entire room follows.

And then he leans down.

And he kisses me.

Soft and possessive, hand tight on my hip.

And Andrew Hart stands there like a king watching someone else sit on his throne.

As we move through the crowd, heading upstairs so we can have a higher ground, Dallas appears beside us like a shadow.

"He's fucking pissed," Dallas mutters, and Ellison gives him a practiced smile before he sips his drink.

"I noticed."

"He's losing it in front of all of these people," I whisper, keeping my smile on my face.

"Yeah, well, he's getting sloppy. He couldn't even keep his face neutral during my toast. He's the one that looks deranged. Not us."

"You're insane," Dallas huffs out a humorless laugh.

His eyes shift past Ellison toward something behind him, and then he meets Ellison's gaze.

"Andrew is talking to a man by the front. Make sure you see him."

Ellison turns slightly to the side and places his wine glass on a passing waiter's tray, and he cuts his eyes toward Andrew as he does it.

"Got it," Ellison murmurs.

"I don't like him," Dallas grits out.

"I don't either. Keep your eyes on him. I don't want him getting too close to Sage."

"Surely he's not stupid enough to try something on me in front of all these people." I look between the both of them, and when I realize they aren't saying anything back, my smile falls a little.

"He isn't going to try something on me in front of all these people, right?" I whisper again, voice a little panicked.

"If he does, we'll handle it, baby," Ellison smooths, reaching over to brush my cheek right there in front of everyone in the room.

"Handle it how?" I whisper-yell, and he just tilts his head at me.

I know what that look means.

"There's a lot of people here, baby," I whisper, using a pet name since I can't call him by his real name here. I wouldn't dare call him Adrian.

"A lot of dead people if they get too close to what's mine-oh, John!" Ellison's voice slips into something more pleasant as he reaches out to shake another man's hand.

They launch into a full conversation about some security venture at a business downtown, and I tune it all out.

I sweep my eyes over the room, and I meet Andrew Hart's.

He's staring straight at me, eyes cold and full of hatred.

And I make sure that I hold his gaze as I slip my hand back into Ellison's.

He tugs me closer, wrapping my arm around his waist so I can lean on him, not even realizing that Andrew is watching.

I look back, and Andrew's face is red. He's not calm at all.

He's standing right there in the middle of the room, posture rigid, sweating with fury, staring at me.

Like he can rip the baby out of my stomach with his eyes alone.

And then a noise hits somewhere downstairs.

Sharp and sudden.

It cracks through the air like glass on hardwood.

Heads turn immediately, including mine.

The music keeps playing, but the illusion of calm slips, just for a second, like the curtain was dropped.

I feel it before I understand it.

Ellison's hand tightens at my waist, and Dallas stills beside us.

And then, in that brief moment of chaos, while the attention is slipping away from me...

A man steps forward.

Too close.

And far too fast.

His shoulder clips mine with intent behind it, and the force of it is enough to make my breath leave my lungs.

My heels slip on the linoleum flooring.

The edge of the staircase is suddenly there.

Open and waiting.

And for one sick second...

The world tilts.

And my hand flies out for something... for anything.

My stomach clenches so violently it feels like my body knows before my mind does what could happen.

What they could take.

What they would take.

And then Ellison moves.

His arm locks around my middle, brutal and absolute, jerking me back against him so hard my spine hits his chest, so hard I can feel the heat of him through the fabric.

He holds me tight like he's anchoring me to the earth.

Like gravity itself is not allowed to have me.

There are gasps all around us.

And the man stumbles forward... like it was an accident. Like he lost his footing. Like he didn't hit me hard enough to push me to my death.

He recovers with his hand on the railing, and he tries to turn with an apology already on his tongue.

The gunshot is deafening indoors.

It detonates inside the mansion, inside my soul, inside the fragile mask we were trying to hide this night with.

The man drops where he stands at my feet.

There's a sharp sound of glass shattering where his wine splashes on the flooring.

And stunned screaming from someone nearby.

Everything freezes.

Everything.

And Ellison lifts his gaze, sweeping the room with terrifying calm, like he's counting.

As if he's asking, silently, who else wants to try.

A man shifts beside us, and Dallas is already there.

A gun appears at the back of his skull like it manifested out of pure contempt. "Uh uh," Dallas murmurs, almost bored though there's tension in his entire body.

The second man freezes completely.

And Ellison turns his head slowly, his expression empty.

Not blank.

But empty.

Like something human stepped back so something violent could step forward instead.

And he walks closer, unhurried, as though he's taking a walk through the park.

As though Andrew's house is just another battlefield he's standing in.

"Were you going to touch my wife too?" Ellison asks, his voice low.

The man's mouth opens, and his eyes widen... because he knows he's not in a good spot.

He was expecting us to fumble.

He was expecting Ellison to hesitate.

"No—I was—I wasn't—"

"Let me guess," Ellison tilts his head. "You were just following orders?"

"I'm loyal to the—"

Ellison's lips twist, and it isn't a smile.

"I was just following orders!" The man's voice rises in terror.

"Yeah?" Ellison nods his head like he gets it. "Follow this."

The second gunshot somehow feels louder than the first because the room is already dead silent.

The man crumples forward like a puppet with its strings cut.

And Dallas steps back like it's nothing.

My heart is pounding so violently I feel sick.

The blood is pooling on the floor in front of me, and my heart is racing just as fast as it spills out.

Ellison turns back to me immediately.

His hands find my face.

And it's not panicked.

Not frantic.

His hands aren't shaking like mine.

A smear of blood has kissed my cheek.

Ellison's thumb brushes it away slowly, with quiet disgust, like the sight of it offends him more than the bodies gushing at our feet.

His eyes lift, and they meet mine.

And for a second... for just a fucking second, I see it with frightening clarity.

My trust from before...

I could never lose it.

Ellison is not my father.

Ellison is not Andrew Hart.

He is something more.

And he is devoted to me.

His entire life... devoted to me.

That look in his eyes, the sickening, devoted, ravenous look... is for me.

He holds my gaze for just a moment until I take a shuddering breath in, and then his hand slowly falls.

He turns on his heel, smearing the blood on the flooring.

His back is nearly touching my chest, like he's shielding me from anything else that wants to touch me.

And when he speaks, his voice carries without effort.

"Let me remind you of the toast I made," Ellison says firmly.

He turns and looks at Andrew Hart.

"I will do anything necessary," he continues, not even blinking as he stares him down. "To protect my child."

His gaze drops briefly back to me.

"And my beautiful wife... who looks better in black than in blood."

He holds his hand out, and I slip my trembling one into his palm without hesitation.

And he helps me step around the gleaming blood spreading on the floor.

No one moves.

No one breathes.

And then he looks around the room, a deadly glint still in his eyes, taking in the fear and the stares and the blood dripping down the staircase, cascading toward the lower level, where Andrew Hart now stands at the bottom step.

"Please," Ellison says smoothly, as if nothing has happened at all.

"Keep enjoying your night in the Hart family name."

His eyes do not leave Andrew.

"In the name of our legacy."

Ellison reaches out to the buttons just outside of the elevator.

He presses it and the doors slide open.

He turns his head slightly, his theatrical courtesy returning like a mask.

"Ma'am," he murmurs to me, gesturing to the elevator.

And somehow... the smile slips right back onto my face.

I step inside and Dallas steps in right behind me.

Ellison snaps his fingers at the men standing just outside of the elevator, both pale and shaking.

"Clean this up."

"Yes, sir," they answer instantly.

Because blood is managed.

And Ellison has demanded it.

He steps into the elevator in front of me, and my hand jerks forward on instinct to grab his.

The doors close.

On the blood.

And the bodies.

On Andrew Hart's control.

And the truth that everyone in this room has finally seen.

The heir has arrived.

And God helps anyone who forgets it.

www.ingramcontent.com/pod-product-compliance
Lightning Source LLC
Chambersburg PA
CBHW030242030726
47493CB00023B/439